Homer's Odd Sea Odyssey

Homer's Odd Sea Odyssey

Jay Dubya

www.bookstandpublishing.com

Published by
Bookstand Publishing
Pasadena, CA 91101
4928_4

ISBN 978-1-956785-24-1

For Homer (but not Jethro)

Other Books by Jay Dubya

Adult Fiction

Black Leather and Blue Denim, A '50s Novel
The Great Teen Fruit War, A 1960' Novel
Frat' Brats, A '60s Novel
Ron Coyote, Man of La Mangia
Pieces of Eight
Pieces of Eight, Part II
Pieces of Eight, Part III
Pieces of Eight, Part IV
The Wholly Book of Genesis
The Wholly Book of Exodus
The Wholly Book of Doo-Doo-Rot-on-Me
Thirteen Sick Tasteless Classics
Thirteen Sick Tasteless Classics, Part II
Thirteen Sick Tasteless Classics, Part III
Thirteen Sick Tasteless Classics, Part IV
Thirteen Sick Tasteless Classics, Part V
So Ya' Wanna' Be A Teacher
RAM: Random Articles and Manuscripts
Mauled Maimed Mangled Mutilated Mythology
Fractured Frazzled Folk Fables and Fairy Farces
FFFF&FF, Part II
Nine New Novellas
Nine New Novellas, Part II
Nine New Novellas, Part III
Nine New Novellas, Part IV
One Baker's Dozen
Two Baker's Dozen
Shakespeare: Slammed, Smeared, Savaged & Slaughtered
Shakespeare: Slammed, Smeared, Savaged & Slaughtered, Part II
Suite 16
Time Travel Tales
Snake Eyes and Boxcars
Snake Eyes and Boxcars, Part II
UFO: Utterly Fantastic Occurrences

Young Adult Fantasy Novels

Content Chapters

Background

The ancient Greek Homer did not invent the popular game of baseball. The slow-motion, boring sport was actually organized by a fellow named Abner Doubleplay.

The poet/bard Homer, reputed to have been blind, is credited with organizing the Odyssey, the epic tale of the Greek hero Odysseus, who had been punished by Poseidon (Neptune, the sea god) for ten-long-years after the Trojan War. Homer had lived around the time when alphabets and writing were being developed (around 1,000 BC), so his epic poem was later recorded by educated scribes and exists today in its present form.

Around 1184 BC, King Odysseus was returning home from the *Trojan War* to Ithaca, his native island, off the coast of Greece. The hero had an armada of twelve ships upon leaving Troy, and his famous confrontation with the contemptible Cyclops was one major episode in a ten-year mis-adventure after the war. King Agamemnon of Mycenae, and his brother, King Menelaus of Sparta, had led the great expedition of a thousand Greek ships and 50,000 warriors against the Asia Minor city of Troy. The *Trojan War* had taken ten-long-years to fight, and the lengthy conflict was finally won when Odysseus, a brilliant schemer and ball-breaker, had two Trojan horses built, and then had the Greek warriors situate the structures outside the main gates of Troy. The city was strategically located at the Hellespont Channel between Greece and Persia (now Turkey).

The first wooden horse contained fifty horny Greek harlots that exited down a hidden ladder, and then proceeded to service the Trojan guards (after distributing to them ribbed-clothed prophylactics, which the dunderhead Trojan soldiers naturally wore over their sandals instead of over their reproductive organs). While the Trojan guards were humping and pumping the nymphomaniac Greek whores, a dozen Greek soldiers descended the hidden ladder to the smaller second *Trojan Horse,* and quickly killed the fifty Trojan guards while the sexpots were busy screwing and happily climaxing inside the fifty insatiable Greek harlots.

The hero Odysseus had ingeniously thought-up the ideas of the dual *Trojan Horses* because the perpetual schemer wanted to return to Ithaca and pump his old lady, Queen Penelope, whom the itinerant king had heard was being wooed by two-dozen or so totally worthless suitors, walking around the rugged island with massive hard-ons.

The *Odyssey,* like the *Iliad* (the story of the *Trojan War* and the Fifty Trojan Whores), took ten additional years to complete, so intrepid Odysseus was destined to go twenty lousy years without porking and sodomizing Penelope, his faithful wife. The Greek hero and his Achaean crew sailed twelve ships from Troy and six-thousand-soldiers across the wine-dark Mediterranean Sea, which tasted more like salty vinegar, and because of that definitive fact, Odysseus creatively called the body of water *"the odd-sea"*.

Greek Name	Roman Name
Zeus	Jupiter
Poseidon	Neptune
Hades	Pluto
Athena	Minerva
Hera	Juno
Aphrodite	Venus
Apollo	Apollo
Hermes	Mercury
Ares	Mars
Cronus	Saturn
Hephaestus	Vulcan
Artemis	Diana
Odysseus	Ulysses

Chapter 1

"GODDESS ATHENA VISITS ITHACA"

B rain-dead-but-awesome Ancient Muse, speak to me now of that intrepid hero who had wondered and wandered all over known creation after pillaging and looting the corrupt bordellos and brothels of Troy. This major mage explored many cities and citadels around the Mediterranean Sea, where Odysseus learned their unique cultures, and while sailing upon the treacherous waves, the brave explorer suffered many torments from mentors and tormentors alike, as the Greek mariner struggled to save his own existence and lead his crewmen (warriors and worriers) back home.

But though the courageous King of Ithaca desired to salvage his doomed sailors, Odysseus, swimming in his own frustration, could not rescue or salvage his rowers from either drowning or from being devoured by famished monsters. The obstinate jerk-offs all died from their own stupidity; the totally greedy and ambitious imbeciles. As a pertinent example, the avaricious dumb-fucks feasted upon the sacred cattle of Helios Hyperion, who was the jealous god of the sun. And so, the vindictive, small-dicked giant snuffed-away their slim opportunity of ever safely arriving back to Ithaca. So now, Athena, the well-endowed virgin daughter of Zeus, will explain to us the entire epic adventure of Odysseus, beginning anywhere her egregious mind wishes.

To supplement this lengthy poem's mystery that pertains to Odysseus, the other more-obedient Greek kings and warriors, including all those who had escaped being utterly destroyed while plundering Troy, were now safely returned to their island homes, facing no more wicked dangers from engaging Trojans in battle, or devastating threats from the unpredictable, and sometimes belligerent sea.

But regrettably, dim-witted Odysseus, who after two decades being separated from Ithaca, still-longed to be reunited with his gorgeous, sex-starved wife Penelope, and the plagued fellow was quite determined to reach his ever-deteriorating palace. Currently, in this wholly truthful account, the daring adventurer was being held captive in a hollow, dank cave by that mighty, sex-starved nymph Calypso, the immortal bitch being a hormone-driven, ignoble goddess, who vindictively desired to vicariously

1

screw Odysseus every single hour of every single day as her enslaved, infidel paramour.

But as the various annual seasons progressed and advanced in succession, the correct year finally arrived in which, according to what the mentally-retarded main Olympian gods had once secretly ordained, the journeyman King was scheduled by Zeus's decree to venture back to his native home in Ithaca; not that the bad-luck-merchant would be free from troubles even there, especially among his horny, rebellious, straight and gay island residents. To add to the drama, most of the normally apathetic Olympian gods pitied troubled King Odysseus; that is, all except contemptuous Poseidon, the sea deity who characteristically maintained his disreputable anger against mortal, ambitious Ithacans. And to amplify the ongoing dilemma, the trident-carrying sea god did not relinquish in demonstrating his ruthless animosity until valiant and persistent Odysseus eventually, through sheer human determination, stubbornly reached his native island destination.

"What the Hades is my brother, Poseidon, King of the Sea doing, pretending to be a pathetic landlubber in Ethiopia?" Zeus (Jupiter) asked his don't give a shit Olympian family. "Does he have water on the brain? Is he learning to dance the Wah Watusi? Why is my wet-behind-the-ears sibling being so pedestrian, behaving like a very lost human ambler?"

"No, Father. Forget all about the Watusi! Our sea god relative, my uncle Poseidon, is learning the essential step gyrations from local African crab trappers as to how to expertly dance 'the Fish'!" Athena (Minerva) maintained. "Your just-mentioned account indicates that you're into the art of anachronism, and your ridiculous statements are living proof that you've been gloriously time-traveling into the decadent future."

But simultaneously, at *that* momentous moment in classic mythology, zany Poseidon was preoccupied and engaged in partying like Dionysus (Bacchus) somewhere in remote Africa; the sea-god's thrilling expedition taking him amongst the wild-and-crazy Ethiopians, with Poseidon's illustrious presence being a long way off from the magnificent temples atop sparkling Mt. Olympus. The other bored and intoxicated gods had already gathered inside the great white marble hall of their Olympian King, Omnipotent Zeus.

Among all the arrogant, self-centered potentates, the mentally-challenged father of gods and men was the first to address the obnoxious, insolent audience. In his immoral, immortal heart, Zeus was momentarily recalling the recent murder of royal asshole King Aegisthus. Insane Orestes,

King Agamemnon's celebrated son, had conveniently killed and butchered mentally unstable Aegisthus. So, with the deceased mortal ruler's memory kept in mind, Omnipotent Zeus now addressed his fully lethargic kin.

"It's excessively disgusting how these puny humans blame us kind-hearted gods for everything from their mild skin rashes to their lethal venereal diseases," Zeus lectured inside his mansion's radiant throne room. "The wily knuckleheads residing down on Earth falsely state that their abundant maladies originate from us innocent Olympians, when in fact, the pure truth is that the ludicrous nincompoops, through their own adulterous foolishness, bestow upon themselves harsh difficulties and consequences, most of which incidentally have not been officially devised by the reliable dictates of infallible Fate," Zeus unclearly emphasized. "Now then, my fellow Olympians; there was an absurd numbskull who had existed down on Earth named Aegisthus, but the sex-driven ignoramus selfishly possessed for himself the gorgeous wife of King Agamemnon of Mycenae. Aegisthus wound-up brutally murdering acclaimed Agamemnon, the pure-hearted son of all-too-kind Atreus. And then, Orestes, son of King Agamemnon, murdered Aegisthus, with the abominable assassination transpiring right inside Atreus's atrium."

"Father, what happened next in that ongoing saga of hate and murder?" insisted curious Athena. "It is my understanding that tragedy often begets more tragedy in continuous, redundant cycles among the devious mortals!"

"And to add more detail, my beautiful Daughter; sex-addict Aegisthus had maliciously butchered Agamemnon's corpse into tiny fragments, immediately after the renowned leader of the Greek navy triumphantly arrived home to the mainland from miraculously conquering Troy over in Asia Minor. That very deliberate kill and mutilation violation definitely was not prescribed by the potent whims of infallible Fate. Aegisthus knew all along that his vile and demented evil act would ultimately establish the idiot's total ruin. The morally deficient dip-shit was then soon butchered by Orestes, the deranged son of King Agamemnon, who, as you all know, had gallantly led the Greek expedition against Troy!"

"Did you have any personal enmity towards the slain Aegisthus?" Athena inquired of her Almighty Father. "Was the aberrant king on your personal elimination list?"

"I resented the fact that *that* weird-fuck mental case occasionally wore purple garments during important palace events, and as you're well-aware Daughter, purple is the chosen color of the gods and is limited to *our* use only," Zeus verbally related. "Other than that intolerable behavior of wearing the color purple, I conceded and allowed Eternal Fate to decide Aegisthus's final demise."

"Who gives a canine's crap about these miniscule, insignificant and mundane human affairs?" challenged the handsome chariot god, Apollo. "A deplorable human butchery enacted in imitation of a previous deplorable human butchering. Lord Zeus; in all candor, I have more nobility in my little pinky than does the brightest and best of that terribly deranged mortal species residing down on Mother Earth!"

"You are more than *a chicken,* Apollo, so stop acting like a foul fowl! So now, back to my history lesson," Zeus gruffly replied, resuming his lengthy exposition. "Yes, my inattentive heavenly family. That silly earthly fool, regal Aegisthus, has satisfactorily paid in full for everything he had deserved in the form of revenge. First, the power-hungry villain had viciously crushed Agamemnon's balls with a heavy sledgehammer. And next, the vile aggressor had painfully castrated the aged victim with his already-bloodied rusty sword!"

Athena, possessing gleaming eyes promptly answered Lord Zeus.

"Son of famed Titan Cronos (Saturn), and genetically inferior and brain-dead father to us all; you who rule on high from your high-chair, er, I mean throne; yes indeed, Father; I now understand the story. Thanks to Orestes's need for retribution, deceased Aegisthus now lies stone-cold dead, experiencing a personal destiny he had initially himself caused. May any other guilty man who does similar to what Aegisthus had evilly attempted also be quickly destroyed!"

A copycat murder!" Zeus interrupted Athena. "Aegisthus killed King Agamemnon, and Agamemnon's son Orestes killed Aegisthus in quite a similar manner!"

"But dear Father; my vulnerable heart remains tremendously tattered. I remain worrying about the fate of wonderful Odysseus; my very special, ill-fated, and extremely confused explorer, who has had to endure and struggle with a frustrating series of horrible disasters for so many years; my mortal champion's defiant activities are still occurring far away from his former friends, and also far-removed from certain often-visited amorous prostitutes. I adamantly believe that faithful Queen Penelope is unaware of her husband's adulterous conduct practiced over his twenty-year absence from Ithaca. Yes, Father; ten years fighting like a valorous Spartan against the Trojans, and ten years being punished by your cruel, heartless brother, Lord Poseidon!"

"Get to the point, Daughter Athena," Zeus angrily replied. "Or else, I'll gladly dry-up your virgin pubic love garden for all eternity! In *my* dominant Universe, might makes right, and quite apparently, Athena, I happen to control all of the might."

"Maybe so, Daddy. But you and Uncle Poseidon savagely punish ethical Odysseus while you completely ignore the other less-moral Greek inhabitants who constantly call you a dizzy dumb-dick and a flagrant fuck-head! Why are you so ambivalent? Can't you see that you are biased against certain mortals, but you tolerate multiple misdeeds from others?"

"Daughter; describe your defense of this primitive caveman Odysseus whom you so admire, while I still enjoy a degree of patience," Zeus nastily retorted. "Honestly, I have less patience than the average mortal physician does, ha, ha, ha! In the future, a low-intelligence asshole named Hippocrates will certainly envy my incredible patience!"

"Well, Pop. The itinerant King of Ithaca is now being held hostage on a little-known island; its topography being surrounded by the moody Mediterranean Sea," Athena informed the assembly of gods. "The extensive body of water forms the mythological ocean's naval navel. And there, Big Daddy, within the lush semi-tropical forest landscape, lives a voluptuous, minor goddess, Calypso, who intentionally prevents her disconsolate captive, my stellar hero Odysseus, who is being egregiously held against his free will, from ever escaping or leaving her rather obstinate authority."

"So, Athena, in a million words or less, what's so damned special about this very ordinary fellow, Odysseus, King of Ithaca?"

"I absolutely adore brave Odysseus," Pallas Athene adamantly answered. "My favorite hero yearns to once again see the smoke and pollution rising from Ithacan chimneys. And the weary victim's spirit presently longs to be immediately defeated by imminent death. Yet, despite *that* overwhelming, grotesque adversity, Great Olympian Almighty Zeus, your occasionally sympathetic heart does not adequately respond to the punished Greek King's incessant pleas and appeals. Now Father; did not Odysseus obediently and respectfully offer, in honor of your immense glory, spectacular sacrifices that had been exhibited upon Troy's arid desert plain, situated beside the moored Greek ships. If so, Father Zeus; why are you so fuckin' angry with afflicted and beleaguered Odysseus? Are your enormous hemorrhoids again acting-up, or what?"

Cloud-gatherer Zeus then answered his recalcitrant Daughter and cynically declared: "My beloved child. How could I ever forget god-like Odysseus, pre-eminent among all mortal men for his reputed intelligence

5

and for his benign offerings to us immortal gods, *we* who hold dominion over wide Heaven and inferior Earth? But my vengeful brother, Earthquake-shaker Poseidon, the stubborn and powerful sea god, is still furious about *that* injured Cyclops, the monstrosity known as Polyphemus, the mightiest of the Cyclopes, whose singular eye Odysseus had violently destroyed during a brief physical encounter."

"But Father. Why is the ogre Polyphemus and his missing private eye so important to you?" Athena detected and asked. "It is true that Odysseus had made a spectacle out of the hideous villain!"

"Thoosa, the notorious and promiscuous sea nymph, bore ugly Polyphemus in childbirth," Zeus recalled and stated. "The minor deity was a radical daughter of that irresponsible Phorcys, who commands the restless deep seas. Sex-craving Poseidon, down in those dark hollow caves, often had twenty-four-hour daily social and physical intercourse with the sultry bitch."

"I wish that Thoosa should have had genetically damaged Polyphemus aborted," Athena sternly argued. "That Cyclops has been a menace to civilization, and also any seamen who might get shipwrecked on the monster's formidable island. The death of all intruders and trespassers is the only special justice that vile Polyphemus ever administered!"

"The blinding of Polyphemus is the principal reason why Earthshaker Poseidon, father of the Cyclops, makes Odysseus futilely wander and squander his impotent life all over my creation, venturing from island to island," Zeus articulated. "But vindictive Poseidon has not yet released your hero, the hard-headed voyager. So, Pallas Athene, who doesn't own a palace; I insist on this strategy; come now, my subordinate Olympic family; let's together consider the King of Ithaca's eventual return, so that the perplexed leader can successfully journey back to Ithaca and reunite with Queen Penelope and his only son, Telemachus. I predict that Poseidon's notorious animosity will soon relent. My ocean brother can't successfully fight me, along with my allied Olympian family, all by himself; not with all of us aligned against his mounting wrath."

Athena, goddess with the sensational gleaming eyes, proudly and quickly replied to her father's monotonous oration.

"Son of Cronos and father to us all; your enviable wisdom vigilantly rules the stars and constellations of heaven above. Let's urgently dispatch the swift flying Hermes (Mercury), killer of Argus, as our personal courier, sending our messenger god over to the island of Ogygia, so that our trustworthy postman can quickly tell that fair-haired nymph Calypso of our firm decision; which is that bold Odysseus will now leave and complete his extraordinary voyage back to Ithaca."

"Well now, Daughter. Your solution must end, as usual, in a satisfactory, fairy tale conclusion," declared Zeus. "If your imaginative plan fails, and this witch Calypso does not cooperate, then I promise that I'll further punish Odysseus by having the addled blockhead shit out of his pecker and piss from his asshole. Or, in another scenario," Zeus threatened, "I might shoot a bolt of lightning up your favorite hero's fat rear-end and effectively cauterize his colon and also his large intestine. Then, your mortal champion could neither shit nor piss out of his sealed-up anus!"

"I'll deftly zoom-off to distant Ithaca and urge the King's son Telemachus to initiate action. I'll instill admirable courage inside the young man's heart," Athena informed, "so that the son of Odysseus will call those long-haired Achaeans destroying his property to assembly. Telemachus will then intrepidly address the bevy of covetous suitors, who keep on butchering his father's flocks of sheep, and also keep randomly slaughtering the King's bent-horned cattle. I'll soon surreptitiously send vernal Telemachus on a secret mission to sandy Pylos, and then off to Sparta, where the pure-hearted lad can learn all about his brave father's remarkable exploits along with his new-found journey home."

After Athena convincingly spoke, the gorgeous goddess gracefully tied her lovely sandals upon her dainty feet; the famed immortal, golden sandals, which reputedly carry Zeus's daughter as fast as stormy winter wind gusts across the ocean seas and over endless tracts of land masses. Athena raced-down from Mount Olympus's lofty peak, sped across the land and sea to Ithaca, and then just confidently stood there, at Odysseus's outer gate, located before the in-need-of-repair palace.

Standing erect outside the musty structure's threshold, the resolute goddess's right hand was still firmly gripping her gleaming bronze spear, imitating the general appearance of Mentes, a noteworthy foreigner who ruled the fierce Taphians. At her position before the dilapidated palace, audacious Athena encountered the egocentric suitors still pursuing the hand of enticing Queen Penelope, the devoted wife of King Odysseus, whose fidelity remained strong, despite her beleaguered husband being away for twenty long years.

Those narcissistic, competing troublemakers, all cowardly parasites, were obviously enjoying themselves playing ancient checkers, and arm-wrestling right outside the huge wooden entrance doors, and all the while merrily sitting-down and laughing upon soft, thick hides of cattle skins.

Little time was left for abandoned Queen Penelope to willfully surrender to gruesome reality, and agree to marry one of the malignant suitors, since her nomadic husband had been away from Ithaca for twenty long years.

Chapter 2

"STELLAR TELEMACHUS"

At the in-shambles Ithacan Palace, Telemachus observed Athena first, well-before the others males, the rabble consisting of dangerous and horny suitors. The attracted and distracted adolescent moved-up near the goddess's position and then softly spoke to her; the youth's inspired words seeming to have majestic wings, which instantly impressed his immortal Olympus visitor.

"My cordial welcome to you, most enchanting stranger. You must enjoy my humble hospitality. Then, after you have consumed some sumptuous food, you can tell me exactly what you might need."

After saying those polite introductory words, congenial Telemachus awkwardly led gorgeous Athena into his father's ramshackle palace's main hall. The youth courteously sat his vivacious visitor into a dust-laden chair, which twenty years earlier had represented a beautifully constructed work of intricate craftsmanship. Beneath Athena's golden sandals, the all-too-pleasant host rolled-out a utilitarian linen mat, and then set in place a flimsy footstool for his guest to rest her feminine feet. Beside her curvaceous body, the amiable lad drew-up a second lovely-but-archaic decorated chair for him to sit and squirm around while dealing with his pulsating erection. The boy's bizarre sexual fantasy was interrupted when a female servant entered the quarters and carried a fine gold-gilt jug, and soon proceeded to pour fresh water out into a silver basin, so that the new acquaintances could eagerly scrub and wash their sweaty hands.

"I'm sorry to admit that I cannot afford for you, kind lady, food, drink and golden thrones like those items enjoyed by the immortals, supposedly existing atop fabled Mt. Olympus," Telemachus apologized. "I sometimes myself imagine that I'm a god and an intimate friend of Hermes, Apollo and Hephaestus (Vulcan)."

"Your provisions are indeed adequate for little old me, a modest suppliant traveling around Greece under the protection of Almighty Zeus," Athena logically replied. And then the 'down-to-Earth' visitor considered further evaluating her freckle-faced host. 'This fucked-up junior jerk-off isn't even enough an intellectual challenge for me to waste my precious time. Telemachus probably doesn't even have signs of hair growing around

9

his tiny dingle! I can't stand me shrinking-down to being a six-foot-tall human facsimile. I felt much more supreme and confident up on Olympus being my standard fifty-foot height.'

Beside the two oddball chamber-sitting occupants, the woman servant set-down an expensive, polished table. Then, the silent housekeeper carried-in newly baked bread and placed the loaf down before Telemachus and his immortal guest. The valet next laid-out a selection of spotted and speckled fruits, drawing freely on supplies that she had scrupulously kept hidden in a side storeroom, concealed away from the parasitic suitors' lustful scrutiny. A longtime palace carver sliced-up many different cuts of meat, and graciously provided slabs upon two cracked and stained plates. Then, the elderly, gray-bearded slicer abandoned his cutlery duties, left the room and found and brought-out tarnished golden goblets, as another lowlife herald entered the dismal area and served the pair sour wine.

Then, one after another, the conceited suitors sauntered into the vast dank chamber. The leeching slobs sat-down upon a variety of reclining seats and upon ugly, uncomfortable high-backed chairs. Available heralds, with nothing better to do, poured water out into mugs for everyone seated inside the enormous chamber, in order for them to wash their hands, and thereafter, laconic women piled assorted wicker baskets full of stale bread onto dirty tables, while young lads filled dull goblets up to their brims with putrid-smelling, cloudy red wine.

The suitors reached-out with their greedy hands to help themselves to the somewhat-diseased fruits that had been placed in front of the morally-bankrupt laughing assholes. When each and every scumbag had satisfied his vast need for mediocre food and sour drink, the freeloaders' degenerate hearts and tongues demanded something more in the form of lap-dancing and risqué song, lewd entertainment elements that the weirdo dregs regarded as the finest joys that the dreadful derelicts regularly associated with their marathon mooching habits.

Next, an enterprising herald handed a splendid lyre to Phemius, so the timid musician was forced to sing in front of all the ignoble scum-wagons. Upon the strange-sounding strings, the musical bard plucked the prelude to a romantic love song about a kinky royal queen lamenting having monthly menstrual and minstrel agony.

But then Telemachus, leaned his dandruff-filled head and scalp over, close to enchanting Athena, so that no other occupant inside the room could listen, and the want-to-get-laid youth murmured:

"Dear, kind, well-endowed stranger, and also my utterly attractive guest. These ruthless men here; yes, the deplorable freaks spend all their time like this, with disgusting songs and horrendous music. It's easy here for the depraved suitors, because the lazy, raucous shits gorge themselves on what belongs to someone else, and the fuck-heads devour my father's wealth with complete impunity; the dastardly creeps mock and malign a noble patriarch whose white bones may well be lying upon the barren mainland somewhere, vilely rotting in the pouring rain, or perhaps disintegrating deep inside the apathetic sea, being tossed around by uncaring waves. If these vermin in our midst ever saw my famous father returning to Ithaca, they'd all be praying to possess swifter feet, rather than accumulating more wealth in amassed gold, or finer clothing through excessive bullying." Telemachus paused to clear his raspy throat, and then continued to communicate his bullshit evaluation to Athena. "But by now, honored suppliant, I suspect that some evil fate much worse than mere acne has furiously killed blithe-hearted Odysseus, and for us, his dependents surviving here within his decrepit palace, there is no particular consolation; not even if some earth-bound immortal should arrive in this forsaken place and announce that my father will soon arrive. But tell me this information, well-mannered stranger, and please speak candidly. Who are your people? What city do you come from?"

'This especially naïve, young fool is even more of a dolt than I had originally suspected!' Athena assessed. 'I can tell by his gestures that this immature jester only desires to rape me and have juvenile sex, the rookie teenage dunce! That's all I need to have happening to me right now; his dumb-ass, over-excited, premature ejaculation shooting high into, and harmfully contaminating, my virgin vagina!'

Then Athena, goddess with the gleaming eyes, plausibly answered her new acquaintance:

"To respond to you, my suave gentleman, I will indeed speak openly. I can tell you that my common name is Mentes, a son of the wise Anchialus, who is the fearless king of the Taphians, who are highly-skilled rowers, and who absolutely love the oar. My dependable ship is securely docked in a berth some distance from your one-donkey town. But come, my eminent friend; speak openly, and tell me the irrelevant gossip that I request knowing," Athena urged. "What is this peculiar feast that I'm presently witnessing all about? Who are the mentally unstable members of this uncouth and sloppy gaggle of disheveled men, the freaks all appearing to be ridiculing you? And why do you need to be grotesquely exposed to all this

11

colossal, belligerent mayhem? Is this a fucked-up bachelor party gone amok?" Athena wondered and asked. "Or, is it a raucous, low-budget university fraternity drinking fiasco? It seems clear enough to me, my callow host, that this vulgar event is no meal where each participant brings and offers his own fair share, and I can plainly observe with open pupils that the riffraff mob gathered here in this dreary room is guiltlessly acting in a totally insulting, overbearing, perverted way, while egregiously dining in a corrupt manner inside your unsophisticated palace."

Noble Telemachus then felt compelled to reply to Athena, anonymously pretending to be the unkempt philosopher Mendes: "Inquisitive stranger; since you've questioned me about the lunatic matter that your keen eyes perceive, I'll tell you the honest-to-Zeus truth. The house in which you sit was once well on its way to being rich and famous; at that time in the past, my father, kind Odysseus, was alive and active among his appreciative people. But now, the whimsical gods, practicing their malicious plans, have sinisterly changed all that phenomenal family history completely upside-down. The contemptible dwellers residing atop Mt. Olympus make sure that merciful Odysseus stays in obscurity, where nobody roaming this accursed planet can actually see him."

"Whose fault is responsible for this horrible chain of events that you cite?" Athena asked. "If I were you, I'd rather be a leper or a terminally ill cancer patient!"

"The mercurial gods, argumentative visitor, have not dealt with other men in a similar manner as the insane assholes have arbitrarily dealt with Odysseus," Telemachus maintained. "But it's not him alone who makes me sad and cry-out my frustration and disillusionment in utter distress. For now, the erratic gods have brought me more intolerable grief. All the best young men who rule the neighboring islands, Dulichium and woodsman Zacynthus, and that criminal Sameo, as well as those who lord *that* barren western land situated here in rocky Ithaca; indeed, my distinguished guest; those black-hearted scoundrels are all now wooing my mother and ravaging my soon-to-be-inherited house."

"Please describe your mother's unenviable plight?" Athena requested. "How is she ever enduring such mounting aggravation?"

"Queen Penelope is trapped within an unfortunate circumstance where, after twenty-years of insufferable unhappiness, she won't turn-down a marriage that she detests, but my mother can't bring herself to make the final choice," Telemachus explained. "Meanwhile, these mendacious, suitors are disdainfully feasting on my home's assets, and the villainous rogues soon will be the death of me as well. These boisterous hoodlums are wickedly dismantling my father's august legacy, and bankrupting my mother and me in the process."

Those glaring and salient revelations divulged by Telemachus made Pallas Athena angry, and the livid goddess disclosed to her host:

"It's quite lamentable that your famous father Odysseus is still wandering all over creation when you and Queen Penelope need him here so much in Ithaca! Your mighty patriarch could easily lay his powerful hands upon these disrespectful suitors and strangle their annoying throats right out of their skinny necks! Listen now, besieged Telemachus, to what essential strategy I'm going to confidentially reveal to you," Athena beckoned. "Tomorrow, you must summon the encroaching Achaean suitors to an assembly and forcefully address the filthy bastards, dynamically appealing to the sympathetic gods of Mt. Olympus as divine witnesses. Next, Telemachus; imperatively direct the fucked-up suitors to go back to their shoddy, rented shanties. As for your sorrowed mother, Penelope, if her heart is honestly set on getting married to one of these garrulous dirtballs, then allow your' mom to return to where her compassionate father lives, for he's an imaginative savant of great abilities and of tremendous hidden, emotional power. Your understanding grandfather will smartly organize the intended marriage and arrange the specific wedding gifts, as many dowry contributions as befit a well-loved, slightly used, non-virgin daughter," Athena stressed. "Now, dear Telemachus; as for yourself, if you'll diligently listen, I have some super-wise, noteworthy advice. Set-off down south seeking fortuitous news concerning your father's fate, for Odysseus has been absent from Ithaca for so long. Some living mortal perhaps can provide you with tangible knowledge of his whereabouts, or you may fortunately hear a voice emanating from Lord Zeus, who often enjoys bringing mortals favorable news as a diversion from his eternal boredom."

"Well, kind stranger; who the hell do I have to see down south?"

I recommend, dear Telemachus, that you first journey to Pylos and eagerly consult with elderly and sagacious Nestor. After you've been there vegetating in Pylos, proceed in haste to Sparta and conscientiously confer with fair-haired, bullshitting King Menelaus, the last one of all the bronze-clad Achaeans to arrive safely home to the mainland after the ten-year Trojan War."

"Your thorough instructions seem easy enough to remember, suave guest. I'll be as cool as a cucumber when I vegetate in Pylos and Sparta. Do you have anything else of importance to convey?"

"Yes, Telemachus. I strongly suggest that you must not continue acting like a spoiled, feckless child; for indeed, craven son of Odysseus; the time has evolved where you're now too old to be weakly conducting yourself as an embarrassing, impotent wimp."

Prudent Telemachus, who in his ignorance actually believed that the traveling goddess was a genuine male cross-dressing transvestite, then constructively answered glamorous Athena:

"Stranger, you have been speaking to me as an authentic and caring friend, even though, before today, I didn't know your' ass from either Prometheus or Pandora. Indeed, you've spoken to me just like a father would advocate for his own disobedient offspring. And what peculiar wisdom you've just communicated! I'll always cherish and never forget your' fabulous counsel. But please come now," Telemachus attempted persuading. "Though you're eager to be off to yonder harbor, stay here for a while so that we can intimately learn about each other in a touchy-feely manner. Once you've enjoyed your naked bath with us both splashing-around in the nude, your fond heart, being a spectacular oracle with four auricles, will soon be fully satisfied. But since you insist on departing, I now instruct you, amiable stranger, to swiftly exit these premises with jubilant spirits, and be off to your awaiting ship."

"You demonstrate the fake valor of Apollo along with the brass balls of Hephaestus!" Athena shrewdly admonished. "I must confess, young and ambitious Telemachus, that you're a fast-read, unenviable, shallow-minded asshole!"

"Furthermore, anonymous guest; as a wonderful surprise, you'll be carrying with you an expensive gift that I wish to contribute to your safe passage home," the simple-minded youth stated. "The alluded-to object is something truly and positively magnificent, which will be my appreciative gratefulness to your sage guidance. In fact, the valuable item is a rather sentimental heirloom, dear guest; the aforementioned prize being the sort of present that a friend would often give to one whom he regards as *his* valued kindred comrade."

Goddess Athena, with the gleaming eyes thought, 'Wow! Perhaps it's a terrific wooden dildo without splinters, or maybe a carton of used, unsanitary napkins!' Then, the delighted guest visiting the ruinous Ithacan palace replied:

"Since I'm eager to depart this outrageous barn of yours that you preposterously describe as a palace, Telemachus, please don't dare keep me as a disenchanted hostage a moment longer. And whatever sensational gift your heart suggests you'll afford me as your loyal friend, kindly present the designated merchandise to me when I eventually come back here to again visit your trashy dump. Pick me out something truly beautiful. I guarantee that your intelligent choice, son of King Odysseus and Queen Penelope, will earn you something desirable that will be even more worthy and stellar upon my return."

With that phony rhetoric being communicated, Athena with the gleaming hazel eyes, departed the decrepit mansion, and after exiting, flew-off like some wild famished sea bird in quest of its next meal. In the Ithacan lad's immature heart, the merciful goddess had inserted both necessary courage and strength. In the process, clever Athena had made Telemachus recall his father's fantastic audacity, which the hero often employed against impending adversity in the form of mortal enemies and insidious monsters. Inside his miniature, underdeveloped, cerebrum, frail Telemachus could vividly picture his apparently feminine guest, just as a sense of amazement suddenly invaded his vulnerable heart. In his wildest chauvinistic conjecture, the teenager envisioned his recent visitor as a cross-dressing god (and not a goddess). And so, the inspired youth moved away from his typical shyness and uncharacteristically mingled with the throng of antagonistic suitors.

The famous minstrel Phemius was currently performing his rehearsed tune at the Palace, as the demented two-dozen villains sat in silence, vaguely listening to the fucked-up lyrics. The phlegmatic vocalist was nostalgically singing of the return of King Agamemnon (brother of Menelaus), and his victorious Achaeans to Mycenae; that bitter trip which Athena had personally prescribed and guided when the weary warriors had sailed home from distant Troy.

Meanwhile, in her upstairs room, the daughter of Icarius, wise and devoted Queen Penelope, heard the minstrel's inspired military verses. The wife of Odysseus cautiously descended the towering staircase from her room, but her appearance below was not alone; two female servants followed Her Highness to the source of entertainment.

When beautiful Penelope reached the vicinity of the avaricious suitors, the Queen stayed beside the doorpost in the formerly well-built room, and a small blue veil across her face hid her attractive features. On either side of Odysseus's wife, her two attendants waited. With tears streaming down her cheeks (the ones on her face), sensitive Penelope respectfully addressed the popular singer.

"Clown show Phemius; you know all sorts of other ways to charm an audience besides your stupid propensity of masturbating in public, but right now, I'm specifically referring to paying homage to extraordinary actions performed by gods and men, which dumb-ass singers like yourself often celebrate. As you listlessly sit here, frog-throated Phemius, gently sing one of those monotonous Trojan War lyrics that I've just suggested, while these condescending suitors drink their putrid wine in absolute silence."

"You wish for me to sing a song of praise about the Greeks defeating the Trojans? Queen Penelope; the suitors might not savor such lyrics!"

"Don't keep vocalizing that painful song you've been chirping, which always breaks the heart pounding here in my chest, and makes my sensitive ovaries ache, for, more than anyone present within this dingy hall, I'm weighed-down with ceaseless grief and excruciating abdominal cramps which I cannot endure. I clearly remember, always, with such yearning, my dear husband's clean-shaven face and hairy crotch. Odysseus was a husband whose fame has spread like syphilis far and wide throughout Greece and central Argos."

Instead of Phemius replying, surprisingly, newly-sensible and inspired Telemachus answered Penelope and uttered:

"Mother, why begrudge this talented singer delighting us in any way. His mind should inspire him to adroitly activate his larynx in the manner he so chooses? One can't deny the minstrel his natural propensities. It seems to me that it's Zeus's lousy fault for all the horrible tragedies that affect men. Yes; the renegade chief god thwarts decent laboring men, limiting the success of each and every breathing mortal asshole, whatever the jealous god's supreme whim at that moment so desires. There's nothing exclusively inappropriate with this dissonant fellow's singing of the evil fate of the doomed Danaans, for brazen men instinctively praise the song which the idiots have heard most recently," asserted Telemachus, effectively articulating his newly-discovered adult independence.

"Where did you ever acquire your new-found courage?" Penelope asked her suddenly transformed son. "Have you visited Delphi without my expressed permission?"

"Your heart and spirit, Mother, should accept the literal interpretation of the disillusioned minstrel's song. Now venture-up to your rooms and keep busy there with your own favorite work, namely the family spindle and the fruitless loom. And instruct your more faithful servants to leave your preoccupied misery, and industriously attend to their separate duties. Talking politics is men's concern, and exchanging gossip is the matter of chattering women. Yes, Mother; your every focus should be on the safe return of your husband, King Odysseus, but his return should also be of special interest to me, since in this house, I'm now, by default, the only one who is in charge."

Astonished at her son's amazing mature speech, Penelope retired back up to her own chambers, keeping her son's strident nomenclature lodged deep inside her suffering heart. With her attendant women, the Queen climbed up the rickety stairs, veered in the direction of her private rooms, and there wept for her beloved missing husband, and his massive manhood, until gleaming-eyed Athena cast sleep upon the matron's heavy eyelids.

Inside the Ithacan palace's shadowy halls, the rambunctious suitors then started to create a loud uproar, with each jerk-off shouting-out his desperate hope to lie beside and then pork Penelope. Knowing their mutual, sinister motive, shrewd Telemachus boldly addressed the pernicious fuck-heads:

"You, frantic suitors of my precious mother's snatcheroo, who display such abundant arrogance, let us for now cooperate and together participate and delight in our imminent banquet. But I caution; there is to be no more exuberant shouting, for it is grand and more satisfying to the ear to listen to an excellent singer as accomplished as this ball-breaker, Phemius," Telemachus daringly maintained. "The minstrel's feminine, high-pitched, alto voice sounds like a god's perpetual orgasm."

"Where have you learned such defiant articulation?" a scar-faced suitor challenged. "You dare to defy us, even though you have no hair under your scrawny armpits!"

Telemachus completely ignored the wise-ass suitor and aggressively proceeded with his startling narrative. "But in the morning, let us all again assemble here, and sit our asses down for an important meeting. I will emphatically speak and tell you dumb-fucks, in a firm manner, to immediately depart my home."

"Why do we have to meet tomorrow morning to hear such nonsense when you've just told us what you plan to say?" the same egomaniac sarcastically vociferated a logical criticism.

Penelope's all-too-confident, recently transformed son was not distracted from continuing his stern narrative. "Listen shit-heads; prepare your un-delectable feasts elsewhere, and engage in dinners that eat-up your own possessions, and not mine. I recommend that you totally reprehensible freaks move your asses from house to house and from shanty to shack. If you think it's better, and would prefer that one man's livelihood should be consumed by your gross and parasitic nature, without paying any compensation in return, I'll simply notify the immortal gods to ascertain if mighty Zeus will devise, on my behalf, a suitable and devastating act of brutal retribution. And finally," Telemachus lectured. "I pray that if you' asinine retards are destroyed inside *my* palace, I wish that your instantaneous demise will not be avenged by any of your cowardly relatives or descendants presently living in and around Ithaca."

Queen Penelope's son finished his marvelous dissertation, much to the chagrin of his rather-shocked enemy audience. The gathered suitors all bit their lips, astounded by the youth's forceful language. Then, Antinous, son of heinous Eupeithes, summoned the wherewithal to answer the upstart:

"Telemachus; you who have yet to enter puberty. I suspect that the gods themselves, it seems, are decisively teaching you how to be a braggart by prompting you to deliver rash and dangerous speeches. I do hope that Almighty Zeus, the volatile son of Eternal Cronos, does not appoint your inexperienced testicles as king of this isolated and poverty-stricken island, even though this piece-of-shit eyesore we're standing in is your unavailable father's accursed legacy to you."

The repulsive suitors then switched their focus to performing intimate gay dancing routines, and to later singing faggot-related homosexual lyrics. The frenzied cabal of dumb-fucks entertained themselves until the darkness of evening fell under the New Moon. Then, each of the regurgitating perverts retired to his own downtown shack or shanty to vomit and sleep.

Telemachus casually strolled-up to his remote quarters, situated high above the wild courtyard vegetation. Enjoying a spacious view, and then on his way to bed, the lad's hyperactive mind was much-preoccupied about confronting the dastardly suitors the following morning.

Accompanying Telemachus, Eurycleia, the youth's personal servant who was suspected by area residents of being a devious pyromaniac, and was also believed to be an old flame of Odysseus, held two blazing torches. Of all the female household slaves, Eurycleia was the infatuated whore who had loved Telemachus most, for she had nursed him as an infant with her massive, flabby breasts. But now, the servant strongly desired to steal the adolescent's valued virginity.

Telemachus opened the doors to his grimy suite, sat-down upon his straw mattress, and pulled-off his soft tunic, giving the faded apparel to the scheming old harlot. Then, the horny, dry-crotched bitch left the room in a melancholy frame of mind, closing the door in despair by frenetically pulling its silver handle to express her stifled sexual frustration. Telemachus lay there upon his bed and deeply pondered, and several hours later, covered-up his gaunt form with a nasty-odor sheep's wool; the lad's foggy mind was reflecting-upon his upcoming exciting journey to Pylos and Sparta, which Pallas Athene had earlier proposed and described.

Jay Dubya

Chapter 3

"TELEMACHUS PREPARES FOR HIS VOYAGE"

A s soon as rose-fingered early Dawn appeared upon the eastern horizon, Odysseus's one and only dear son anxiously jumped-out of bed and hurriedly dressed. The wacky kid carried a sharp sword hanging from his shoulders that he had won at a summer carnival concession, and gingerly laced-up lovely feminine sandals upon his shiny feet. At once, the new man-of-the-house asked the gay-voiced heralds to summon all of the long-haired, radical Achaeans that were aimlessly lounging-around to a scheduled assembly.

The heralds issued the call to meeting, and the Achaeans answered with shouts of "Fuck you!" But for some inexplicable reason, the loafers, all wearing sandals, gathered quickly for the announced parley. When the complaining rabble had quieted-down, Telemachus stepped inside the chamber and nervously convened the meeting. Among the crazed maniacs in attendance, heroic wrinkled Aegyptius, an old-but-revered curmudgeon, suffering from chronic arthritis, and also being a sight for psoriasis, was the first to speak.

"You other Achaean inhabitants of Ithaca, pay strict attention to the irrelevant cow manure I have to say. We have not held a general meeting or 'brain-dead conference' ever since that propitious day when dumb-ass Odysseus sailed-away from here with his twelve hollow-hulled warships. What captain has made us gather now? What's the puny punk's reasoning? Does the brazen novice wish to tell us that his father's defunct navy has bankrupt the land? Has this nincompoop Telemachus heard some female gossip about the Greek army's fate, and will give us false details about our vigilant soldiers' journey home, or is this impromptu seminar some other fucked-up, immaterial business that he'll bring-up and awkwardly attempt discussing with us?"

Inspired by Athena, Odysseus's emboldened son stood and spoke, talking first to Aegyptius, whose hyperactive asshole was having a major bowel movement:

"Old, feeble and doddering Aegyptius; the person who called the suitors to this decisive meeting is presently not far-off, as you will quickly comprehend. I did summon your asses to this room, and I'm proudly standing before your squinting eyes with knees that do not knock. For I'm now a mature individual whose brain suffers more mentally than you' miserly old farts ever will. But in all truth, I have no reports to reveal of our returning army pretending to be a navy, and consequently, no vital military details to pass-on to you morons; nor is there any other pertinent public business I intend to mention or discuss. The primary issue now is my own weighty need, for upon my household here, troubles have fallen like a thousand quivers full of heavy arrows, in a catastrophic double sense. Do you dimwits now fathom my rhetoric?"

"Who wants to hear your contrived bullshit?" bellowed a critical suitor standing in the rear. "Your expendable verbal crap smells lousier than Aegyptius's decaying, stinking asshole!"

But inspired Telemachus was neither thwarted nor discouraged by the vile invective and the obnoxious shouting that ensued. "First and foremost, I believe that my noble father Odysseus has possibly perished. Yes, the great archer, the spouse of Queen Penelope, who was once your privileged king, and also my kind father. And then there's an even greater prospective problem that persistently haunts my psyche, which will quickly and completely shatter this entire house. And my whole livelihood will be destroyed."

"Who gives an airborne shit besides Aegyptius, here, about your vulnerable psyche; about your father's fate; about your shoddy palace, or about your mediocre inheritance!" a second more-vocal suitor sarcastically hollered.

"Lazy and bellicose leeches," Telemachus firmly countered. "You are the deadbeat sons of those sailing champions possessing admirable nobility; yes, those mighty warriors, your patriarchs, under the command of Odysseus, might still be returning from Troy. But you, their ungrateful descendants, are constantly pestering my mother for her hand in marriage against her will. From past experience, I judge that you' disreputable dregs are not sufficiently brave enough to journey to her father for permission to wed."

"That fucked-up custom is obsolete!" yelled a third impostor. "Who gives a shit except Aegyptius? Ha, ha, ha!"

"Elderly, Icarius, Penelope's aged father, lives in his ancestral home, and is still fully capable of competently arranging a bride price for his treasured daughter, and then giving her to the rogue amongst you whom he likes best," Telemachus expressed. "Yes; the lucky asshole among you who pleases the old codger the most will get to wed Queen Penelope. But instead, you' leeching derelicts casually hang-around *my* house, day after day, butchering my cherished oxen; slaughtering my well-fed goats, and screwing *my* celibate sheep. You' disgraceful fucks are indeed dispensable liabilities to humanity. Your vile mouths keep-on feasting and drinking gleaming cups of wine without noticeable restraint or guilt, and without remorse, if I may add. You nauseating fuck-heads consume so much until you vomit all over my tarnished walls, and even regurgitate up to the tawdry high ceiling. My home is being demolished in a manner that is not right, ethical, or moral. You' pathetic scoundrels should all be ashamed of your scurrilous deportment."

Telemachus ceased speaking, and then surrendering to immaturity, threw the royal scepter upon the slate floor, and burst-out of the silent chamber, crying and sulking. Everyone seemed to momentarily pity the amateur orator, so all the dipshits seated in the assembly remained temporarily reticent and unwilling to give an antagonistic answer to Telemachus during his swift exiting from the chamber.

But Antinous, ready to exploit the opportunity, was the only one in the gallery motivated to verbally respond.

"Telemachus; you' conniving juvenile delinquent wannabe'; your boastful spirit is entirely too unrestrained. How you haughtily carry on, attempting to shame us into submission, since you so desire to blame your myriad failures upon us. But in your depraved and very disillusioned case, we amicable Achaean suitors aren't the guilty ones."

Telemachus turned and asked, "What the hell are you implying?"

"Your own dear mother, Penelope, is the cause of all our' woes," the loudmouth suitor insisted. "The Queen is an expert on how to use deceit to create emotional agony amongst us. It's been three long years now, and soon it will be sixteen terrible seasons since your devious mother began to deceive the hearts pounding within our Achaean chests, along with the blood pulsating inside our throbbing erect peckers."

"Antinous, even though points are for pinheads, get to the point!" Telemachus demanded before sobbing.

"The Queen gives false hope to each one of us; she makes fake promises to everyone, and constantly sends-out obscure and indecipherable messages to deliberately distress our eager egos. But indeed, Penelope's intent is different than her cryptic narrations. In her evil mind, your distraught mother has contrived another mischievous stratagem. She had a large loom set-up in her upstairs quarters and commenced weaving a mammoth tapestry, very enormous in dimensions. And your mother improvised her deceptive weaving thread, that was quite thin and non-binding. Then, Penelope had the unmitigated audacity to announce to us the following arcane twisted word: "Young men and old farts; those of you who are my suitors and tailors; since I feel that my wonderful husband Odysseus is now possibly dead, you must wait another while, although you are all keen for me to marry and be humped and pumped by one of you' horny bastards. But first, I must complete sewing a huge wall tapestry, for if I don't, my current weaving lessons would be fully wasted and done in vain. I'm sewing a tribute shroud to honor my father-in-law, failing warrior Laertes, for I've heard through the grapevine that a lethal Fate will soon strike Odysseus's father's lily-white ass. Then, none of the Achaean women dependent here, and in my employ, will be thoroughly annoyed with me because a man who once possessed so many riches, along with a most-fantastic fadorkenbender between his skinny legs, would lie in state without sufficient money to even pay for an ordinary sacred shroud."

"That bullshit is precisely what Penelope had stated," impetuous Antinous maintained. "I am not lying, because I am standing!"

Then, the fucked-up antagonist again clumsily quoted and paraphrased Penelope's lengthy commentary, but this time, his caustic remarks were addressed to frustrated Telemachus, who had just fully re-entered the palace hall.

"And Telemachus, our proud suitor hearts have mutually agreed about a certain practice performed by Penelope. And so, each day your obsessed mother weaves at her great loom, but every night the distrustful conniver sets-up torches in wall sconces and pulls her day's work apart. For three years now, your coy mother nefariously fooled us Achaeans with this devious unraveling trick. We positively trusted her. But as the seasons progressed and passed, the fourth year of delay had arrived. Then, one of her women who knew all the details spoke to us about her clandestine method, and we slyly surveilled and caught the Queen undoing her intricate weave."

"You fault my mother for being a perfectionist?" instinctively Telemachus argued. "You contemptible liar!"

"So naturally," Antinous continued his sarcastic commentary. "Becoming wise to your mother's scheme, we righteous and benign gentlemen compelled Penelope to complete the unscrupulous sewing enterprise against her obstinate will. The suitors now say this, so that you, naïve and quixotic Telemachus, deep inside your gullible heart, will fully understand as all Achaeans staying on this primitive island already know; send your mother back to her quarters to complete her impractical tapestry weave. Divulge to Penelope that she must marry whichever eligible wooer that her father Icarius decides and discloses. But we suitors are not returning to our native islands, or even traveling to someplace else like Persia or Africa; that is, not until Queen Penelope decides to marry a deserving macho Achaean of her own choosing."

Prudent Telemachus considered Antinous's testimony and then vehemently replied:

"Self-indulgent Asshole; there's no way I shall dismiss my charitable Mother out of this shabby palace, against her volition; Queen Penelope is the one who bore and nursed me inside my bed-sized cradle. As for my father, I've experienced valid dreams that he's being held captive in a distant land by a horny, promiscuous nymph. It would be hard for me to compensate for Queen Penelope, returning my mother to wealthy Icarius, with me providing a suitable reverse dowry, as I obviously would have to do if I stupidly sent her back to the greedy bastard."

"You previously said that you honored tradition," Antinous challenged Telemachus as the other suitors indulgently laughed. "Are you deliberately trying to be ambivalent?"

"Listen carefully, Antinous; if I did not pay the hoary loansharking prick compensation, then Queen Penelope's influential old man would treat me badly, and some observant deity on Mt. Olympus would initiate other troubles and crises, since my mother, as she ventured from this house back to her former protector, Icarius, her humiliating return to her father's estate would compel the dreaded and furious Furies to directly intervene in *our'* dilemma."

"More rhetorical bullshit," Antinous vehemently objected. "Utter religious nonsense spewing from your juvenile lips!"

"Jealous men like yourselves would automatically blame me for *their* debacle, too," Telemachus boldly argued, regaining his composure that had been inspired by Athena. "That's why I'll never issue such an insane, ludicrous order concerning my mother. But to you suitors I make *this* appeal. Just provide me with a swift ship and twenty veteran mariners, so that I can serenely make an arduous journey to sandy Pylos, and next to militant Sparta, just to determine if I can discover some accurate news about my father's highly-anticipated voyage home."

"What the hell would such a futile trip solve?" Antinous retorted. "More expensive daft delays?"

"If I hear from dependable sources that my father is still living and advancing towards Ithaca, I've concluded that my fortune could hold-out here in Ithaca for about one more year, although it's very hard for me to be frugal with you' voracious assholes sponging off of my ever-dwindling estate Now, if I learn from Nestor and King Menelaus that Odysseus is dead and gone, I'll reluctantly return to my dear native land, build my father an extravagant tomb, and there perform as many funeral rites as are customarily appropriate. And after that responsibility is completed, or should I say that 'duty' is enacted, I will agree that my mother must choose a suitable suitor."

Telemachus strongly conveyed that specific declaration, and soon enthusiastically dissolved the meeting. The confused suitors slowly dispersed, each one going to his own ghetto house.

Soon thereafter, Telemachus walked away, pacing along the ocean shore, thinking about his many duties and obligations. Once the troubled youth had washed his hands in gray, stagnant salt water, the determined lad addressed a prayer to his personal mentor, Athena:

"Oh, hear me, you who yesterday visited my ramshackle mansion as a transgender god, and persuasively ordered me to embark from Ithaca in a swift sailing ship across the murky seas, with my designated mission to learn about my father's great voyage after being away from this miserable island for two decadent decades. My father's incredible success is what the selfish Achaeans are intentionally preventing from happening; most of all, especially with the horny suitors brazenly exhibiting and stating their evil objectives out loud."

As Telemachus solemnly and somberly expressed his prayer, divine, impeccable Athena appeared to him as an effeminate male, but this time the lad's immortal guidance counselor was looking and sounding just like the wise sage Mentor. Disguising her regular voice, the creative goddess spoke-out like an accomplished ventriloquist, with insightful words floating on heavenly wings:

"Telemachus, you must not procrastinate beginning that essential excursion I wish for you to make. I'm a grateful friend of your father's notable past, and I'm so much of an appreciative confederate that I will accommodate your *special needs* by furnishing a super-fast vessel, and as a tremendous incentive bonus, I'll personally accompany your simpleton ass as you visit Pylos and Sparta."

"What should I do?" Young Telemachus asked, his emotions mired in a quandary. "I've never ventured outside of Ithaca before!"

"Now then, young Fool; you must go home to your room, pack a few satchels, and politely mingle with the dumb-fuck suitors. I'll go through town and quickly round-up a non-inebriated crew of loyal, non-mutinous associates, all volunteer sailors with vital marine experience," Athena explained. "In a seaport such as impoverished Ithaca, I'll choose from the many leaking ships, both new and old, and select the finest, non-leaking tub for you to function as the captain, and when that ship has been made sea-worthy, and is fit to raise sail, we'll together launch it, with our currently unemployed mariners, out into the wine-dark sea."

Being motivated to commence his information-gathering expedition, Telemachus descended deep into the palace's storage rooms and instructed palace servant and sex-addict Nurse Eurycleia to locate some fancy adult toy supplies ready for his imminent voyage. The enthralled youth swore to the sex pervert, possessing the dried-up honey-well, to keep confidential secrecy about his impending voyage.

Telemachus next stridently marched down a dank corridor into the destitute dining hall, once more loaded to capacity with the hellish company of criminal suitors.

Then, sympathetic goddess Athena, with the signature glittering eyes, delved deep inside her suspect cranium and conceived a new-found plan. Looking like a facsimile of Telemachus, the sometimes-creative goddess roamed and traipsed all throughout the poor city endeavoring to organize a respectable sailing crew. To every crewman Pallas Athene encountered and enlisted, the recruiter-impersonator issued the same mundane instruction, which was to conserve the sailor's strength by not ejaculating the seaman's semen, and disclosing to each euphoric mariner to responsibly meet alongside the chartered ship at dusk.

Next, the crafty goddess, supernaturally disguised as Telemachus, asked Noemon, fine son of the blowhard Phronius, for his swiftest ship, and the penniless gambler was quite happy to oblige when the transvestite benefactor handed him three gold coins. Then, soon thereafter, the sun went-down on the western horizon, and all the cobblestone and gravel roads became dark. Using her awesome mental powers, Athena dragged the fast ship down into the placid harbor, and again exercising her magical Olympian faculties, the disguised goddess readily stocked the merchant vessel with substantial supplies, featuring all the utilitarian materials that well-decked boats usually have stowed on board. And finally, the immortal shape-shifter adroitly moved the ship to the port's outer edge. It was there at dusk that Athena's unrivaled cunning assembled that rag-tag group of unlikely companions. The goddess mystically filled their limited hearts with abounding spirit, renewing each man's ambition and self-esteem.

Next, in truly impressive military-like order, bright-eyed Athena imperatively commanded Telemachus to venture outside the decaying Ithacan palace and stand erect by the main entrance to the spacious hall. In her inimitable voice and radiant form, the lad's counselor somewhat resembled the political idiot, Telemachus' other mentor, Mentor:

"Telemachus, your well-armed companions are already sitting beside their newly fabricated oars, waiting for you to launch this historic expedition. Let us now be off, so that we don't delay this nonsensical, non-productive trip a moment longer."

With those magnificent words, Pallas Athene quickly led the way, and Telemachus followed his patron's fart trail. Then, with Athena ascending the plank and arriving on board ahead of him, Telemachus anxiously clambered on deck, too. The pair eagerly sat upon a sturdy bench at the "Pride of Ithaca" stern.

The experienced crewmen untied the stern mooring ropes, and then clambered on board the stellar vessel; each well-trained sailor moving to a plank-seat beside an oar. Bright-eyed Pallas Athene magically arranged a fair breeze for the shipmates to enjoy their labor, which constituted a strong West Wind blowing gustily across the wine-dark sea.

As the "Pride of Ithaca" majestically sliced through the rhythmic swells on its way forward, around the bow began the familiar great chorus of splashing waves. Then, all night long, and well beyond the sunrise, the majestic vessel continued sailing toward Pylos on its well-planned journey.

Chapter 4

"TELEMACHUS, NESTOR AND MENELAUS"

A weak week later, Telemachus had reached Pylos and was coolly welcomed and soon dismissed by Nestor, King of Pylos, and also the venerable dean of Pylos University. Nestor provided an ancient, wobbly-wheeled chariot for Telemachus to journey to Sparta, and the King/Dean sent his delinquent teenage son Peisistratus to accompany the Ithacan, just to have the little prick be out of his sight for several months.

"You mean I've sailed all the way to Pylos and you have nothing to report about my father's fate?" Telemachus bitched. "Not one bit of news, or even a rumor! What a freakin' bummer this is!"

"Look, naïve delinquent! Don't waste my valuable time. Now get the hell out of here. I'll have my sex-crazed son go joyriding with you and wish that you both never return! Hopefully, the wheels will come off the rigged chariot, and you'll both be hospitalized somewhere between here and Sparta!"

"What more important things do you have to do rather than granting me a short interview?" Odysseus's son wanted to know.

"I'm a hundred and twenty-seven years old, and right now, I have to figure-out how to die!" Nestor vehemently yelled. "Now hit the dirt road! On your way to Sparta, try yelling-up to the clouds, 'Apollo is a chicken! Apollo is a chicken!' and see what the fuck happens to you!"

Telemachus and Peisistratus, Nestor's leave-the-nest son, after taking three unnecessary detours and getting wildly lost each time, eventually arrived a month later at Menelaus's palace in Sparta, where a small feast was prepared for the two by the famous king and his beautiful wife Helen, who ten-years-before had been smuggled to Asia Minor by Paris, a Trojan prince. And thus, the re-capture of Helen by Menelaus was the principal cause of the Trojan War, with the aggressive Greek kings' combining their forces and sailing a fabulous naval expedition of a thousand warships and 50,000 soldiers to impractically retrieve the lustful whore. During the meager Spartan-type dinner, Menelaus and Helen talked about incomparable Odysseus's major strategy contributions at Troy.

Then, one of the men attending to the needs of Menelaus, faithful Asphalion, poured fresh water onto the visitors' hands and sticky fingers, and the traveling junior jerk-offs, Telemachus and Peisistratus, with the encouragement of Menelaus and Helen, ravenously reached for the week-old food that had been meticulously spread-out for their consumption. The Spartan King soon initiated the dinner conversation.

"Amuse me, callow son of Odysseus. Have you grown any amount of hair under your armpits?"

"No, King Menelaus," Telemachus modestly confessed. "But conversely, my skin has produced a thick blond tuft of hair atop my left shoulder, and also a dense brown fur patch on top of my right one."

"That's quite insignificant, and it doesn't add one iota to my overall empirical knowledge," the King commented. "Are you mature enough to eject a quantity of sticky, white juice from your erect dingle? I noticed that it required four minutes for you two visiting imbeciles to simply wash and scrub your palms!"

"Indeed, King Menelaus!" Telemachus exclaimed. "Young prepubescent Peisistratus and I had halted our squeaky chariot near a babbling brook just outside metropolitan downtown Sparta to take dual pisses. Then, I succeeded in shooting a volume of white fluid from my personal junk, but impotent Peisistratus could only blast-out erratic air blanks out of his semi-erect pecker!"

Queen Helen, showing a modest degree of mild mortification, covered her petite mouth with her right hand in response to the male bonding verbal exchange.

But Menelaus's wife soon regained her confidence and composure. Reputed to being a daughter of Almighty Zeus, the wily queen thought of something special that would allow the two adolescent guests to enjoy additional hospitality. Very discreetly and furtively, the Queen quickly dropped into the sour wine the jovial pair were sipping a potent drug that had the reputation of relieving men's pains and bothersome irritations, making the imbibers forget their many troubles. A drink of that powerful elixir, once mixed-in with potent wine, would be more intoxicating than the fabled African Lotus flowers. And the brain-addling mixture would guarantee that no man, or horny punk teenager, would let a tear fall upon his cheek for one whole day. Even if the consumer's mother and father had died during an earthquake; or even if wicked men brandishing sharp swords would be hacking-down the gulper's brother and his son, the killings would have no effect on the mesmerized drinker.

Helen had mastered the utilization of magical healing potions, like the aforementioned drug, which she'd obtained from Polydamna, wife of Thon, who came to Sparta from Egypt, where that heathen country, so rich in grain, produced the greatest crop of drugs and African aphrodisiacs. Many of these secret formulas, once dissolved, are quite beneficial, and many others are poisonous and lethal. Each person living in Egypt was rumored to be a quack physician whose knowledge of those potions surpassed that of every other human group, including the horny Trojans, who incidentally never practiced birth control.

When Helen had stirred-in the drug and ordered the dining room servants to again serve the tainted vinegar-wine to Telemachus and to Peisistratus, the King's devious wife rejoined the conversation and pleasantly spoke-up once again:

"Husband Menelaus, son of Atreus, whom gods both cherish and despise, and also you two mentally challenged nutcase sons of noble men; since both good blessings and bad omens are arbitrarily decided by capricious Zeus, you two dumb-dicks should now sit and eat this fast food with us. After that, your host, the local steak and burger king and I will together enjoy listening to your fascinating horse-shit stories."

"But I'm not here in Sparta to spin tales and myths to you two royal freaks of nature," Telemachus immaturely argued. "I'm here to learn about the fate of my adventurous Old Man!"

"Learn to conquer your glaring adolescence and strive be become more diplomatic," Menelaus cautioned Telemachus. "Become more contrite and less trite. Learn the difference between being adult and being a dolt! I do believe that you two royal assholes are both wet behind your ears and must endure daily an enormous flood of water on the brain!"

Helen felt compelled to interrupt her fearsome husband. "During our conversation, I'll tell you two smart-asses one ordinary thing I think is within the realm of being suitable. I'll not speak of, nor could I recite, everything about glorious, steadfast Odysseus. The famed Ithacan warrior managed to tackle immense hardships and dynamically thwart the Trojan enemies at every turn. But there's that time when the fucked-up Achaeans were in such distress, and undaunted Odysseus prevailed in his quests, and did so much for his erratic subordinates to survive, right in the homeland of those screaming, out-of-control Trojans, too! Enduring savage blows, and with your father's body being horribly battered, invincible Odysseus threw a ragged garment upon his wounded shoulders, so that the bigger-than-life champion looked like a mere ragged slave to the Trojans. Your father, Telemarketer, er, I mean Telemachus," Helen suavely corrected, "then ingeniously skulked along the main streets of that totally hostile city."

"Evidently, my father imaginatively concealed his Greek warrior status to the Trojans," Telemachus alertly remarked. "He had done the exact same thing to me when I was a kid, because I never knew what the hell he' honestly looked like, either!"

Helen then resumed her informative exposition. "Your father Odysseus sagely hid his own identity, slyly pretending to be a commonplace tinker, or a typical dreg, or even a vagrant begging for alms or copper coins. No Trojan there ever suspected his creative duplicity," Helen elaborated. "I was the only one in Troy who had recognized him, in spite of his terrific disguise. I questioned your father, but his skill in deception made my interrogation elusive. Still, when I escorted Odysseus inside King Priam's palace, I thoroughly bathed him in hot oil, rubbed his alluring manhood with myrrh, and helped him to dress after he shot a fantastic amount of sperm juice onto the high ceiling," Helen shared and ejaculated. "I was so enthralled with the size of his sexual apparatus that I instantly swore a solemn oath not to reveal to any Trojan that my mendicant guest was the great Odysseus of Ithaca; that is, until he'd reached the swift ships and the numerous Greek Army huts that had been constructed on the beach. During his massage, your incredible father told me all about the upcoming Achaean plans."

"About the legendary Trojan Horse? Was my father wearing jockey shorts, or his regular dependable diaper?"

"Don't be so impertinent! I'll get to that!" Helen chastised. "Then, soon after our chance encounter, your father's long sword slaughtered many Trojans, and Odysseus boldly returned to his countrymen, bringing to the craven Achaeans, a full report on the layout of Troy's main streets. Trojan women began to cry aloud when the Greeks invaded through the city gates, but I was fully glad. My heart, by then, had changed to ally with the marauding Greeks, led by my husband's brother, King Agamemnon of Mycenae. In my grieving heart, while still in Troy, I was sorry for that brief blindness that conspiring and untrustworthy Aphrodite (Venus), goddess of love, had brought upon my soul, when the intrusive troublemaker had mysteriously led me there, far from my own native land, abandoning my child, and my own husband Menelaus, who lacked nothing in terms of good looks and wisdom."

"Did you ever have sex with my father when you bathed his entire body?" Telemachus bluntly asked Queen Helen, while his acne-faced companion, drugged and drunken Peisistratus, sat there with his eyes crossed and his mouth wide open.

"Interesting question!" Helen of Sparta, formerly Helen of Troy, answered. "King Menelaus here is the only man who has ever penetrated my lush blonde-haired, pink-wet love tunnel. But I did administer really good oral sex to Odysseus, whose manhood was so huge that instead of me being deep throat, I suddenly choked and became deep esophagus!"

"What about your romantic relationship with Prince Paris of Troy?" Odysseus's only son and heir brashly requested knowing.

"That was just a foolish romantic fling, and nothing more," Helen replied after sighing. "Prince Paris had visited Menelaus's palace while on a political visit to Sparta. I recognized right away that the handsome fellow was very cute and attractive. But then Paris wooed and persuaded me to elope with him to Troy, and that stupid mistake of mine caused my husband and his brother Agamemnon to organize a major military campaign against Troy. Your father Odysseus was one of the Greek kings involved in the invasion!"

In reply to Helen's account of events, fair-haired Menelaus added: "Yes, indeed, dear wife; everything you say is genuinely true. Before now, I've come to understand the minds and plans of many crazed warriors. I've roamed many foreign lands, but these eyes of mine have never seen a man to match the exceptional integrity and dignity of your patriarch, King Odysseus."

"Then, Queen Helen; you're the cause of the fucked-up Trojan War. I'm glad to learn that fact," Telemachus revealed. "The Greeks weren't just greedy pirates and marauders sacking and plundering the city's wealth. But King Menelaus; please tell me more about my father's activities at Troy?" the young guest uttered before burping.

"How I loved your dad's chivalrous ball-breaking; his steadfast heart, and his remarkable fighting ability!" Menelaus frankly related. "And what about the things which that forceful man, your father, endured while designing and later stealthily contriving the infamous Wooden Horse? Achaea's finest men were crouching-down inside the large, fabricated structure, which in reality, omened a lethal fate to the dumb-fuck Trojans. Then, you, my spouse Helen, loyal to your immaculate heart, approached the marvelously constructed 'Horse', perhaps being instructed by some anonymous god who wished to give an inglorious defeat to the small-dicked Trojans."

"Did you feel trapped inside the horse's hollow stomach?" Telemachus obnoxiously asked and then loudly belched. "Were you about to suffocate or faint?"

"Look, junior jerk-off!" Menelaus vehemently yelled. "Stop farting out of your mouth! Show more discretion and culture, and give me sufficient time to accurately relate the entire weird sequence of events."

"I'm sorry for being so insolent and defiant," Telemachus apologized and soon hiccupped. "I value my tiny testicles, so I'll remain quiet while you piously smother me with your ludicrous and outrageous propaganda."

"So why are you lustfully staring at my breasts with such possessive eyes?" Helen asked half-intoxicated Telemachus. "Quite honestly, you look-like you haven't yet even learned how to work your stick!"

"My father always told me that I should study abroad, and that's exactly what the hell I'm doing right now!"

"And, where you walked, dear Helen," King Menelaus continued his boring litany, "noble Deiphobus followed the path of your enchanting footsteps. You deftly circled around the tall Wooden Horse three consecutive times, and then you raised your soft hand and felt the diameter of that hollow trap. Your melodic voice called-out, naming the best undigested occupants among the concealed Danaans hidden inside the horse's abominable abdomen, and you spoke-up exactly like the voice of each soldier's Greek wife. I was there, sitting inside with wise Odysseus, right smack in the middle. We heard your siren call, Helen. Two of us fanatical interior combatants, Diomedes and myself, were eager to get-up and wildly charge outside the wooden wonder, and we also felt prompted to answer back your alluring beckoning from where we were sweating and huddled inside the artificial equine."

"Then you and father weren't exactly horsing around?" stupidly joked Telemachus. "Were you and father wearing jockey shorts?"

King Menelaus totally ignored his young visitor's inane-absurd remark. "But fortunately, idiot Telemachus, perceptive Odysseus stopped us from entering imminent danger. Diomedes and I wished to scream-back imprudent replies, but your nimble-witted father aptly held our destructive compulsions in check. All of the scared-shitless Achaeans sitting with your father and me managed to keep their chatty mouths shut, except for that fucked-up scamp Anticlus, the only one who was about to raise his voice and who felt a death-wish to answer Helen's alluring summoning. Odysseus instinctively clapped his hand firmly upon Anticlus's mouth and held the numbskull in a gorilla grip before then puncturing the stupid shit's already-abused testicles with a sharp dagger. In short, hero Odysseus and I deftly kept our dual grips upon Anticlus's neck and upon the rogue's bleeding balls until Athena, I suspect, escorted you, Helen, away to ultimate safety."

Then, naive and intoxicated Telemachus belched again and replied in a dumb-ass stammer: "Menelaus, son of Atreus, and leader of the militant Spartans, and also truly loved by moody blues Zeus. That interesting Wooden Horse incident you've just described is more painful still; it could not save my revered father from bitter death; not even if the heart inside his hairy chest had been made of cast iron, just like his stomach. But come; send my comatose comrade and me off to bed, so that Sweet Sleep can bring us relaxing joy."

After Telemachus requested lodging for Peisistratus and himself, Helen instructed her servants to set-up mattresses within the drafty corridor and spread-out lovely purple blankets over the cushions, with rugs on top, and over those items some woolen cloaks. The women left the hall with blazing torches after skillfully arranged the beds. A drunken herald soon led the two inebriated guests to their appointed Spartan accommodations.

And so, the traveling Prince from Ithaca and his coughing colleague Peisistratus slept there inside the cold palace vestibule, which wasn't exactly a comfortable ancient Greek bread and breakfast scenario.

"You would think that King Menelaus would've had the courtesy to have his two guests sleep in Atreus's second atrium here in Sparta instead of us having to snore like muddy swine out here in this nasty corridor!" Telemachus complained and shared with his non-attentive, drunken companion. "On second thought, Peisistratus; we should be glad that we're not sleeping in the infamous Mycenae atrium death chamber."

The next morning, Menelaus arrived inside the chilly corridor and gave his two lethargic and groggy listeners a long account of his travels in Egypt, especially his adventures with the Old Man of the Sea, with the death of the lesser Ajax (who was an expert sword fighter who wanted to deter gents that were avowed enemies), and the king's lengthy speech also encompassed the death of his brother, Agamemnon, in Atreus's other atrium. Menelaus invited Telemachus to stay for several days longer, but the neurotic lad declined, futilely grieving of painful bed sores and of agonizing bedbug bites.

Meanwhile, back in Telemachus' crime-laden and rebellious Ithaca, the bewildered and agitated suitors gathered outside Odysseus's palace, enjoying themselves in recreation by throwing spears and discuses on level ground, with all the excessive arrogance that the raucous contingent usually displayed. The two men who led the worthless leeches, hostile Antinous and handsome Eurymachus, were sitting there smoking marijuana in the high weeds; the despicable pair, by far being the best of all the competing suitors. Noemon, Phronius's stuttering son, came-up to them to pertinently question Antinous.

"Fellow Achaean Antinous; I have a grievance to share. In our black hearts, do we truly know or not know the day Telemachus will be coming back from sandy Pylos? The punk fugitive had left Ithaca, taking a splendid ship, of which I am a principal investor, which I now need the vessel to make the abbreviated trip across the harbor to anchor at spacious Elis."

When Noemon finished his short spiel, the suitors were amazed at the boat owner's spunk. The eavesdropping buffoons had no inkling that Telemachus had traveled to Pylos, land of Neleus, and still had believed that the dim-headed fool was visiting the sickened flocks on his various squalor-laden estates. Antinous, son of Eupeithes, then spoke to the delirious throng of unhappy residents (from mainland Mycenae) that had been transplanted to insular Ithaca. Antinous was extremely angry, and his black heart was filled with intense rage.

"Here's the perfect depiction of the definition of the ugly word *trouble*", the head-suitor articulated. "In his overbearing way, that scheming, yellow-bellied snake Telemachus, with this ridiculous voyage of his, has now achieved significant success from recent reports I've received. And we permitted the dumb-fuck to venture-out to sea, fully believing that the motley cretin would never ever see his expedition through. So now," Antinous resumed his objecting rhetoric. "Provide me with a swift ship and twenty able, nautical comrades, so that I can watch and prepare for the asshole's eventual return. I'll set a surprise ambush as the simpleton traitor navigates his passage straight through the strait dividing Ithaca from rugged Asteris."

Antinous carefully selected twenty of the best-available remaining sailors in Ithaca. The crew marched-down to the shore and dragged a swift black ship out into shoulder-deep water, where the unhinged maniacs climbed aboard the vessel and sailed-away on the southern sea, all the while, contemplating and plotting the bloody slaughtering of unwary Telemachus.

Well out into the harbor lies rocky Asteris, where ships could easily moor and hide. The nutcase Achaeans impatiently waited there at Asteris and carefully organized their secret ambush of naïve Telemachus.

Chapter 5

"ODYSSEUS LEAVES CALYPSO'S ISLAND"

As rosy Dawn stirred from her bed beside Lord Tithonus, bringing light to superior eternal gods and also to inferior mortal humans, the occupants of Mt. Olympus were restlessly sitting in assembly, and among them, presided high-thundering Zeus, whose awesome power was supreme. Talkative Pallas Athene was reminding her immortal family of all the excellent stories depicting Odysseus's multiple troubles, and the empathetic deity was concerned for her favorite hero as the Ithacan King passed his days inside nymph Calypso's dark cavernous home.

"Father Zeus, let no sceptered earthly king be prudent, kind, or gentle from now on, or should you think about and consider my champion's consequential fate. Since you are immortal and supernatural, you're bored with life and only derive pleasure in torturing and humiliating trivial humans with your unfair power advantage. Let your ruthless brother Poseidon, instead, always be cruel and treat men with rancor, since few mortals in human civilization now have any fixed memory of Lord Odysseus, who favorably ruled his people, and was a kind and gentle father."

"Daughter; tell me more about this obstinate pawn on my gaming-board, this Odysseus," Zeus asked Pallas Athene. "Where on Earth is the charlatan at this moment?"

"Father, beleaguered Odysseus lies suffering extreme distress on that dreadful island where nymph Calypso is the sole authority. The immortal bitch keeps her captive as hostage by exercising magical force, and her helpless victim is unable to sail-away in even a hand-made timber raft. And now, some jealous, diabolical suitors are setting-out to kill his only son, whom the King of Ithaca fondly loves. The naïve adolescent has embarked way down south to Pylos and Sparta to gather news about his extremely exploited father."

Atop glorious Mt. Olympus, cloud-gatherer Zeus then firmly answered his distressed-but-beloved daughter.

"My overly concerned child; did you not concoct this ongoing bizarre Pylos and Sparta plan yourself, so that once the wanderer made it back to Ithaca, the mere avenger could take-out his animosity against those diabolical suitors? As for acne-faced Telemachus, you should use your granted skill to return him to his native land unharmed, and *that* easy task exists well-within your inherent power. If you act with dispatch, I assure you that the scumbag enemies of your insignificant Odysseus will quickly scurry back to Mycenae, on the Greek mainland, with the Ithacan King's vile antagonists voyaging inside a leaky merchant ship without ever achieving even minimal success at defeating your favored hero."

Austere Zeus next imperatively instructed Hermes:

"Swift-footed winged Messenger, Hermes. I command that you inform the fair-haired nymph Calypso of my firm decision that I must appease Athena, and that she should immediately release this Odysseus person from her custody, so that the brave King of Ithaca can use his ingenuity and courage to eventually arrive back home. However, the faltering, weak fellow will obtain no guidance, special assistance, or divine intervention from the gods, but his only viable option for escape is independently sailing-off upon a well-lashed wooden raft."

Once Almighty Zeus finished speaking, Hermes, the legendary killer of Argus, nodded and obediently obeyed his superior's imperial demand. At once, the messenger god laced-up his lovely golden-winged sandals upon his magnificent manicured feet; the eternal footgear which carried Zeus's private courier across frontiers as fast as stormy winter blasts of wind.

When the energetic messenger swiftly reached Calypso's remote island, Hermes rose-up above the violent violet sea, and easily drifted and glided onshore, until his flight conducted the golden-helmeted Olympian in proximity to an enormous cave; the residence of the fair-haired, promiscuous nymph, Calypso.

Hermes found the exotic nymph standing there, being comforted by a huge fire blazing above an enormous hearth. From far away, the smell of split cedar and burning sandal-wood spread like hypnotic aroma all across the tiny island. Calypso's enchanting voice was singing love renditions inside the colossal cavern, as the notorious, whoring witch/bitch moved in a rapid quandary all around; back and forth, before her cherished spindle loom. All around inside the unusual cave, contrary to conventional logic, wonderful cypress, oak, maple and alder trees were in splendid bloom, despite the lack of sunshine.

Long-winged strange birds were actively nesting inside the miniature deciduous forest, and owls, hawks, and chattering sea crows, who spend their time out on the water, also squawked and abounded. A garden vine, fully ripe and loaded with delicious-looking grapes, trailed and thrived in the dark shadows throughout the lengthy cave.

From four fountains, situated close to each other in a row, clear, clean water streamed-out into basins in various directions, and on every side of the natural enclosure, soft meadows displaying a variety of flowers spread-out in full colorful array. Even a major Olympic god, who lives forever, would be amazed to enviously gaze at the extraordinary spectacle, and Hermes's normally cold heart instantly filled with warm pleasure.

Lord Hermes marveled upon witnessing the entrancing entrance sight. But after the rare visitor's spirit had objectively contemplated *that* rather exceptional scenery with wonder, Hermes hesitated, but soon ambled inside the spacious cavity. And Calypso, that lovely goddess with the two-pound clitoris, when she saw the courier's heavenly face, was not ignorant of whom her unexpected guest was, for the Greek gods are not unknown to one another, even though the home of some minor immortal might geographically be far away from Olympus.

But Hermes did not find Odysseus inside the cave because the lion-hearted war champion sat lamenting, weeping and cursing upon the shore, his misery breaking his mental state with sorrowful tears and groans. As pathetic Odysseus's eyes looked-out upon the restless sea, Calypso was inviting Hermes to sit-down upon a lustrous, shining chair, with the nymph's immediate purpose having the courier explain the nature of his unanticipated arrival. Then, vivacious Calypso interrogated Zeus's only delivery service.

"My dear Hermes, honored and welcome guest; why have you come here with your golden wand, not the one between your legs, but the one held in your hand. You have not been a visitor before to this remote porno haven. Tell me exactly what concern is on your mind. My heart desires to perform whatever you request, and I hope it's munching on sweet pussy, or us turbulently getting laid like two warthogs in heat."

After that brief introductory speech, Calypso carefully arranged an exquisite banquet table laden with ambrosia, then mixed-in red nectar, the combined formula, the secret food of the gods, that when consumed together, allotted and guaranteed the supernatural, immoral beings, total eternal immortality.

And so, the messenger god, famed mythological killer of Argus, ate and drank the wonderful elixir. When his meal was over and the mixture had comforted his famished intestines and pacified his throbbing erection,

Hermes stated his answer, speaking to Calypso with these rather urgent words:

"Enchanting Calypso; you're indeed a renowned goddess of wonder. Since you've questioned me, I'll tell you the truth as I know it. Almighty Zeus has commanded me to fly here against my flexible will. My superior says that you have here under your jurisdiction an ordinary man, more unfortunate than many others, who had fought for nine crucial years around King Priam's immoral city. In the tenth year, the Greeks had destroyed and plundered Troy, and soon left Asia Minor to return home to their various towns, villages and cities. Now, Almighty Zeus is commanding you to send this unfortunate fellow, Odysseus of Ithaca, off your fucked-up island as soon as possible."

The Olympic gods' great messenger tersely announced those declarative words and quickly departed the premises with a limp dingle bobbing nowhere. The regal nymph Calypso, once she'd heard and fully comprehended Zeus's stern decree, dashed-away to find great-hearted Odysseus, who still was a dashing old man who was not dashing anywhere. The witch's sprint soon engaged her already-married hostage upon the shore, sitting upon a rock in a heightened melancholy frame of mind, all alone by the thundering sea waves.

The well-stacked, dazzling nymph no longer gave his abused soul joy. At night, Odysseus slept beside Calypso inside the immense cavern, as the hostage was forced to do; not of his own free will, although she herself was capable enough to screw his ass all the way to High-Olympus. Moving-up close beside her despondent captive, the lovely goddess, daydreaming about Odysseus pumping the poop out of her during animal-like intercourse, gently spoke to her depressed prisoner:

"Poor man, against my obdurate will, you'll spend no more time grieving on this desolate island, wasting-away your meaningless life. My heart agrees that the time has come for me to send you off into oblivion. So, come now; cut long timbers with a dull-bladed axe I shall provide, and construct a large, primitive raft. Build a deck high-up on it, so that your nautical craft can topple upside-down during a torrential sea tempest. Your improvised raft can carry you across the misty and dangerous sea. I'll reluctantly supply your floating timbers with all the food, water and red wine you'll need, clueless idiot, to adequately satisfy your nautical wants and needs."

The lovely-but-saddened, sex-starved nymph finished speaking, and then quickly led her human slave from the shore with a distraught mental attitude. Odysseus followed in her mud-laden, barefoot steps as the minor goddess and the Ithacan King entered the nymph's vast hollow. The famed wanderer sat-down in the same chair from which Hermes had recently risen, and the kinky nymph set upon the fine table a smorgasbord of sumptuous food and potent drink, the sort of delectable morsels and beverage which mortal humans generally consume.

Calypso grabbed a wooden chair and took a seat opposite godlike Odysseus, and her eunuch male servant entered and placed ambrosia and nectar, the secret edibles that made the gods remain immortal, right beside her lustful grasp. The pair of diners reached-out to partake of the other tasty foods that had been spread-out for their culinary satisfaction.

When Odysseus finished consuming his traditional appetite for ordinary meat, fruit, and wine, beautiful and divine Calypso was the first to speak after his regular meal. Starting with preliminary small-talk, the conversation gradually changed to the subject of nymph's actual modus operandi.

"Admirable Odysseus; I'd love that you satisfy my deepest fantasy and vigorously pump the poop out of me upon yonder mattress. My overwhelming lust for having wild sex with you still dominates my total immortal soul. I can't get laid with any of my fifty-three eunuch servants, who obviously don't have the balls to screw my gushing wet, pink honey-well. Forget me getting laid by you, mortal Odysseus. I can't even get marmalade on this boring and depressing, fucked-up desert island."

"Immortal Calypso; all of these difficult and lonely months I've stayed with you inside your massive cavern, and I had to listen to your cornball singing when you made me shrink my body under your low-set bar and dance the fuckin' Limbo and not the Calypso, which I really preferred doing all along," Odysseus opined and replied. "I mean, gorgeous, eternal chic. How low can you go, without raising the fuckin' bar!"

"Nobly born mortal son of Laertes; yes, you, resourceful Odysseus, now still wish to get back to your own lackluster native land without delay. In spite of every nuance, I wish you well as you stubbornly return home to endeavor changing the current squalor of your former luxurious palace into its former magnificence. If your heavy heart recognized how much distress Fate has in store for you, before you ever reach your miserable homeland," Calypso emphasized, "you'd elect to stay here and keep this homely cavern with me. My hot pussy craves your marvelous tool, which I admire when you take a piss, even with your fabulous pecker being limp."

"I respect your sexual addiction," Odysseus commented, "but I have more drastic family concerns plaguing my mortal and inferior brain than

41

merely desiring to frenetically pump your fantastic ass into yonder mattress. Now Calypso; do you have some sort of irrefusable proposal for me to evaluate? You sound very much like my deceased great-godfather. Do you have a tremendous offer to propose that you believe I can't refuse?"

"Well, Odysseus, here's the full agenda in a nutshell. You'd never die on this island, and every day, you will enjoy mad, passionate sex with me for all eternity. I have the ability to make you immortal, even if your obdurate will dictates otherwise. I realize that your limited spirit yearns to be reunited with your earthly wife, Penelope, who after twenty years of separation from you, your aged spouse now features a smelly, dried-up cunt. I can boast that at present, I'm far more beautiful than she is, but in terms of basic logic, it's simply wrong for mortal women to ever compete with an impeccable goddess such as myself in either form, libido or beauty. I've just thoroughly described my distinct advantage over your middle-aged wife? Handsome man; do you not now discern the wisdom of my keen observations? Speak to me."

Resourceful and clever Odysseus then rather explicitly answered Calypso's curious entreaty:

"Mighty sex-starved goddess; I promise to manufacture a functional dildo for you to use after my departure from this hellhole island you call home. Please do not be angry with my final decision to leave your benevolent custody," the captive king explained. "I myself know very well that Penelope, although intelligent, is only mortal, and not your match, either to look-at, or for she and me to fuck like minks as if there's no tomorrow. Although my wife is quite attractive, she is no rival to you in either stature or in beauty. But sad Penelope, just like myself, is a human being, and quite obviously, you're a fantastic and well-endowed goddess. You'll never die or age, but my spouse and I certainly will someday kick the pottery. But still," Odysseus insisted. "I wish, every moment of every breath I take, to return to my home that's probably now overloaded with tiny-dicked freeloaders who want to screw my wife's nasty, dried-up love tunnel. The fucked-up assholes only have the wherewithal to think with their tiny dicks and not with their miniscule brains!"

"You skillfully argue your case like Zeus himself would advocate!' Calypso maintained and complimented. "Do you not wish to become immortal like myself? I have the ability to provide you with that wonderful secret!"

"When I analyze your general deportment and tremendous loneliness, Calypso, I pity your chronic boredom and monotony. Those elements are the debilitating curses of enduring immortal existence, and of suffering eternal emotional grief. There are no life-threatening challenges in your existence, but on the contrary, I wholeheartedly value limitations and obstacles, which represent the thrill and fun of living through. Even if out there on the treacherous, wine-dark sea, some obnoxious god breaks my balls and rips my anatomy apart, I'll persevere and continue pursuing my lofty goals and dreams. I assure you, dear goddess, that I'll assiduously persist in my striving for civilized fame and fortune."

"Then Odysseus, you are refusing my offer of immortality? Why do you prefer death and being with aging Queen Penelope to living here with me forever on my pleasant island?"

"Who the hell wants to live forever without any hurdles to overcome, or any hardships and impediments to conquer? Look, Calypso. The fun in life is dealing with the problems that life offers to humans. What mortal wants to be bored forever, which is a terrible curse persistently annoying the gods? Beautiful Goddess: you know not the challenges, the hardships, and the difficulties that humans experience daily. Believe it or not, those are the things that make human life interesting. The heart beating inside my mortal chest is quite prepared to bear any affliction inflicted by either Zeus or Poseidon. I've already had so many perplexing physical troubles and mind-boggling riddles sent by those two Olympian bastards," Odysseus insisted, "and I've labored so hard through formidable ocean waves, along with wicked Trojan warfare. Let what's yet to come materialize before my eyes, so that I can resist their rather precarious advances."

Just after role-model Odysseus dramatically finished his fantastic oration, the familiar sun went-down upon the western horizon, and the sky grew dark as pitch. Both the mortal man and the immortal goddess slowly ambled into the vast cavern's inner chamber and lay-down there to obtain their mutual nightly sleeps. Although Calypso really never had to eat, rest or sleep, the nymph enjoyed vicariously pretending to be Queen Penelope.

As soon as rose-fingered early Dawn appeared in the eastern sky, Odysseus quickly dressed himself in a tunic and cloak, and the disappointed nymph adorned herself in a long white shining robe along with a lovely woven, see-through, dress. Calypso gathered the ordinary tools that brave Odysseus would require for his departure, handing him a huge axe, the instrument, made of a double-edged bronze blade, with the object possessing a finely-crafted shaft of durable olive wood. Next, the sorrowed nymph provided her former hostage with a polished adze, whatever the hell that piece of fucked-up equipment happened to be. Then, in a dejected and dismal state of mind, Calypso slowly escorted her about-to-be-freed captive along the familiar path down to the edge of the island, where tall coniferous trees grew, alongside alder, poplar, and oaks that seemingly reached and touched the upper sky.

"The dry wood from these most excellent trees will afford you the material you need to build your means of transportation upon the wine-dark sea," the goddess sadly lectured. "Whatever floats your boat, Odysseus. Whatever floats you boat, er, I meant to say 'raft'," Calypso reiterated and corrected.

Once the frustrated nymph had shown her human companion the location of those towering trees, inconsolable and utterly bored Calypso, returned back to her cavern home with her head crestfallen. Odysseus then aggressively began cutting and chopping the appropriate trees to obtain the best woods needed for his upcoming, strenuous voyage. The adamant fellow worked incessantly and as quickly as he could, and amazingly, took-down twenty trees in one afternoon.

Calypso, feeling sincere compassion inside her lonely emotional state, brought her Platonic lover an auger (not an augur), so that her dedicated-to-duty masculine protege could bore the timbers, deftly fasten them to one another, and tighten the beams with provided pins and ropes. After that job had been completed, the industrious king fabricated a functional mast with a yardarm fastened to it, and then the on-the-task amateur craftsman carved-out a long steering oar, acting as a rudder, to effectively guide the raft. Calypso, again returned from her shadowy cavern and brought her fantasy lover woven linen to weave and produce a viable sail, which the industrious craftsman manufactured very skillfully under her magical guidance.

On the assembled sail, the prospective mariner tied bracing ropes and sheets. Then, fatigued to the point of unbearable exhaustion, the weary builder levered the flimsy raft off the slanted beach and dragged his gaudy creation down to the shining sea.

By the fourth day of the mortal enterprise, expending incredible toil, the problem-solving artisan had completed all of that required arduous work. So, on the fifth day, beautiful Calypso gingerly bathed her prized mortal, and then administered a memorable, exaggerated farewell blowjob; dressed her "male doll" in sweet-smelling clothes, and took Odysseus to the place of his raft, ready to leave her secluded island, and against her wishes, probably to never return. The gorgeous goddess had stowed on board the flimsy wooden platform sacks full of dark wine, fresh water and plenty of nourishing guacamole.

Calypso also handed Odysseus a small urn containing six ounces of aromatic pussy juice, to both inspire and remind the evacuee of his lonely island goddess acquaintance, and of his distant grieving, heartbroken wife. The goddess, through her awesome powers over nature, afforded her hero a warm and favoring wind, and Lord Odysseus was quite happy as the ancient mariner masterfully set his sails to catch the stiff breeze that Calypso had provided.

The mixed-feelings hero sat beside the steering oar, and used his reputed skill to guide the raft smoothly out of the tranquil harbor. Sleep did not fall across his eyelids as that night, the self-appointed navigator perceptively watched the constellations: the Pleiades, and the late setting Bootes (which erroneously reminded the raftsman of Calypso's solid boobies). In sheer desperation, Odysseus's voice boomed-out to the night sky, "Shake, shake, shake; shake shake, shake; shake your Booties, shake your Booties!" And next, the on-a-mission raftsman was viewing Ursa Major, the Great Bear constellation, which men call "the Wain", always turning in one place like a confused, spinning, fucked-up Ithacan suitor.

The vigilant helmsman's keen eyes perceptively kept a vigilant acknowledgment of Orion, the only star cluster that never takes a bath, or even a decent meteor shower. In regard to the volatile ocean, kind Calypso had told her male companion to keep the star Orion to his left as his course drifted-away from her island across the burgeoning, foreboding sea.

The courageous adventurer sailed for ten days upon the restive water, and then, safely for seven more, and using elementary arithmetic, on the eighteenth day, shadowy hills miraculously appeared, where the land of the Phaeacians, like a large shield riding upon the vacillating misty sea waves, lay very close, according to Odysseus's severe glaucoma condition.

Poseidon watched Odysseus sailing across the choppy waves, and the envious sea-god's spirit grew enraged, and his massive testicles suddenly became swollen. So, the spiteful nutjob's angry head actively communicated with his own angrier heart:

'Something's gone radically wrong in this uncanny scenario!' Poseidon conjectured. 'More than likely, my asshole brother Zeus must've changed what he was planning for this bizarre dumb-dick Odysseus, while I've been far away partying and enjoying mermaid lap-dancing among the Ethiopians. For now, the diminutive mortal's primitive raft is drifting hard by the land of the Phaeacians, where he'll temporarily escape the great non-nostalgic sorrows which have come over him; and so, inevitable Fate's will shall aptly ordain,' Poseidon evaluated. 'But still, even right now, I think and believe that I should further punish and pulverize this asshole's insolent defiance, so that the meager shit-head receives his well-deserved fill of troubles.'

Then, the contemptuous sea god seized and waved his magic fork and easily drove the separate sky clouds together. Utilizing his awesome three-pronged trident, Zeus's erratic brother stirred-up the formerly passive waves into a turbulent frenzy. The sea-god's anger and fury brought-on blasting tempests from every kind of stormy wind, concealing land and sea with gloomy clouds and wicked downpours; so soon, darkness fell from heaven, soaking and drenching vulnerable earthly inhabitants all over the globe. And East Winds clashed with South Winds, while West Winds, in a rage, smashed straight into ornery North Winds, until all living upon planet Earth got wind of what the fuck was happening.

Odysseus's fragile knees buckled and gave way, with his defeated spirit falling into a doom and gloom mode, and in great distress, Poseidon's nemesis cried-out, standing upon his vulnerable raft, addressing his tormentor and the sea god's invincible trident. "Fork you. Poseidon. Fork you! I'm facing a horrible disaster, a veritable twelve chariot crossroads' collision!" Odysseus imagined and yelled skyward. "How is all this unbearable adversity going to end-up for me? I'm afraid that everything that the bitch Calypso had predicted has now materialized as ugly truth, especially when she told me that while out to sea, before I arrived safe and sound back to my native land, I would experience more than my share of demanding troubles along with formidable obstacles."

As the weary rudder manipulator uttered those all-too-honest words, a massive wave charged forward like a ferocious incensed bull, swirled all around the unprotected raft, and then, from high above, crashed-down with a tremendous thud. Odysseus let go his grip upon the steering oar, and his body flipped into the raging sea; his plight being a long distance from the wildly bouncing raft. Fierce gusts of howling winds suddenly savagely snapped the mast in half, precisely along its middle.

Then, astute Athena, Zeus's empathetic daughter, thought of something rather phenomenal. The goddess blocked-off the pathways of every wind but one, and soon mentally ordered all of the gusty East, West and South blowhards to stop, and the compassionate goddess deftly checked their combined force. Being roused, the swift North Wind broke the waves in front, so that divinely-inspired Odysseus might yet make contact with the people of Phaeacia, men who loved the oar, and who cherished avoiding death while defying Fate.

"Oh Fate!" Odysseus loudly screamed to deaf ears in high heaven. "That was definitely the worse blowjob I've ever had!"

So, for two solid days and two whole nights, the ancient mariner floated and swam upon the tossing ocean waves, his vanquished heart being saturated with countless thoughts of welcomed death. But when fair-haired Dawn gave rise to the third morning, the intense wind died-down, the tempestuous sea grew calm and then still, and everything again seemed to be copesetic. Odysseus was raised-up by a large swell, and as the weary swimmer quickly glimpsed ahead, his eyes could see a land mass close by. Poseidon's human foe kept rapidly doggy-paddling until the sea god's human rival reached the mouth of a fair-flowing river, which seemed to him, the exhausted swimmer, the best place to stumble ashore.

There were no rocks upon the sandy beach, and the desolate place appeared sheltered from the accommodating North Wind. From hazy memory, Odysseus recognized the familiar, flowing river from an archaic map still-imagined and etched deep inside his cerebral recall. With both knees bent, the fatigued castaway let his strong hands fall, because the sea had crushed his heart along with his grip. All of the mortal's weatherworn skin surfacing his entire body (including his treasured scrotum sac) had become swollen from his intense ordeal. The defeated king lay there upon the pure white sand, out of breath, virtually an ungrateful escapee from drowning.

Close by the tiding water, the sea-survivor crawled-about, and finally discovered a place featuring a wide-open view. So, the discarded raftsman crept-forward like a curious animal on the prowl, peering-out beneath two bushes growing from a single source. One of the shrubs was an olive tree; the other a wild thorn. Alert Athena then poured-out much-needed sleep across the fellow's eyelids, so now the exhausted trekker could find necessary relief, a quick respite from his persistent troubles.

Odysseus's final thoughts before shutting his heavy eyes and slumbering into complete rest were, 'I may be a disillusioned fool, but who the fuck wants to live forever in a state of perpetual boredom! Fork you, Poseidon! Fork you!"

Jay Dubya

Chapter 6

"ODYSSEUS AND NAUSICAA"

While much-enduring Lord Odysseus soundly rested, lying in his new beach environment, being overcome with weariness and welcomed sleep, Athena flew-off to the land of the Phaeacians, to their principal city, and vaporized her form inside the palace of the king, Lord Alcinous. The goddess's prime objective was to cunningly arrange a safe journey back to Ithaca for brave Odysseus. Zeus's daughter moved into a wonderfully furnished room where a comely young girl slept, just like an immortal goddess, in both form and loveliness.

The slumbering teenager was Nausicaa, child of great-hearted Alcinous, whoever the hell he was. Like a frantic wind gust, Athena slipped-over to the young girl's bedside, stood there beside her head's brown tresses, and lowly whispered in the girl's ear. At that moment, the goddess's appearance mystically changed to look like Dymas's daughter, a young lesbian girl of the same age as her frequent companion mate, Nausicaa, whose heart was well-disposed to her cherished friend. Utilizing that clever disguise, bright-eyed Athena softly uttered:

"Nausicaa, how did your mother Queen Arete bear a girl who is so careless and who keeps a room so unkempt? Your fine clothes are lying and strewn-about upon the dirty floor, here untended. Soon enough, you'll have your wedding day, when you must dress-up in expensive robes and give the apparel, while standing nude, to your wedding groom, as is your country's ridiculous tradition. You'd better be a bisexual, or else you'll suffer an unhappy future being penetrated by a stiff penis every hour of every day for the remainder of your marriage!"

'Who the fuck is whispering in my ear?' Nausicaa thought in her deep sleep. 'I already have one fucked-up lesbian girlfriend, and the last thing I need is a second annoying bitch!'

"You know," Athena, in needless disguise, mentioned. "It's little things like tidiness that help to make a worthy reputation with *our* people, and also please your honored mother and father. But apparently, you don't give a tiny rat's turd about anything that requires self-discipline. At daybreak, let's together diligently wash-out the wrinkled clothing. Early this morning, politely ask your revered father to provide you with a commonplace donkey cart and his best mules, so that you can carry the bright covers, the heavy robes, and the family sashes to the distant laundry rocks. That use of the donkey cart would be better than carrying your burdensome load of garments on foot, because obviously, the dirty washing tubs are located some distance from the town."

When rose-colored Dawn on her golden throne arrived and woke fair-robed, lazy Nausicaa from her extended slumber, the fat girl was curious to learn more about her rather-peculiar dream. So, the spoiled brat sped through the house, located her apathetic father, and against her selfish nature, lovingly spoke:

"Dear favorite parent; can you kindly prepare a high wagon with quality sturdy wheels for me to use, so I can carry my fine clothing out and wash my abused garb on the distant riverbank? My attire is lying in a heap inside my room, all dirty upon the grimy floor. And as is your fine habit, it's appropriate for you to wear fresh-washed garments on your person, so I intend to imitate your fine example, especially when you're meeting with our city's leading politicians while legislating impractical laws in council."

"Why Nausicaa," her distracted father answered. "What has inspired you to abandon your sloven ways? I'm both shocked and stunned by your willingness to finally act responsibly!"

"You have five worthless sons living in your house," the seemingly-transformed daughter declared. "Two are married, but three are young assholes still unattached, and the lazy dolts always require freshly-washed clothing when they go-out dancing and romancing at the downtown strip clubs. All these are matters I must seriously think about. Now Father; I plan on washing the entire household's clothing down at the river basin."

Nausicaa declared those unusual matters because she felt ashamed to remind her father of her own happy thoughts of possibly getting married to a transvestite male. But the parent fully understood all that related bullshit and replied, saying:

"I have no objection to your unorthodox request of providing my strongest mules for you, or any other things you so desire, as long as you marry a man with a donkey dick and a huge bank account. Go on your way and get pregnant with carrying sextuplets, for all the hell I care. I need to get you, and the massive aggravation you engender, out of this fuckin' home as soon as possible. At your disposal, my slaves will get a four-wheeled wagon ready with a high box frame attached on top."

Once the elderly patriarch announced that concession to Nausicaa, the king called-out to his domestic slaves, and the fearful jerk-offs enacted exactly what their owner commanded. The obliging dumb-fucks prepared a smooth-running wagon exclusively designed for dun mules; the laborers led-up the animals, and then yoked the tamed mules to the improvised cart.

Nausicaa, pretending to be an adult, brought her fine clothing from her room, and the spoiled brat situated the various items inside the polished wagon. Household slaves gathered and packed the other dirty attire into the awaiting donkey cart. The girl's impressed mother, Queen Arete, loaded on board a box containing all sorts of tempting high-calorie foods that would instantly fatten-up the already-corpulent three-hundred-pound, spoiled-rotten teenager.

The conscientious mother then included some rare delicacies, too, and generously poured some month-old vinegar into a goat skin for her obese daughter's personal consumption. The still-mesmerized girl awkwardly climbed onto the wagon. Soon, employing a clatter of hooves, the king's mules moved ahead, carrying discardable clothing along with the dream-influenced girl, who was being accompanied by her regular attendants, who also were devout lesbians, dancing nightly at the popular downtown strip clubs.

When the jolly traveling party eventually reached the stream of the fair-flowing river, the giddy gay girls gathered-up the clothing from the wagon, carried the garb in their arms down to the murky stream, and then trampled and stomped the disposable apparel inside the often-used washing trenches, each motivated bitch trying to work more quickly than the others in order to later go behind the nearby beach shrubs and munch on each other's hairy bushes.

Once the aberrant teens had cleansed the clothing and scrubbed-off all the pussy juice and semen stains, the gay gals laid the laundry-out in rows along the shore, placing the garments where deposited waves beat and surfed upon the rugged coastline.

When the aroused lesbian chicks had bathed themselves and rubbed their curvaceous nude bodies well with greasy black oil, obtained from inside the ground, the young dames ate a meal beside the river mouth, waiting for their clothes to dry in the sun's warm rays. Once the naughty hussies had finished consuming their food and actively eating each other's crotches, Nausicaa and her perverted attendants, still naked from the neck down, removed their head scarves to more effectively play catch with an immobile sea urchin that had lost its will to live.

But when the spoiled princess threw the substitute beachball, Nausicaa accidentally missed her prospective target, and the quilled sea animal landed near the deep, swirling river.

The pissed-off attendants shouted sharp, dissonant protests, incidentally rousing Odysseus from his powerful slumber.

'That loud screaming is evidence of massive trouble occurring in this alien country,' Odysseus's brain hypothesized. 'What the fuck are those insane imbeciles shrieking about? Are these felines violent and untamed monsters without any sense of civilized justice, just like the mythological Cyclops? Or are the sirens simply hostile to random strangers? In their mini-minds, do the bitches fear the gods? Some young woman's shouts just rang-out around me; I don't need this weird shit; they're probably fucked-up nymphs like insane Calypso, who are living along steep mountain peaks and by the local river springs and grassy meadows,' Odysseus's skeptical brain assessed. 'Forget these raunchy, hysterical, emotional female dumb-clits! Could I somehow be near rational men possessing logical human speech? Well, come on now; I'm going to have to find-out this weird conundrum all by myself.'

With those all-too-nebulous thoughts, Odysseus crept-out of the thicket. In his strong hands, the veteran wanderer snapped-off a leafy branch from a nearby bush to hold across and conceal his impressive, naked groin area. Then, stepping forward, the slightly-embarrassed itinerant king emerged from the thicket, moving just like a stealthy mountain lion relying on its own cunning and strength. That's precisely how clever Odysseus was making his way out of the brush to face those fair-haired, lesbian girls, whom his instinct believed to be warlike Amazon fanatics.

The pathetic castaway, being mostly nude, was in dire psychological distress; but, caked with sea brine, the trespasser was an absolute fearful sight to the chatty lesbians, when after also being startled, Odysseus dropped his foliage camouflage and thus exposed his limp, foot-long, dangling dingle.

The delirious servants ran-off in fear, and anxiously crouched-down here and there among the jutting sand dune and beach cactus, thus piecing their delicate assholes along with their sensitive, dipshit pubic lip slits. The only one who did not rush-away was Alcinous's appalled and hypnotized only daughter.

So, the recent visitor to Phaeacian shores quickly used his legendary cunning and spoke to Nausicaa with soothing language, but the lesbian girl stood motionless and stared wonderingly at Odysseus's awesome, dangling fadorkenbender.

"Oh, you divine chubby beauty queen; I come here as a harassed and bewildered suppliant seeking your pity. Are you an exotic goddess, or an erotic mortal being?" the eccentric castaway praised. "If you're one of the gods who hold status in wide heaven, I think that you most resemble huntress Artemis (Diana), daughter of great Zeus, by mere virtue of your loveliness, your stature, and your oddball portly shape. If you're human, and since I'm a confirmed fibber who often prevaricates, I insist that your parents are thrice-blessed, and thrice-blessed are your shit-eating brothers, too, if you're lucky to have any male jerk-offs in your family," Odysseus wildly exaggerated.

"Your Greek sounds like absolute geek to me," Nausicaa criticized. "What's that salami hanging between your legs? It looks like pregnant pepperoni!"

"In their warm hearts, your lucky parents must glow like candles with pleasure for you always, when their delighted eyes see a child, such as yourself, moving-up into the adult phase of the life dance. But the happiest heart, more so buoyant than all the rest, belongs to the lucky groom who, with his stellar wedding gifts, will lead you home to merrily feed your hungry black cat," Odysseus stupidly joked. "These eyes of mine have never gazed upon anyone like you, either fruitcake man or vegetable woman. As my gaze marvels at the magnitude of your fantastic pulchritude, I'm gripped with ethereal wonder."

"What the fuck are you talking about?" Nausicaa yelled back. "A farting asshole makes more common sense than your phony lingo does!"

Odysseus was not deterred by his listener's brash criticism. "In Delos, I once observed something like this awkward situation," the nervous King of Ithaca proceeded with his peculiar narrative.

"Are you a recently escaped mental patient?" Nausicaa asked. "Your words sound stranger than strange!"

"A palm-tree sapling had grown beside Apollo's sacred altar in Delos," the sea survivor continued his recollection. "I had ventured there, with many others in my illustrious company, to attend a religious pilgrimage, but Fate had planned for me so many forthcoming Zeus-forsaken troubles. But when my eyes noticed that very special shrine, my understanding became quite astonished," Odysseus explained to the disinterested girl.

"Are you one of those nutcase greenies I often hear about?" Nausicaa asked. "The environment is perfectly okay without you' idealistic assholes and your destructive ideas ruining my general happiness!"

"I had never before perceived such a lovely tree springing from the Earth," Odysseus continued his boring monologue about his experience in Delos. "And, fair damsel, that's how I'm amazed at your fabulous facial and physical appearance; I'm lost in wonder, and very much afraid to clasp your knee. Do you perform oral sex? My conscience will not permit me to get laid with a hefty heifer, but I desperately need a decent blowjob."

"Listen to me, you dumb-ass mendicant randomly deposited upon this country's coastline," Nausicaa lividly replied. "Tell me some more fascinating bullshit so that I can get colitis and shit all of the constipation out of my anus hole."

"A great distress has recently overtaken me," Odysseus, still naked, proceeded to articulate. "Just yesterday, my twentieth day afloat upon the savage sea, I had miraculously escaped the wine-dark wrath of enraged Poseidon and his devastating Trident. Before that encounter, massive waves and swift-driving storm winds carried me from Calypso's Island of Ogygia to where I stand right this moment. And now, another anonymous, demented god has tossed me onto shore here, so that somehow, I'll suffer a litany of mysterious hardships in this strange location as well," the plagued traveler attempted to explain.

'You're so full of shit that you must have more than one asshole!" Nausicaa suspected and stated. "I guess, at least three!"

"For you see, fair young lady. I don't think my progression of problems will end right now. But, divine area queen, or whoever the hell you are, have bountiful mercy on my unenviable circumstance. You're the first mortal I've approached, after so much grief, and I do not know any prominent people living in your seemingly barbaric land."

"How can I render assistance?" naïve Nausicaa asked. "Do you need a good spanking? I sometimes randomly practice sadism and masochism, you know!"

"Kind child; help me by showing the direction of the nearest town. Give me some oily rag to throw around my personals, perhaps some useful wrapping you had brought for the clothes when you came here to wash," pleaded Odysseus. "As for you, despite my lack of heavenly influence, may the whimsical gods grant everything that your heart and ovaries desire. May you achieve a serene husband with a massive dingle, a luxurious mansion, and mutual harmony and melody with the two of you singing in your temple choir."

Skeptical, white-armed Nausicaa then replied:

"Mentally challenged Stranger; you don't seem to be a wicked or perverted heterosexual. Olympian Zeus himself gives happiness to both bad and worthy men, each one receiving just what Zeus desires them to deal with. But now you have reached our backwards land and primitive city. Despite our inferior education system and obsolete culture, we are aware of the gods' Law of the Suppliants, and we feel especially obligated to render aid and comfort to all visitors to our land who seek food, clothing and shelter before resuming their stupid-shit travels," Nausicaa divulged. "I'll gladly show you directions to the town, and I'll tell you the name our country bears, for we are the isolated Phaeacians, residing in antiquated Phaeacia. As for me, I am the daughter of the national criminal-politician, King Alcinous, and unfortunately, Phaeacian power and strength depend upon his warped brain and his reprehensible judgment."

When Nausicaa abruptly finished speaking, the naughty daughter of King Alcinous and Queen Arete called-out to her fair-haired attendants, still practicing sixty-nine in the dense beach bushes.

"Stand-up, you proud lesbians. Have you run-off because for the first time, you've seen a grown man's dangling dingle? Surely, you don't think he is our well-endowed contemptible enemy? So, girls, give this stranger adequate food and drink. Bathe his foreign ass and testicles in yonder river; select a calm place which offers our guest some nice shelter from the blustery wind."

Nausicaa briskly finished dictating the specific instructions to her obedient gay servants. The entire company stood-up in the bushes and called-out their mistress's command to one another. The garrulous troop took Odysseus aside and escorted their sandy guest to a sheltered spot, and two at a time, performed quality fellatio on the very happy fellow. In fact, one of the more proficient and talented servants, identified as Connie Lingus, was able to perform true to her name.

Then, after thoroughly enjoying their new-found pleasure, the gay dolls set-out appropriate clothing for the sea survivor to wear; a cloak and tunic; and next the bitches gave their new friend a gold flask full of smooth olive oil so that grateful Odysseus could wake-up oily the next morning. The blithe contingent advised the displaced king to bathe in the flowing river in order for his massive erection to shrink-down to its normal, limp, foot-long length.

When the castaway had washed himself all over and rubbed-on the soothing oil, Odysseus dressed into his newly-acquired clothes. The young girls gazed at him in wonder, imagining what it would feel like having his long, thick manhood penetrating their eager-beaver vaginas.

Without further delay, Nausicaa and several of her lesbian companions climbed-up onto the donkey cart, and then the driver shouted-down:

"Get-up off your ass now, muscular Stranger, and venture into the town. I'll show you the way to my wise-ass, er, I mean my wise father's house, where, I assure you, you'll get to meet all the finest jerk-off power brokers of Phaeacia. You seem to me to have a sophisticated, cultural background, so I suggest that you urgently act as follows. While we are moving through the countryside, past many farms, and past bulls and cows copulating in their muddy pastures, walk fast alongside my faithful attendants, directly behind the stubborn mules and the antiquated wagon. I'll cautiously lead the way from my position on the driver's bench."

"Can't I sit inside the wagon with you and enjoy the scenery much more?" Odysseus protested. 'I didn't grow a donkey dick simply by walking behind a donkey cart, you know!"

"No, you totally ungrateful suppliant!" Nausicaa rather sternly reprimanded. "You'll walk past a fine olive grove to meet and communicate with the goddess Athena. Don't ask me how I've come to know this esoteric bullshit! The grove, situated near the road, is planted next to a clump of popular poplar trees. There's a dysfunctional fountain, with lush meadows abounding all around it. My father has a fertile vineyard at that remote place, within a mile's shouting distance from the town. I know all of this absurd family vineyard nonsense simply because I heard it through the grapevine."

Nausicaa then decisively cracked her shiny black whip, striking the docile mules, and quickly left the area of the flowing river. The donkey wagon moved briskly forward at a rapid pace. Using her judgment and noteworthy skill, the girl steadfastly and slowly drove ahead, so Odysseus and her talkative servants had to trot forward and keep-up on foot. Just at sunset, the contingent reached the celebrated grove, wholly sacred to Pallas Athene. Odysseus sat-down there and quickly made a prayer, appealing to great Zeus's daughter for assistance.

Chapter 7

"ODYSSEUS AT THE COURT OF ALCINOUS"

Lord Odysseus, who had endured so much tribulation, prayed there at the groovy grove, while two strong mules transported Nausicaa and her entourage back to her father's palatial home. Then, after successfully lighting a fire and offering a sacrifice of a dozen overripe oranges to Athena, Odysseus got-up from his knees and set-off on foot for the designated town, finally making his way to erudite King Alcinous's splendid mansion. The Phaeacians, men with dense eye cataracts who were celebrated for their armada of merchant ships, did not see the new pedestrian's approach into the tranquil city, mostly because Pallas Athene would not permit such observation or surveillance to occur. In her heart, the radiant goddess truly cared for the besieged Ithacan King, so Zeus's daughter defensively cast around her favorite mortal hero a mysterious, mystifying mist.

Above the high-vaulted home of pusillanimous and self-serving King Alcinous, there persisted a fabulous radiance, as if originating from the sun, or the then-visible moon. Bronze walls extended-out well-beyond the threshold in various directions, funneling into resplendent inner sanctuaries.

The entire architecture exhibited an eye-appealing, azure blue, enamel cornice. Gold-plated doors blocked the main entrance from trespassers, especially door-to-door-salesmen, from entering into the well-constructed edifice. The bronze threshold boasted silver doorposts set inside, and the closed portal featured a silver lintel. The handles were of glimmering gold, and on both sides of the entrance door stood solid gold and silver dogs, ageless, immortal creature representations that would not grow old, created by the lame blacksmith god Hephaestus's matchless artistry; the sensational animal statues were specifically designed to symbolically guard and protect the magnificent palace of great-hearted Alcinous.

Lord Odysseus, who had endured so much adversity, stood there and gazed-around in awe. When his heart and eyes had sufficiently marveled at the superlative entrance, the wary visitor, with the help of Athena, moved like a vapor quickly past the threshold, further into the mansion's interior.

The long-suffering King of Ithaca, his form still enveloped in the camouflaging mist that had been poured around him by the benevolent goddess, proceeded through the central hall until his invisible feet came to where Queen Arete and King Alcinous were preoccupied, alternately arm-wrestling and judo flipping. With both his tanned, muscular arms, Odysseus embraced the knees of Arete, who immediately enjoyed a major orgasm as the rush of adrenalin within her system enabled the Queen to easily defeat her husband, with his right-hand slamming and severing-in-half the table being utilized. At that wonderful and outstanding moment, the miraculous mist surrounding the castaway dissolved in a totally magical fashion, and Odysseus's appearance became visible to Nausicaa's slightly-embarrassed royal parents.

All the old-fart Phaeacians who were witnessing the arm-wrestling competition were struck dumbfounded, as the stunned politicians intensely gazed-upon the newcomer, their shallow minds overcome with wonder at the sight of the intrusive alien. Odysseus then made the following unique entreaty:

"Arete, daughter of godlike Rhexenor. I've come to you and to your husband King Alcinous, with my hands embracing your skinny kneecaps, in supplication to you and your benign mercy. I am an exhausted wanderer who has undergone much terrible hardship for ten-long-years all around the volatile Mediterranean Sea. And to those hoary spectators here, I also beg your undivided indulgence."

"What's going on here?" King Alcinous exclaimed. "How did you get through the locked security doors?"

"May the gods grant your other guests happiness in their personal lives," Lord Odysseus proceeded with his introduction, ignoring King Alcinous's concerned inquiry. "May each individual in attendance within this chamber generously pass on abundant riches within their households to all their blessed children, illegitimate bastards and horny bitches, too. And furthermore," Odysseus bullshitted. "May all you noblemen present in this huge room receive the finest honors and awards given by the richer residents of your most excellent city. Please rouse yourselves to heightened pity to help me travel home to my faraway kingdom of Ithaca; for me to get back quickly to my native soil, so that I might right the great evils that prevail within my traduced domain. For a long time now, I've been in great distress and away from friends and my nuclear family, people that I dearly love."

When King Alcinous heard those rather extraordinary words, the gullible asshole stretched out his hand, reaching for Odysseus, not ever suspecting that His Majesty could be successfully being duped by his wise and crafty, uninvited guest. The dim-witted host raised-up his visiting suppliant from the hearth, and asked Lord Odysseus to relax, and later, when the guest had gathered adequate strength, review for the monarch's pleasure his extensive tale of woe. Then, royal Alcinous called-out to his herald:

"Pontonous; please prepare wine in the mixing bowls, and then serve large portions to all people assembled in this hall, so that we may pour libations out to Almighty Zeus, who loves lightning, thunder, tidal waves, blizzards and nasty hurricanes, for Poseidon's brother accompanies all pious suppliants to our isolated island, and allows them to suffer immensely in their separate struggles."

Once Alcinous completed those imperative sentences, Pontonous meticulously prepared fifty-gallons of the honey-sweet wine, and poured-out the precious drops for libation into every extended cup. The gathered connoisseurs mumbled, grunted, and gulped, after falsely making their traditional offering, and quickly chugged-down their fill of the very rare and absolutely delicious wine, the moochers immediately demanding seconds and thirds.

Then, sinus congested King Alcinous addressed the rowdy, drunken revelers:

"You ridiculous Phaeacian government counselors and esteemed kindergarten administrative leaders, pay attention to me, so that I can verbally enunciate the concepts that the heart pounding inside my chest commands. Now that all of you have finished drinking and exchanging irrelevant anecdotes, I advise that you drunken corrupt bastards all return to your individual domiciles and get some much-needed rest."

"When can we have more wine?" an intoxicated old coot loudly asked. "I might not live to see tomorrow!"

"In the morning, we'll summon an assembly with even more of our senile elders in attendance, and we'll entertain this implausible stranger here inside my palatial home, and also sacrifice choice offerings to the apathetic Olympic gods. After that ritualistic travesty is completed, we'll think and assess how we intend to send this scruffy castaway off and away from our responsibility, so that this discouraged stranger, with us escorting him to the docks, without further pain or effort, may reach his native Ithaca, no matter how far distant from here that little-known, son-of-a-bitchin', insignificant island may be."

Antinous paused for a minute, evaluated how his speech was being received, and then proceeded with sharing his non-dynamic commentary.

"Meanwhile, this itinerant fellow, who ironically calls himself 'No Man', should not suffer additional harm or trouble, despite the fact that many of you dangerous dunces would take pleasure in assassinating the bullshitting asshole right here and now. After his return to fictional Ithaca occurs, 'No Man' will more-than-likely undergo explaining all those imaginary things he has so far described, including being given a thorough psychological examination to be performed by the local witchdoctor, or by the most available regional oracle on duty. Destiny, along with the dreaded spinning Fates have wickedly woven fantasies into the thread of this man's most complicated mental fabric, and we must wonder why this dumb-fuck ignoramus was ever born into this horribly deplorable world. However, if a deathless verdict comes-down from heaven, then gods are planning something different than my miniature brain can essentially theorize."

"The gods are indeed unpredictable," Queen Arete chimed-in. "As unpredictable as common earthquakes, typhoons, tsunamis and volcanic eruptions!"

"So far, the evasive and unpredictable gods occasionally show themselves to us in their true form, when we cleverly offer-up to their statues a well-received sacrifice," King Antinous lectured. "The divine deities sometimes invisibly dine with us, sitting in the very chairs where we park our fat asses upon. If someone traveling all by himself meets those immortal entities that we fearfully worship, the singular gods often don't hide their true identities, because we are close relatives of their genetics, just like the Cyclopes and the wild tribes of Crazy Giants that reside in caves all over the fucked-up Mediterranean. The only major difference between the Olympians and us is that the dirty knuckleheads have mastered the secret of what constitutes nectar and ambrosia, and we stupid earthly shits don't even have a partial clue concerning the nature of that special magic formula. Nor don't we comprehend what the fuck the nectar and ambrosia concoction really is, or even where the two elusive ingredients causing Olympian immortality can be found."

Resourceful Odysseus then answered the confused monarch:

"King Alcinous; you should not concern yourself about what you've just proclaimed, for I'm not like the immortal gods who hold wide heaven; with the exception of the eternally punished Titan known as Atlas, *that* commentary of mine is meant figuratively and not literally, neither in form nor in shape. In truth, I'm both frail and mortal, just like your dimwit senile politicians seated in this vast room happen to be."

"You dare to insult our integrity?" a farting elder challenged. "Finish-up with your jargon before I shit my diaper a third time! You mentioned Atlas! Why the hell didn't you cite the punished Titan Prometheus, also!"

"Indeed, Phaeacians. I could recount a much longer and detailed story when I have mustered the strength to do so; I'll articulate a gruesome tale enumerating all of the tragic hardships I've had to suffer from the ever-vacillating and capricious gods," Odysseus elaborated. "But first, allow me to peacefully eat my dinner, and although my tortured mind is in great distress, my stomach is extremely famished. For there's nothing more shameless than an unhappy growling belly, which compels a man to seriously think about his indispensable biological needs, even if one's spirit is enduring harsh excruciation; yet, a man must eat first, and reveal descriptions and explanations after."

"Well then, when can we hear your entire story?" King Alcinous demanded knowing. "I hope it's much better and more intriguing than your lackluster preface!"

"Kind Phaeacians; when dawn appears, I will relate my myriad calamities to you. Then, after hearing my incredible, lengthy adventure, you can stir yourselves to send me, in my miserable state, back to my own soil, in spite of all the arduous hardships I've clumsily endured. If I can see my goods, my properties, my slaves, and my large and high-roofed mansion again, then I'll be content to let life end. But I've been away from all of those abstract images for twenty-long-years, and my confused mind conceives all of those matters as perhaps vague, imaginary, contrived; a pauper's many illusions. I presently appeal to your generosity and respect, humbly urging your kindness under Zeus's supreme Law of the Suppliants!"

Once Odysseus finished orating his philosophical elucidation, the naïve, doddering idiots in attendance all approved and applauded his incredible words, and, because the itinerant had spoken so well and so directly to the point, every drunken asshole seated inside the enormous hall of Antinous agreed that their peculiar guest should be assisted and escorted upon his incomparable journey back to his native Ithaca.

Jay Dubya

Chapter 8

"ODYSSEUS IS ENTERTAINED IN PHAECIA"

The following afternoon, King Alcinous addressed his chief government officials and clumsily stuttered to the distinguished-but-corrupt Phaeacians:

"Listen to my review of recent developments, you risk-taking Phaeacian counselors and leaders. I'll tell you what the heart in my chest says, even though the organ has no throat or voice-box. This wayward stranger here, a fellow who yesterday described himself as 'No Man', I do not personally know. I believe that our guest is a world wanderer who might be conveying to us the truth about his voyage here. No Man is asking us our cooperation and mercy to help him to be sent away, back to his uncharted native island, and our inimitable visitor wishes us to grant him his unprecedented request under Zeus's Suppliants Law. So royal officials, let us act as we have never done before with anyone else, and assist No Man to diligently continue along on his intended journey."

"If the weirdo stranger identifies himself as "No Man', is he some kind of female, or transgender, or neuter, or perhaps a tri-gender?" Queen Arete asked her regal husband. "Does the drifter ever use the pronoun 'he'?"

"No man arriving at my palace, including 'No Man', stays for very long, grieving about not getting back home," Alcinous explained to his inquisitive wife. "I'll make my position on this major agenda matter quite short and sweet. If any subject or topic ever unnerves and disturbs me, it's a groaning grown man crying his tear ducts right-out of his bony skull. I mean, we have to get rid of this 'No Man' character because taking care of him might be the start of a debilitating welfare system; an unnecessary tax burden on all of us businessmen!"

Alcinous spoke and soon led the smaller-sceptered regional kings in discussing the very strange matter. A herald was dispatched to find the missing forgetful singer so that the committee's decision could be captured in both song and history.

Meanwhile, fifty-two hand-picked young men were inanely assigned to scamper-off to the city's distant shore. Once the selected sailors had reached their appointed merchant ship, the chosen crew dragged the black vessel out to deeper water, set the mast and sails in place inside the boat, lashed the rowing oars onto their leather pivots, and then hoisted the standard friendly white sail. That being done, the fledgling mariners moored the ship well out to sea, and then upon completing that elementary task, returned to the great home of King Alcinous. Luckily, the singing minstrel had by accident remembered his scheduled gig and found his way back to King Alcinous's palace.

Hallways, corridors, and courtyards were full of curious residents; the assembled dunces forming a massive crowd comprised of both young and old curious dolts. On their behalf, Alcinous had his regal butcher slaughter eight white-tusked boars, two shambling oxen, and twelve prized sheep.

Those twenty-two prodigious carcasses were carefully skinned and dressed, and then the palace chefs prepared a spectacular banquet for all present to partake. In the interim, the neurotic herald entered the premises, accompanied by the pompous, blind singer, a performer who was particularly loved by the melodic demigod Muse, above all other effeminate male sopranos. The herald, Pontonous, next brought-in a silver-studded chair with a circular hole in its center, which served a dual function of being King Alcinous's favorite seat, and also his favorite hopper.

After the rowdy congregation enjoyed their heart's fill of food and drink, the minstrel Demodocus, inspired by the immortal lyric critic Muse, sang about the glorious deeds of Greek warriors, especially about Odysseus and Achilles, son of Peleus, who had lost his life after his exposed heel/tendon had been lethally penetrated by a sharp Trojan arrow.

When the last morsels of the great array of meat had been consumed, the noble Phaeacians ventured outside upon the expansive, well-kept lawn, and the young men participated in a number of difficult individual competitions. Odysseus astounded all of the local athletes with his superior skill in throwing the discus across the city and embedding the heavy orb into a distant high mountain peak. After the preliminary games had terminated, Alcinous called for a large gathering, where the jovial Phaeacians could demonstrate their unique dancing ability, along with chanting a medley of oddball musical renditions.

Nine incompetent officials, who regularly specialized in organizing each detail of the absent-minded king's meetings, rose from their seats, smoothed-off a dancing space, and then marked-out a circumcised circumference. The hoarse herald stepped-up to the circle, and the raspy-voiced announcer was carrying the clear-toned lyre for fretful vocalist Demodocus to slowly strum.

Around the acclaimed singer stood a dozen pre-pubescent boys in the first bloom of youth; small-peckered, but relatively skillful dancers, whose dainty feet then stuck to the semen-laden, animal blood-strewn, recently-consecrated dance floor. Odysseus marveled at how rapidly those young boys in leotards could move their prancing feet, despite all of the recently ejaculated semen and disgusting dropped animal blood under their sandals.

The minstrel struck the opening chords to his complicated song, and sang about how Aphrodite had been married to the ugly blacksmith god Hephaestus; how the fair-crowned Aphrodite, goddess of love and beauty, lusted for the war god Ares; how in Hephaestus's own volcanic, lava-laden, subterranean abode, Aphrodite and the ugly blacksmith god first had secret sex, and how Ares, the god of war, gave Aphrodite many gifts, while the hostile war deity disgraced the marriage bed of Lord Hephaestus, forcing the goddess of love and beauty to give-up her private business, the very lucrative Aphro-dite Diaper Service.

But then, the trouble-making sun god Helios's spying observed the unlikely pair (Ares and Aphrodite) making love, and the tattle-taler hurried at once to tell disfigured Hephaestus of the illicit love affair. When the god of the forge heard the unwelcome news, the lame listener went to his underground foundry, angrily turning copper and tin over deep inside his furnace, and in a matter of hours, Hephaestus had creatively forged a heavy-duty net that neither mortal nor immortal could ever break or loosen. And the ensnarled victims of the net would have to stay immobile and inactive at the blacksmith god's constant, peeved discretion.

When, in his wild rage, Hephaestus had finished the encumbering snare, designed to trap and incapacitate Ares and Aphrodite, the livid personage entered into the honeymoon room, which housed his and Aphrodite's marriage bed, and the vengeful lame blacksmith adroitly anchored the metal netting around the high bed posts. The crazed lover next hung loops from sturdy ceiling beams above, the net being as intricate in design as the finest possible spider's web.

Once the livid, red-skinned anvil hammerer had set the whole snare in place above the honeymoon bed, according to the minstrel's song, Hephaestus loudly announced to Mt. Olympus that he would be taking an unscheduled trip to Lemnos, a well-built citadel that was his favorite retreat.

Seeing his immortal rival depart to Lemnos, wily Ares rushed over to Hephaestus's below-ground dwelling, eager to again have passionate adulterous sex with fair-crowned Aphrodite. The goddess of love and beauty had just left the presence of her father Zeus, and was sitting-down upon a soft-cushioned lounge chair. Ares charged inside the underground dwelling, and anxiously grabbed Aphrodite by the hand.

"Come, my dear; let's go together to bed and make insane, hog-snorting love together. Hephaestus is not home, and I'm hornier than Hades, both the god and the place. No doubt your hideous-looking husband has gone to visit Lemnos and communicate with the pornographic Sintians; yes, those evil creatures who speak like barbarians and who sloppily and ravenously eat luscious pussy like demented cannibals."

To lustful Aphrodite, having sex with Ares seemed quite delightful when compared to having any kind of intercourse (including verbal) with Hephaestus. So, the in-heat duo raced-off to bed and lay-down together. But then the metallic net that had been craftily fabricated by Hephaestus's great skill collapsed around the horny adulterers, so the immortal sinners could not maneuver their limbs, shift their bodies and genitals, or even move their smelly bowels. After a while, the trapped twosome finally realized that neither of them could possibly escape their very tight, confining entanglement.

Upon his returning to the screaming scene of marital infidelity, Lord Hephaestus stood inside the bedroom doorway, and gripped by ascending rage, the jilted husband yelled-out a dreadful cry to lofty Olympus, shouting to all the bored and disinterested gods: "Father Zeus, and you other narrow-minded, so-called sacred gods who live forever; come witness what has transpired within my modest volcano residence. Ares, the destroyer of cities and civilization, is quite handsome, having healthy limbs, while I had been born deformed and grotesque. I'm not to blame for my hideous appearance that has even frightened Medusa the Gorgon, and has made the snakes jump like grasshoppers out of her terrible, dandruff-infected scalp."

Sensing a dire emergency, the gods quickly gathered inside the bronze-floored Mt. Olympus Whorehouse Temple. Earthshaker Poseidon arrived, and speedy Lord Hermes, too. The archer and golden chariot god Apollo was the third to answer Hephaestus's call of anguish. But the female goddesses were all far-too-modest, afraid, and ashamed to participate in indicting fellow female Aphrodite, so the ravishing beauties stayed at a distance.

Hermes attested that Ares's misdeed should be punished, and Apollo agreed, saying that Hephaestus was a more important deity than was Ares because the abused blacksmith god had constructively made all of the swords, shields, sandals, helmets and other valued materials for the other key Olympians.

So, in conclusion, according to the minstrel's recollection, the male gods honored the shared statement between Hermes and Apollo, and soon thereafter, everyone on Olympus returned to their normal, everyday monotonous activity, while the punished war god was forced to spend several future peaceful centuries aimlessly ambling about the lackluster streets and alleys of a foreign city called Buenos Ares.

Then, Lord Odysseus, originally disguised as and professing to be "No Man", was cordially requested to address the relatively enthusiastic gathering:

"Mighty Alcinous, Queen Arete, and most distinguished officials among all men in this unparalleled land; you claimed that your dancers were the best in the known world, and now, indeed, what you have indicated is indisputably true. When I gazed at the effeminate faggots, er, I mean 'talented boys' dancing with the stars, I was lost in wonder, thinking that I'm watching a pack of graceful human gazelles having queer aerial sex in full motion."

At Odysseus's exaggerated and phony words, powerful King Alcinous felt a great delight, and at once commanded strict imperatives to his Phaeacian master sailors.

"Leaders and counselors of us illiterate Phaeacians; listen intently, even though there are no tents in this room in which to hear any fuckin' thing being mentioned. This remarkable Stranger possessing 'No Name' seems to me to be a rare mortal specimen exhibiting an uncommon wisdom that evidently transcends life itself. So, come now; let's give him our offer of friendship, as is only right and proper," Alcinous insisted. "As we all know, with the exception of eminent 'No Man' here, twelve honorable kings are rulers in our land and govern it inefficiently, and I myself, of course, am the lucky thirteenth, making us a unique baker's dozen. Let each one of us loyal patriots donate a fresh cloak and tunic, newly washed, and a money-exchange talent of pure gold for the benefit of our honored guest's departure from our jagged shores. All of this civic duty we should put together very quickly; our immediate preparation is to be rendered so that this nomadic stranger has his honorable gifts in hand, and meanders-off to dinner and wine with a joyful heart."

All those adult dolts present in the large room agreed with Lord Alcinous's stupidity, and consented that the thirteenth king's proposal should swiftly be executed, and not "No Man". Then, every one of the pecker-head aristocrats assigned a personal valet to find and bring forward the castaway's redundant clothes and money presents to be used at sea.

As the hot sun went-down in the western sky, the splendid gifts were carried-in and taken to Alcinous's spacious meeting room by worthy-unheralded heralds.

Nausicaa, whose incomparable fat ass was a horrendous-looking gift from the gods, stood inside the exit door of that well-built hall and stared at Odysseus, feeling a genuine sense of wonder. The portly teenager was compelled to utter winged words to him:

"Farewell, fair Stranger with the lengthy, impressive dangling dingle. Once you have successfully returned to your own distant country, I sincerely hope you'll occasionally remember me, since you owe me your fuckin' life."

Then Odysseus, presently masquerading as that fantastically resourceful fellow "No Man", candidly replied to the obese lesbian girl's audacious opinion.

"Nauseating Nausicaa, daughter of great orator King Alcinous and laconic Queen Arete; may Hera's loud-thundering husband, Zeus, grant that I see the day of my return when I eventually arrive at my native land to reclaim what is rightfully mine. There, I will pray to your happiness all my days, as I would to a god. For you, fat girl, your solicited sacrifices indeed saved me my beleaguered life; for I'm a traveling man, who has made a lot of stops, all over the known world!"

Completing his perfunctory remarks, Odysseus finished speaking and casually smiled. Then, the honored guest sat his ass down upon a soft chair right beside gas-farting King Alcinous, as Demodocus, who was inspired by the god Apollo, resumed singing his story at the point where the plundering Greeks, having burned their beachhead huts and ascended on board their well-oared ships, were sailing-off, away from Troy.

Magnificent warriors, led by glorious Odysseus, were furtively hidden inside the already-fabled wooden "Trojan Horse". City guards had hauled the massive structure inside the gates near King Priam's Palace, their "impregnable citadel". While groups of idle soldiers sat and conversed around the huge artificial equine, the guards were confused about exactly what they should do with the weird "gift from the gods". Three quite very different options existed in making their final decision.

The first was to split the hollow, wooden stomach apart with pitiless bronze swords. The second choice was to drag the heavy structure over to the distant cliffs and push the Wooden Horse from the heightened rocks into the sea. And the third method of disposing of the eyesore monstrosity was to let the awesome artifact stay inside the city gates and be worshipped as a superb offering to the Olympian gods. The impressive object would serve as a wonderful shrine that would assuage Zeus's notorious anger against mortals everywhere. And that third decision is precisely what the indiscreet fools finally agreed upon, for it was their ultimate fate to be totally obliterated once the military clowns had pulled within their city walls the gigantic Wooden Horse, inside which lay hidden all the finest Greek heroes. Obviously, Troy was doomed to inevitable death, collapse, and historic devastation.

Then, after reviewing his popular song version of the demise of Troy, the bard Demodocus proceeded to sing about how the bold Achaean warriors had left their hollow hiding place, lowered their bodies upon a rope hanging from the horse's interior, and easily overpowered the drunken guards, thereafter opening the city gates and allowing thousands of Greek soldiers to swarm into doomed Troy and wildly plunder the wealthy Asia Minor metropolis.

The bard maintained that the hero Odysseus, in a similar fashion to Ares's quarrel with the ugly blacksmith Hephaestus, went to the home of Deiphobus, where, the ferocious King of Ithaca engaged in a most-horrendous fight. The Greek swordsman emerged victorious, thanks to assistance received from Pallas Athene, who truly admired her champion's integrity and courage.

Odysseus, still role-playing the assembly scene as anonymous "No Man", was moved to sob and weep as the wayward warrior recalled his participation in destroying Troy by designing and inventing the legendary Wooden Horse. But "No Man" kept his tears well-hidden from the oblivious Phaeacians; that is, all except Alcinous, who, as the respected city leader sat there beside anonymous "No Man", and the King was the only individual sitting in the mosquito-infested chamber who had perceptively noticed his esteemed visitor sobbing and weeping honest-to-goodness sighs.

So, the observant lucky thirteenth king spoke-out, firmly addressing his "Old Salt" Phaeacians, ardent lovers of the sea:

"Listen to me speak, you lunatic Phaeacian counselors, and you listless lethargic leaders. Let talented Demodocus now cease from playing his clear-toned lyre, for the song he's singing does not please all his listeners in attendance at this exceptional conference. Since our godlike minstrel was first moved to sing, as we were dining like starving gluttons, our visiting guest has been in emotional pain, and his mournful sniffling has never stopped. 'No Man's heart, I think, surely overflows with grief in his recollection of the falling of Troy. Some of you might suspect that 'No

Man' is sorrowed because his people had been allied with the Trojans, but I'm inclined to truly believe the reverse, opposite scenario."

All of the gathered city noblemen, like typical, low intelligence politicians, enthusiastically applauded King Alcinous's supreme words. The thirteenth ruler didn't hesitate to continue his extraordinary oration.

"Please tell me your actual name, 'No Man'. What do your people call you inside your residence: your mother, your father, and the assumed others in your' nuclear family. Explicitly, reveal to us dumb-dicks assembled in this chamber of your country and of your people, and of your city, too, so that a sea-worthy Phaeacian ship can transport you there, using what available maps we've acquired to chart your passage."

"I promise to tell your assembly everything," pledged Odysseus. "Gosh; I truly wish I knew everything, but I don't! But I shall tell you some-things I remember!"

"And now 'No Man', divulge to us all the pertinent information, and calmly speak the truth. I learned in pre-school that the word 'travel' is derived from the word 'travail'. Where have you journeyed and where have you visited while suffering-through your perpetual wandering?" Antinous asked. "Before I recommend that you be provided a ship transport back to your native island, I demand to know what other fucked-up countries have you toured? Please describe to us all of the people and all of their well-built towns you've personally experienced in your abundant adventures and near-death misadventures; whether those cultures are cruel, unjust, and wild, or if the other unknown places you've visited welcome strangers, and if the inhabitants fear the same gods as we do within their mortal hearts and souls."

Chapter 9

THE LOTUS EATERS"

Resourceful Odysseus then replied to Alcinous:
"Lord King, most renowned of local men; I say that there's nothing that provides one more delight than when joy seizes entire groups of drunken men who sit in proper order within a massive hall; feasting, farting, belching, and enjoying the lyrics of a talented minstrel. Indeed, fine tables have been presented throughout this stately chamber, laden with bread, fruit and meat," Odysseus commended. "All these provisions transpiring as the well-trained steward draws wine out of the ten-gallon mixing bowls, moves around, and pours the tasteful liquid into our empty cups. To me, this stellar arrangement seems the finest thing there is that is practiced among mortals."

Odysseus paused for a moment to organize his next thoughts into rational speech. "But now gentle noblemen, or should I say 'noble gentlemen'; your hearts and minds want to ask about my plentitude of grievous sorrows, so I, a grown fellow, can weep and moan more than I had done before. What phenomenal exploits shall I tell you first? Where do I stop? For the heavenly gods have given me so much accumulative distress," Odysseus further related. "Well, I shall begin my preface by telling you my actual birth name. Once you know my true identity, if I escape the painful day of impending death, then later I can welcome you into my kingdom as my honored guests, though I will then be living in a once-majestic palace that is far away from your' more-than-mediocre island."

"Cut the dramatic bullshit," an intoxicated Phaeacian bellowed. "Who the fuck are you?"

"I am the famous Odysseus, son of Laertes, and well-known to all Greek-related civilizations for my deceptive methods and for my accomplished skills. Proudly speaking, my reputation stretches all the way to Heaven, and also down to Hades. I lived in my palace in Ithaca, land of both sunshine and moonshine."

"Everyone in this immense hall has heard of Odysseus," a second unconvinced attendee boomed. "How the hell can we know that you aren't a quack impostor?"

"From far away one's eyes view a scenic mountain there on Ithaca; thick with whispering trees that hold no secrets. Mount Neriton, and many islets lying around its summit, exist close together. It's a rugged landscape, and the fruits and vegetables grown in the hard soil nurture fine young warriors. But now, avid listeners, I'll speak of the unhappy journey I've encountered, which mercurial-minded Zeus, allied with Fate, with the cooperation of that bastard sea-god Poseidon; yes, the three supernatural entities arranged for me a series of very traumatic events when I attempted to return to Ithaca immediately following the ten-year Trojan War."

"How did you manage to piss-off those vindictive deities?" a third listener asked. "You must have a death wish ascending to the tenth power!"

"From plundered Troy, my twelve ships with fifty men rowing on each, were carried by the strong southern wind to Ismarus, land of the bellicose Cicones. My six-hundred warriors raided and destroyed the primitive city, killed many of the fanatical cavemen, seized and screwed their crotch-diseased screaming women, and captured a trove of treasure, which my attentive subordinates eagerly divided-up."

"Then the stories that claim that you Greeks were pirates and looters appear to be absolutely true," a fourth critic yelled. "Why the hell should we trust a plunderer?"

"Don't jump the octopus!" Odysseus sharply countered. "Being democratic, I took great pains in requiring that each soldier should receive an equal share of the booty being distributed. Then, I gave orders that we should speedily leave the accursed land on foot, and fearing retribution from the fickle gods, we evacuated in haste. But my greedy crew was quite foolish. The dumb-shits did not listen to my savvy commands. The stupid fucks drank too much wine, and on the barren, shell-laden shoreline, the zany assholes slaughtered many bleating sheep, as well as wildly shambling the native cows having twisted horns."

"I've heard of these Cicones," King Alcinous interrupted. "Those nasty fucks would eat their own young if hungry!"

"Anyway, the remaining fierce Cicones set-off around their island and gathered-up their nutcase neighbors, barbaric tribesmen living further inland. There were more of those crazed cannibals than there were Cicones, and it is my opinion that the fucked-up cannibals were more awesome and ferocious than were the fucked-up Cicones."

Odysseus ceased speaking for a moment, took a deep breath, and then continued describing his exciting monologue to his captive audience. "As I was about to mention, the dual enemies of wild Cicones and their neighboring wilder cannibals, reached us in the morning, attacking thick as falling leaves, showing-up right near where my' own mother ship had been anchored. One of my more ignorant disciples yelled in defiance at the cannibal aggressors, 'Eat me!' And that's exactly what the hell the hungry, primitive mother-fuckers did. My warriors threw our lethal bronze-tipped spears at the fucked-up cannibals, and the rambunctious idiots began munching and chewing on those weapons, also."

Did you capture any of the perverted cannibals and take them back to Ithaca to be exhibited in a zoo?" King Antinous asked.

"No, dear King. But thank you for disrupting my series of thoughts," Odysseus politely answered with a smile. "While morning lasted, and when that sacred day gained age, we Greeks held our ground and beat the boisterous son-of-a-bitches back into the adjacent forest. But as the sun moved to the hour when oxen are normally unyoked, the very insane, dumb-ass Cicones broke-through our established outer defense perimeter, overpowering a dozen or so valiant Achaeans. Of my well-armed companions, six men from every ship had been killed in the savage melee. The rest of us frantically made our escape, avoiding the dual clutches of invincible Death and Fate."

"How many rowers does one of your boats require?" objectively asked Queen Arete. "Tell us the general name of your twelve warships."

"Two rows of twenty-five on each side," Odysseus informed. "The warship is called a Bireme. My remaining warriors hastily boarded our twelve Biremes and frantically rowed-away from there in a total frenzy. Our hearts were full of grief at losing many of our loyal comrades, though the survivors were happy and thrilled that we had cleverly eluded death ourselves. Cloud-gatherer Zeus then stirred-up the turbulent North Wind to rage against our under-manned dozen vessels."

"How did Zeus get wind of your location?" asked and accidentally punned Alcinous.

"Zeus knows all, and you can't keep any secrets from his omniscience," Odysseus replied. "The cyclonic gusts had produced a howling storm, with its pestering rain and swirls concealing both land and sea. And as darkness swept from heaven down-upon us mariners, every rower aboard my captain's ship was so scared that he emptied his kidneys dry."

"Your story is a real pisser," commended a fifth now-fascinated attendee. "Frankly, I'd be too pooped to pee!"

"Nine days of extremely fierce winds drove our Biremes far away from the charted land of the Cicones, and we floated in the dull doldrums across the fish-filled sea. And on the tenth day, we landed where the infamous Lotus-eaters live. These drug-happy people feed-upon the plant's delicious fruit, which has the ability to put humans into a deep trance, where they refuse to continue their journey, and only wish to stay and eat more Lotus flowers."

"I could use some Lotus flowers right here on Phaeacia," King Alcinous remarked. "I often feel a need to escape reality. Nausicaa is enough to drive me to overdose!"

"Unaware of the flowers' drug-addictive properties," Odysseus proceeded with his oration, "we waded ashore and carried fresh water back to our vessels. Then, my companions quickly had a meal by our swift boats, and several began sampling the very palatable Lotus flowers. We laughed and exchanged short stories and tall tales, enjoying our recently confiscated food that had been stolen from the Cicones. But I noticed that the crewmen who had experimented and eaten the Lotus flowers were no longer present amongst our company," Odysseus communicated to the totally fascinated Phaeacians.

"What happened next?" intrigued King Alcinous wanted to know. "Did you establish a chain of apothecaries or drug labs on other islands?"

"No, Idiot King," Odysseus vehemently replied. "I then sent some of my most capable comrades out to glean vital information about the missing crewmen who had eaten the sweet Lotus food, thinking that the flowers were a fine aphrodisiac that allowed the crewmen to get laid among the island's numerous harlots and prostitutes. I carefully chose two of my best sailors to act as spies, and being of a distrustful nature, I sent a third messenger to spy on the initial two spies."

'Three assholes and better than two," a sixth Phaeacian hollered from the rear. "But quite honestly; I'm just happy having two functioning parallel assholes inside my' rear-end!"

"Anyway," Odysseus resumed his bizarre recollection. "The three assholes left at once and soon engaged the Lotus-eaters, but did not marry them. The tribesmen were rather friendly and had no thought of killing my spying companions, but the village witchdoctor gave my dumb-shit spies sample Lotus plant flowers to eat; an exotic fruit, sweet as honey, which made any man who swallowed the seeds lose his desire to ever journey home, or bring back word of the flowers to us, who did not dare venture into the local village. My fucked-up spies were even more fucked-up because the moronic dunces then wished to stay and idly linger there amongst the unmotivated Lotus-eaters, who in fact were immature, idealistic Flower Children, who were uttering absurd jabberwocky such as 'Make love, and not war'!"

"These Flower Children sound like they're more fucked-up than we are!" laughed King Alcinous. "They might have even been naively singing in chorus, 'Give peace a chance'!"

"And so, dear Phaeacians," Odysseus began to summarize. "Feeding on the alluring plant, many of my foolhardy troops were eager to forget all about their homeward voyage to Ithaca; all about their families and kinky whores, and slutty girlfriends."

"Do you have any Lotus flowers for me to sample?" Antinous asked the semi-annoyed speaker. "I need to mentally escape the weight of my heavy government responsibilities, along with my three-hundred-pound lesbian daughter, nauseating Nausicaa."

"No, Dimwit!" Odysseus angrily answered the airheaded King. "Now, please allow me to continue my fantastic story. I, and my undrugged soldiers, forced our companions, the tearful derelict buffoons back onto the awaiting ships, dragged their asses underneath the rowing benches, and tied the frivolous fucks to the different Biremes' oar locks. Then, I issued orders for my other trusty comrades to embark and sail-away as quickly as possible with the utmost speed, in order to facilitate our rapid departure from that rather enticing land."

Jay Dubya

Chapter 10

"THE CYCLOPS"

"**M**y mariners sailed-away from that dumb-shit island with heavy hearts, and a day's rowing later, our small armada reached the country of the Cyclopes, a totally crude and lawless cabal of ruthless one-eyed giants. The uneducated dumb-fucks don't grow any crops or plants, Lotus, or otherwise, by hand; or plow the Earth, but the tribe of stupid-assholes puts their entire faith and trust in the ever-vacillating, immortal Olympic gods."

"These Cyclopes sound a lot like us!" King Alcinous exclaimed. "There must be dumb-shits all over the world!"

"And although the lackadaisical bastards never sow or work the land, but still, every kind of vegetable and fruit magically springs-up out of the soil for their satisfaction, mostly in the form of wheat and barley, along with rich grape-bearing vines. And Zeus provides the cave-dwellers with sufficient rainfall to enable the various crops to mature and grow all on their own. The isolated tribe lives in rudimentary mountain-top caverns, without any council to make community laws and moral decisions."

"Sounds like Nausicaa belongs on their fucked-up island," Alcinous evaluated and stated. "I suppose that lesbians are taboo there, too!"

"Each of the one-eyed Cyclopes establishes his own family laws for himself, for his own wife, and for his children, and the entire culture, or lack thereof, shuns all civil dealings with each other, and also, ignores all contact with the outside world."

"I've heard of this primitive tribe you're describing!" Alcinous remembered and related. "The story goes that an eye doctor was once unfortunately stranded on that formidable island. The cannibalistic tribe sacrificed his ass to the Rainbow Goddess Iris, just before attaching the doomed physician to a hand-cranked, rotating barbecue rotisserie!"

"Now, King Alcinous, after a week of listless drifting at sea, my crew of 'don't-give-a-shit' sailors arrived at the island of the Cyclopes, giant lawless hermits that lived in virtually inaccessible mountain caves. The Cyclopes were illiterate, and never read about themselves in en*cyclope*dias. The mammoth, one-eyed idiots never planted crops or plowed their fields because the assholes were basically lazy, worthless, and indolent shit-heads.

And worst of all, the immortal giants reputedly ate men, but ironically, were not homosexual, but generally celibate, and incidentally, to my knowledge, never ate pussy, either. Although immortal, the race also consumed wild grapes, wheat and barley that grew without any cultivation. That was their basic problem. The Cyclopes lived without cultivation, neither agricultural nor even cultural cultivation. But Lord Poseidon always provided the heinous creatures with ample nectar and ambrosia, conveniently stolen from Mt. Olympus. The Cyclopes voraciously ate the nectar and ambrosia, not knowing what the foods actually do!"

"Humans should keep an eye out for these vicious monsters when voyaging the sea," Alcinous realized and stated. "Perhaps even keep two eyes out would be a better approach!"

"However, in all due respect, King Alcinous, the Cyclopes did learn how to make grape juice, mixing it with semen to have a nice white froth resembling *head* on a cold mug of beer. This outlandish concoction the Cyclopes drank morning, noon and night, so each of the one-eyed monsters always had what looked like a milk mustache showing above his upper lip that in actuality, really was a 'semen cocktail' mustache instead'."

"Inform us more about the Cyclopes civilization, or lack thereof," Queen Arete asked the guest storyteller. "My moronic husband can't understand that if he kept both eyes out for the Cyclops, then my spouse would also be blind!"

"As had been alluded, the Cyclopes had no laws, no councils, no judges or courts, no government, no schools, no Bingo halls, and no legislatures, so in many respects, the ogres were much better off than fucked-up civilized men were. Each Cyclopes was a government unto himself', and the dangerous assholes never helped each other and were often arrogant, antagonistic neighbors. As a result, each Cyclopes had to live a good distance from any others of *his* species; otherwise, the loose society would self-destruct within a year's time. I make no reference to any female Cyclopes, but I have to believe that women existed among that peculiar colony of one-eyed creatures, simply in order to reproduce the idiotic race, evolving from generation to generation."

"What happened when your mother ship landed there?" interrogated a Phaeacian listener. "Did you receive a crazed, hostile reception?"

"Now, I observed that a fertile islet that remarkably wasn't pregnant had been situated about a half-mile from the lawless Cyclopes' Island. I commanded that *my* twelve ships be anchored off that smaller wooded territory, and my guileful mind planned on raiding a cave or two on the larger island to do what we ancient Greeks knew best: pilfer, plunder, pillage, and possibly pedophile little nude, unwary boys and girls."

"Were there any grazing animals to steal?" a second Phaeacian asked. "You suggested that these barbarian Cyclopes had a certain herd mentality."

"Yes; there was a multitude of goats grazing upon the smaller wooded island. The Cyclopes were too stupid to invent or build boats to sail the half-mile distance to bag the wild goats, and the imbeciles were too ignorant to ever attempt to learn how to swim, or even how to wade across the shallow harbor. Fresh water streams abounded on the 'goat island', but the dumb-shit Cyclopes were content living in misery on their less abundant, larger island, and killing and eating their fellow uncivilized cavemen whenever the opportunity presented itself, or whenever the food supply ran short."

"Odysseus; please continue with your very fascinating story," the Phaeacian King instructed. "I'm especially intrigued with gory details involving one-eye monster tales!"

"This looks like a fine island to beach our ships and to search for food and water, I told my second mate, Eurballsourout. We're now safe, as long as there are no fucked-up, hostile human residents dwelling here."

"Don't bother me when I'm trying to flirt-with and feel-up your first mate!" Eurballsourout, the second mate answered me. "Eurshiddenme is really pretty well-endowed!"

"Are you shittin' me?" I challenged Eurballsourout."

"No; my friggin' name is Eurballsourout," the second mate replied. "Eurshiddenme is your goddamned first mate! You oughta' know that common-knowledge bullshit by now!"

"I suppose that when no women are available over the course of many months, men are inclined to become horny homos!" the second alert Phaeacian listener spoke-out to me."

"Now then, most eminent King and Queen. That first morning in the uncharted area, *my crew* and I left the other eleven ships to explore the smaller island for food and water. The troop carried their spears, and bows and arrows, and divided into three *bands* that sang and danced to mediocre Greek folk songs. It was hard labor shooting the wild goats while singing and doing ancient Greek versions of *vaudeville*-type dance routines, so finally my men quieted-down so that the fags were able to stealthily sneak-up upon their intended prey and quickly zap them."

"Altogether, kind King, the hunting expeditions had killed a hundred and eight goats, and then the merry men from all twelve ships feasted, drinking sacks of wine they had stolen from the Cicones, a city of imbeciles *they* had recently marauded and plundered. The Greeks had obtained the 'sacks' of sweet mellow wine when the marauders had thoroughly *sacked* the entire city. Then they 'ran' away. That's how the soldiers had effectively *ransacked* the victimized Cicones' one and only town. But my macho warriors managed to kill most of the village people!"

"From the smaller island, my men could see the campfires glowing inside the Cyclopes' caves, a half-mile distant. I called a military council meeting the next morning to organize a raid on the unsuspecting, dumb-ass Cyclopes, who all didn't care a tiny shit about the outside world, or give a damn if they or anybody else lived, starved, disintegrated or died."

"Stay safe here on this magical island," I had instructed my other eleven crews earlier that morning, before I and *my* vanguard from *my* ship paid a visit to that larger, inhabited land situated over yonder. "I want to determine if the natives are uncivilized savages, or cunning and detestable civilized barbarians like we are."

"Now your story is getting to a climax," a Phaeacian sex pervert in the back remarked. "What happened next?"

"My special bodyguards and I boarded a sleek commando landing vessel, and after loosening the hawser ropes that had been used for mooring the boat, the team clandestinely rowed to the land of the Cyclopes, with visions of committing theft by looting, if random experimental conniving and ordinary trickery failed. After anchoring our landing boat in a remote harbor that was obscured by rocky cliffs, our hit squad of daring attackers furtively climbed-up the steep mountain ridge to an area where we could clearly view an unoccupied cave."

King Alcinous cautioned his councilmen to stop asking preposterous questions, and stated that the idiots should just sit and evaluate Odysseus's spellbinding testimony. "Queen Arete and I will be the only ones allowed to ask questions from here on out," the restless monarch announced. "Now tell us everything your brain recalls from paragraph-to-paragraph!"

"Look at the size of that chair inside that hollow up there!" I lowly marveled to my first mate. "Whatever creature lives there must be as big and as tall as Zeus himself'."

"Yes, Captain," agreed Eurshiddenme, my needed-to-be-castrated first mate. "The monster's dick is probably longer and larger than any of us are tall and wide. The salami on that huge fuck must be a real monstrosity!"

"The cave dweller might not be a human being at all!" Eurballsourout, the second mate, speculated and opined. "He might be half-beast and only part human! The asshole might be even more genetically and mentally fucked-up than we are!"

"Listen men! If you enter into that tall cave, some of you might never see your wives or your children again!"

"The crew-members all looked at each other and shrugged their brawny shoulders. None of them desired to ever want to see their fat ugly wives, or their bratty, parasitic kids ever again, and would gladly die first in a dark cave on an unknown island at the hands of a cruel, indiscriminate brute/monster."

"Listen to this next part, patient Phaeacians. I had selected my twelve 'best men', none of whom were ever in any wedding party, to accompany me the last hundred-feet up to the ominous hollow. The guests' had brought along a goatskin filled with sweet-tasting wine, which had been given to me by Maron, a priest of Apollo, after I had threatened to castrate Maron if *he* did not present a favorable gift of tribute. I often practiced receiving fabulous gifts by intimidation and by extortion."

"Upon reaching the Cyclops cave, the single-eyed monster was not inside, but instead, was out shepherding his hungry flock. My neurotic scouting patrol bravely advanced inside, leaving mounds of wet crap all the way from the entrance to a hundred-feet inside the dreary, dismal cavern."

"Look at those racks loaded with cheese," I whispered. "And the resident of this horrid place has more lambs, hoglets and kids than his pens could ever contain. He must certainly be a very prosperous fellow on this apparently forbidden island!"

"And look," noted Eurballsourout, my second mate. "His pails and bowls are as big as we are, and filled to the brim with milk and whey."

"Get out of my *whey!*" I exclaimed as I stuck my cupped hands into a shoulder-high bowl, and then voraciously drank some of the richly delicious dairy product. *"Whey* to go, Odysseus!" moronic Eurballsourout praised.

"After that trivial verbal exchange, dear King Alcinous, the men then begged me if they could steal some cheeses and a kid each, but I strictly commanded them to just take the cheeses and not get involved in any complicated, felonious, illegal, time-consuming kidnappings."

"Men, we are humble guests in the owner's house," I declared, "so according to *our* customs and tradition, our host should present us with gifts under the Law of the Suppliants. If you recall," I sanctimoniously lectured, "any strangers visiting a person's home while traveling through a distant town or village is to be extended hospitality and generosity. I say we *not* steal the cheeses! Let's wait until the *big cheese* gives us his cheesy cheeses under the protection of almighty Zeus and his Law of the Suppliants."

"I say your logic is really fucked-up," the first mate criticized. "Why should we risk injury, or maybe even death just because *we* honor *our* dumb laws and our fucked-up traditions?" Eurshiddenme adamantly indicated. "I say that this bigger-than-life creature that lives here might not favor us, or honor our asshole laws, gods or traditions!"

"If he's more fucked-up than we are," the second mate emphasized, "then we are undoubtedly in for a very long day, that's for damned sure!" Eurballsourout observed and opined. "Has anyone brought along any knitting needles, yarn and a rocking chair to passively pass the friggin' time away?"

"Now, King Alcinous, in the dark, dank cave my men lit a fire, and then sacrificed some cheeses to the gods before they ravenously ate like blackbirds any of the remaining ones themselves. Some of the soldiers became restless and picked their noses, twiddled their thumbs, squeezed various pimples, and scratched their itchy balls."

"Why do we sacrifice these good cheeses to the gods when we could have stolen them and eaten the pieces ourselves!" the first mate questioned. "Sometimes, we really do some stupid shitty things!" Eurshiddenme perceptively concluded."

"Because, Dip-shit!" I yelled back. "There might really be gods up on *Mt. Olympus* that might be offended if *we* didn't think of *them* first, before considering *our* own selfish, biological needs. And if we start getting our asses kicked by the creature that lives here in this putrid-smelling cave, we might require the emergency services of some supernatural intervention in a fuckin' hurry!"

"But still," the second mate challenged. "If there really aren't any gods on *Mt. Olympus* to be pleased by our offering, then we will have wasted all of that lousy burnt cheese for nothing!" Eurballsourout stubbornly argued. "And besides, what Greek god in his or her right or left mind would ever desire burned cheese that is no longer cheese anyway? You tell me that answer, Captain Asshole! Who the hell wants or needs evaporated or cheesy burnt cheese? A skinny mouse about to die, perhaps?"

"I never thought of that stupid bullshit," I reluctantly admitted. "But who's willing to take the risk if your supposition is wrong? I mean," I philosophically explained. "When's the last time you had one of Zeus's shocking lightning bolts shot-up the center of your smelly, hairy asshole?"

"Great Zeus! I really never thought about such a dreadful consequence!" the second mate exclaimed in a terrified tone of voice. "I don't need to be divinely juiced into reality by that kind of electrifying experience!"

"Merciful King Alcinous," Odysseus proceeded with his lengthy narrative. "An hour later, the horrible Cyclops finally entered his cave, accompanied by an obedient herd of bleating sheep. The monster carried with him a big load of firewood to light near his wooden supper table, still loaded with bowls of whey and slabs of goat meat. The hideous-looking giant flung the heavy timbers onto the ground, and the impact sounded like a wicked clap of thunder, almost scaring the entrails out of the us Greek trespassers' unlucky thirteen rectums."

"Now Phaeacians, the gargantuan Cyclops then used a wooden rod to drive the remainder of his ewes and she-goats inside the cavern, leaving the horny male goats and the rambunctious rams outside to gaily screw one another, rather than penetrate the females of their own species now trapped inside the colossal cave. Then, the ugly fierce behemoth, demonstrating the strength of two-dozen strong, healthy men, rolled a huge stone in front of the cave's entrance, preventing any of the domesticated creatures, along with us Greeks, from escaping to the outside."

"We're trapped inside this freakin' hellhole!" I softly whispered to my frightened crewmembers. "Who says a 'rolling stone' gathers no moss!"

"I think it was the minstrel Mik Jagged that once said *that* weirdo idiomatic expression, and he's the lead singer in a major 'rock' group back in Mycenae!" My first mate aptly replied. "Jagged's quite notorious for inventing silly, meaningless, bull crap aphorisms like *that* hackneyed cliché."

"Quiet Asshole!" I uttered a little too loudly. "Quit farting out of your mouth! That big jerk-off might overhear your zany, nauseous comments!"

"The men's ridiculous conversation echoed throughout the cavern, and soon distracted the Cyclops, who was about to piss a hundred gallons of urine onto a sidewall of the already-stenchy, foul-smelling cave."

"Strangers or Intruders; who is foolishly speaking so loud over there that a deaf person could hear your annoying drivel?" the Cyclops asked in a booming voice. "Are you A) traders, B) rovers, C) soldiers, D) thieves and trespassing pirates, or E), a combination of all of the above?"

"Well, King Alcinous and Queen Arete; we intruders were scared out of our wits until I mustered sufficient courage to address the towering, malicious ogre. "Kind Sir; we are Achaeans returning from the vanquished city of Troy," I proudly began. And Zeus's supreme will has detoured our armada to your beautiful land. We have come in peace!"

"Oh yeah!" bellowed the grotesque one-eyed giant. "You' trespassing dumb-fucks say you have come in peace, but you will soon *not* leave in scattered pieces, after I rip you' puny dirtballs to shreds! Ha, ha, ha, ha!"

"I beg you, Lord," I pleaded with my mouth continuing a little 'bolder' from me, fearfully hiding behind a boulder. "Please show some fear of Zeus's wrath, and demonstrate some respect for the almighty *Olympians*. We have come to your cave as suppliants, under the protection of Zeus, the travelers' god, and the avenger of all foreigners and legal and illegal aliens journeying in distress, while wandering along the world's highways, or sailing upon the high seas!"

"Well, King Alcinous; then the Cyclops laughed lustily and disrespectfully answered: "Stranger; *you* are certainly an ignorant dolt coming to this land so naively. I fear not your asshole gods, and I mock their impotent vengeance," the monster insisted. "I'm much more potent that any of your timid, weakling gods, and I shall now show my great animosity toward you and your absurd laws and customs," the one-eyed brute boasted. "And if your midget god Zeus were to appear in this cave right now, I would pull-down my animal furs from my torso and then directly shit on *his* pointed head while he is standing erect next to me. Ha, ha, ha, ha!"

"You speak quite haughtily for a fellow who merely lives in a friggin' cave!" I idiotically ridiculed my new-found adversary. "For the amount of advanced culture *you* have developed on this wretched island, you must sleep, shit and jerk-off all day long for how much progress you have achieved since the ancient dawn of mythology!"

"The Cyclops didn't like being harassed and chastised by a mere six-foot-tall man, so the deformed Titan figured he would stall for time so that the giant could capture and kill me, his egocentric, intrepid tormentor. "Tell me brave Intruder," the big bruiser replied. "Where is your ship anchored? Is it around the inlet, or is it moored straight off the land?" the frightening monster asked as *he* began systematically searching and sniffing around, attempting to trace the exact location of the little wise-ass mortal that had been mercilessly berating him."

"Well, Your Highness, King Alcinous. I knew that *I* had to think quickly, but I was too foolish to realize that the Cyclops didn't give two flying turds about anything an Achaean king would say. The reprehensible stalker only wanted to discover the location of my voice's origin, and then exterminate the antagonist's vocal cords, along with any targeted companions that might have recklessly strayed into *his* domain."

"Poseidon, awesome god of the sea, forced my ship to crash upon the rocks at the south end of this miserable, forsaken place," I creatively lied. "And the boat is so severely shipwrecked that neither my friends nor I will ever be able to repair the extensive damage to the hull! Thanks to Zeus's mercy, my crew and I have evaded the jaws of death!"

"The formidable Cyclops stretched his grimy, vile hand into the dismal shadows, his fingers reaching behind a prominent boulder, and the ruthless brute clutched two of my' paranoid, crouching crewmen. The creature easily picked-up the pair of warriors into the air, and then smashed my petrified bodyguards' skulls against the rock-solid floor, splitting-open their craniums with their worm-like brains oozing-out. Then, showing no compassion for human dead, the pagan Cyclops ripped each of the two soldiers' limbs from their torsos, just like pulling the legs off a dead crab, and without even heating the fresh meat inside the crackling fire, the fearsome fiend disgustingly gobbled-up the chewed flesh, and spit-out the bones from the victims' appendages."

'Wow!" bellowed King Alcinous. "This story has plenty of thrilling action adventure! I don't know what I'll involuntarily do next: piss or shit my tunic, or maybe begin writing a really tragic play!"

"The eleven human witnesses to the cave carnage knew not what to do except gasp in horror at the totally despicable, cannibalistic act we had viewed, and solemnly pray for the souls of the dearly-departed, who were now also the dearly-separated and the dearly-consumed."

"Then, King Alcinous and Queen Arete, when the carnivorous Cyclops had filled his tank-like stomach, and after he had washed-down his meal with ten gallons of whey, the creature further exhibited his great disdain for trespassing Greeks. The god-sized barbarian lied-down on the ground in ankle-deep sheep shit, resting among squealing goats, and soon dozed-off like a satisfied bear that had gorged itself' with a winter's supply of fat and protein."

"Well, my royal friends and Phaeacian guests; I was profoundly motivated to grab his five-hundred-pound sword and drive it deeply into the Cyclops' inhuman heart, but then my better judgment considered something rather salient. I understood that I was not strong enough to enact that bitter revenge, even with the help of my petrified warriors. Even if I were successful at killing the evil monster by thrusting *his* sword into his evil heart, then surely *me* and my remaining men would never be capable of moving the enormous stone away from the cave's entrance in order for us to exit. So, I instructed my soldiers to simply sit there all night long thinking 'Fuck! Fuck! Fuck!' a hundred thousand times each until shafts of light filtered through the circumference of the cavern's blocked mouth, signaling that morning had finally arrived."

"I'm really enjoying your bizarre story," King Alcinous's wife, Queen Arete, yelled-out. "Listening to your tale is better than watching a massive, in-progress sex orgy!"

"Well, Queen Arete; the Cyclops arose from his deep slumber and then brushed some of the excessive sheep and goat crap off of his fur clothing, and also from his arms, legs and face. The ruthless villain again ignited his woodpile, milked his ewes and goats, and then remembered that he had human trespassers hiding somewhere within the cave's confined perimeter. The disgusting dick-head gathered-up two more of my personal bodyguards and thrust their heads onto the cavern's rock floor, dashing-out their brains with pints of blood squirting into the air in all directions. Then *he* breakfasted as he had supped, licking his fingers that were coated with layers of human blood and smelly sheep shit."

"He just ate two more of my men!" I panted to my' knee-knocking companions. "He's a lawless fanatic!"

"The giant is too uncivilized to even be a homosexual," Eurshiddenme, my gay first mate regretted, "because the Cyclops just doesn't suck dick. He swallows the man's pecker along with the rest of the victimized person in one tremendous gulp! What a fuckin' pitiful waste of humanity!"

"The primitive brute then rolled the huge circular stone back against the cave's sidewall, allowing his ewes and his goats to venture-out into the sunshine to graze and be screwed by the lustful rams, and any other animals of different species waiting outside. Then, the monstrous hulk adroitly rolled the huge rock back from outside the cave as if the twenty-ton object weighed only twenty-pounds. Finally, my shrewd brain had time to plot a plan to defeat the extremely treacherous, unethical foe."

"Let's slice his balls and dick-off and barbecue them over the fire!" mate number one intelligently recommended. "I haven't sampled Greek meatballs in over twenty years."

"No, Asshole," I emphatically disagreed. "This Cyclops doesn't have any wife or kids, nor does the ugly bachelor bastard want any of those fucked-up headaches. His penis and testicles bring him no natural pleasure except maybe by means of masturbation! Boy, I'd hate to be splattered against this solid rock wall by one of *his* prodigious ejaculations!" I neurotically exclaimed. "I hope that's not a *coming* event!"

"Well then, we could pierce his jugular vein with our spears and have him fuckin' bleed to death!" Eurballsourout, my second mate, smartly suggested."

"No, Jerk-off. That would be too damned messy!" I objectively countered. "The brute might have some unknown, contagious venereal blood disease that might kill us a month from now. And besides," I proceeded and argued. "If *he* moves and we miss the jugular while attacking his neck from both sides, we might accidentally pierce his earlobes, and then the berserk giant might get the idea of wearing two of us as decorative earrings. I can't take *that* chance. And furthermore," my machine-mouth elaborated. "We could never roll that immense stone back and be able to escape from this fuckin' cave. We must decisively punish the gargantuan asshole without killing him!"

"This is absolutely great!" King Alcinous complimented. "Please continue."

"I brazenly disclosed a nifty plan to my perceptive subordinates, who wholeheartedly endorsed the proposal after I promised the nine remaining idiots that each one could screw Queen Penelope and munch on her delicious, wet, pink pussy-hole upon their safe return to Ithaca, which *I* naturally believed was quite highly-unlikely to ever really happen."

"The Cyclops kept a great club the size of a ship's mast lying next to one of his sheep pens. I boldly instructed my remaining men to use their swords and cut-off a ten-foot-length of the massive staff, and then carefully shave-down the head until it was shaped into a hard, sharp, wooden point. The beam's tip was soon charred inside the fire as phase one of the 'stake-out' had been satisfactorily completed."

"The mighty Cyclops eventually returned from outside, and after re-entering the dismal cave, again rolled the tremendous stone to effectively block the entrance, keeping us from escaping. The giant next snatched-up two more of my loyal men, and heinously snacked on them just like the horrible animal had done with the other four unfortunate victims."

"That Cyclops must've been one hungry dude just getting off a big weight-loss diet!" King Alcinous commented. "What the fuck happened next? Is it now eye-for-an-eye time?"

"Well," I said to my remaining apprehensive crewmen. "We started-out with unlucky thirteen, and now we've been dwindled-down to a mere lucky seven. Just think men," I eloquently revealed. "This is really to your advantage because now with six men dead, you'll all have more time shafting Queen Penelope, day and night, and chomping on her sumptuous wet pink vagina upon us victoriously returning to Ithaca."

"Boss," said Eurshiddenme, the gay first mate. "We would stand more of a chance of living after drinking a five-gallon jug of hemlock mixed with arsenic than ever having the pleasure of either screwing your beautiful wife, or lapping and buttering-up her moist muffin! And anyway, I would only sodomize Penelope if she's a goddamned practicing lesbian!"

"Showing magnificent, steadfast courage, King Alcinous, soon my aching feet stepped forward with my trembling hands carrying a large bowl filled with the delicious dark wine that the priest of Apollo, Maron, had maron-ated and given me. "Here kind sir," I cleverly offered. "Sip some of this splendid wine I had originally brought to your fine home as a gift, as is the custom of travelers seeking Zeus's protection. My illustrious host; I request that you please drink man's rich beverage to wash-down the taste of man's rich flesh!"

"Well, gathered royal Phaeacians, the heinous Cyclops accepted the bowl and drank-down its fabulous contents, never before tasting wine, because the oversized asshole had never learned how to ferment liquid from grapes and then produce the wonderful substance. "Er, da; that drink tasted very good!" the hideous one-eyed giant conceded. "It tastes much better than grape juice, or even better than pussy juice, I believe. This flavor indeed tastes like the mysterious nectar and the ambrosia that my father Poseidon occasionally provides. I think it is definitely the drink of the gods that will indeed make me even more immortal than I already am!" Cyclops erroneously generalized. "Give me some more, so that I may live beyond all eternity! Ha, ha, ha, ha!" the drunken beast chortled like the demented lunatic that *he* truly was."

"I instinctively filled the huge bowl three more times, and the dumb-fuck Cyclops greedily consumed the fine, smooth-tasting wine, saying that he had never tasted such a wonderful elixir-type laxative. And then, the inebriated ogre asked me outright, "What exactly is your name, oh generous stranger?"

"My damned name is 'No Man'," I wisely answered. "And my mother, father, friends and enemies all address me by that terrific title. I hate my friggin' name with a passion!" I falsely exaggerated. "So Cyclops, watch exactly how you verbally use your smart-assed *No Man*-clature!"

"You're more fucked-up than your fucked-up gods are! Do you know that observable fact, wimpy No Man?" the Cyclops bellowed until the giant nearly started a serious landslide, or a turbulent earthquake outside the cavern. "You're so funny you ought to do standup comedy in an amphitheater without any damned seats! Ha, ha, ha, ha! You should suck a red rooster's red cock, you little cock-sucking dick-licker! Ha! Ha! Ha! Ha!"

"Odysseus, watch what you say to this horrible, ungodly thing!" Eurshiddenme, the first mate cautioned me. "This atrocious creature does not honor any laws and respects nothing that *we* value! Not even pussy or homosexuality!"

"That's right!" Eurballsourout, the second mate concurred with Eurshiddenme. "This big lummox respects 'no man', either gay or fuckin' straight!"

"That's precisely my goal," I honestly replied. "This big, oversized jerk-off is gonna' learn to respect No Man!"

"Then next, oh King Alcinous; the cruel fifty-foot-tall oaf' temporarily cleared his groggy head and declared: 'I'll eat all of No Man's comrades first, and then save *his* tender skin and tiny dick for last. This is the gift I shall give to No Man in exchange for this savory wine from your fucked-up priest's vine! This juice is for Zeus!' the crazy pea-brain laughed and rhymed, as *he* held his half-full bowl up toward the cave's curved ceiling."

"Well, Queen Arete and noble husband. After the repugnant giant bragged and again sarcastically mocked Zeus, my chief deity, the intoxicated Cyclops tumbled-onto, and then sprawled-upon the cave's dirt floor, stoned out of his mind, which indeed was a very mini-mind in proportion to the enormity of *his* total anatomy. The drunken monster became quite animated, and then while lying there, soon belched-up a gallon of wine along with the semi-digested flesh of his last two consumed humans. He next spit the essence of his guts to the posterior area of the mammoth cavern, and the horrible debris splattered onto the faces of the seven remaining Greek survivors."

"I hope he barfs his intestines out and then goes into a deep sleep," I told my loyal men as the not-from-Crete cretin wiped the repulsive vomit from his arms and from his cheeks. "This uncouth Cyclops is gonna' pay for his insolence to our values, and for his defiance of our gods, I insisted!"

"How's he gonna' pay?" Eurshiddenme challenged. "They ain't got no friggin' money system on this freakin' freak show island of demented freaks!"

"I meant that the Cyclops is gonna' be punished for committin' cannibalism and for doing sacrilegious things in excess. Hubris will sentence this impudent, fat, barbaric asshole to a deserving fate," I bluntly asserted."

"This over-inflated shit-head thinks he's a god, so let's smash him with the stake right in his fuckin' *temple!*" Eurballsourout candidly suggested."

"No, Eurballsourout!" I strongly objected. "I have a much better idea to implement!"

"Well, King Alcinous, after the Cyclops finally stopped vomiting all over the damned place in his deep sleep, myself and the remaining crewmen lifted the wooden beam that we had hidden under three-foot-deep sheep and goat dung. The remaining intruders and me, their itinerant captain, again heated the charred tip inside the blazing fire, and after rotating the pole for a full ten-minutes, until the searing beam sizzled inside the roaring flames; then, inspired by Pallas Athene, the enraged entourage ran forward and violently thrust the red-hot spike directly into the center of the Cyclops' single eye!"

"Take that, Shit-head, since you think you are such hot stuff!" Eurshiddenme yelled at his avowed enemy."

"Now, your eye will be a real eyesore!" Eurballsourout frankly added insult to injury."

"The center of your eye has now become one of my *pupils!*" my tongue and throat gleefully shouted. "Now you can't keep an eye out for us any more, you dumb bastard!"

"Yowllllllll! Owwwww!" the enraged Cyclops thundered as the brute was rudely awakened from his drunken slumber. "Hey; I can't see a goddamned fuckin' thing! What's this odd hissing sound coming from inside my eye?" The retard hideously screamed, as the giant twisted and then yanked the sizzling, flaming timber from the center of his scorched and blinded eye."

"Other Cyclopes in the vicinity heard the noisy racket and were curious what the source of the clamor might be. Three of them gathered outside the cave and yelled inside to their awesome, bellicose neighbor."

"What is the matter Polyphemus? What is bothering you? Did you accidentally ejaculate a ten-pound load backwards into your balls, or what?" a somewhat concerned Cyclopes yelled inside the still-closed cave entrance."

"Polyphemus, what has happened? Did you accidentally crush your dick on a rock while slamming-down your enormous sledgehammer?" a second inquisitive giant hypothesized and hollered inside."

"The still-delirious and drunken Polyphemus boisterously shouted from the cave's interior: "No Man is killing me! No Man has fuckin' killed me!"

"Surely Polyphemus, no man is capable of killing a fearsome giant like you," a surprised and amused neighbor replied from outside. "You must be hallucinating. *No man* has the strength or the force to do you any significant harm!"

"Listen fuck-heads. I need your goddamned help!" the wounded and distraught blind giant vehemently answered. "I tell you, neighbors. No Man has attacked and blinded me! No Man has fuckin' attacked and blinded me!"

"Well then, Polyphemus; if no man has attacked or blinded you," the first mountain cave resident concluded, "then what the fuck are ya' complainin' about? Stop annoying us with such bad, illogical, nonsensical riddles! Everyone knows that one puny man can't assault and blind a fifty-foot-tall jerk-off like you! It's just not fuckin' plausible!" the amused Cyclopes neighbor chided. "Just fondle and flog your log, pop a big load, and go the hell back to sleep! See ya' tomorrow, ya' big pouting crybaby!"

"No! Stop! Listen to me!" Polyphemus screamed and shrieked like a berserk maniac. "No Man has blinded me! Do you hear me? No Man has fuckin' blinded me!"

"Why don't you do something constructive like committing suicide!" a third voice remarked from the cave's exterior. "Goodbye Polyphemus; you dumb, melodramatic, thespian fuck! You can't stage a comeback! Ha, ha, ha!"

"Good stuff!" King Alcinous commended. "Please get to the big climax without squirting nasty sperm juice all over my face!"

"Well King, my remaining men laughed incessantly at the blinded Cyclops's very apparent frustration. The clumsy, injured giant sat with his back leaning against the rock wall, regretting that he had been born with only one eye in the center of his head, and now was blinded for the rest of his accursed tenure on our ass-backwards planet. But, as you already know, my stellar reputation has been renowned for inventing clever solutions to difficult dilemmas, and I still had to devise a viable method of escaping the cave and its blocked entrance."

"It was now daybreak, and time for Polyphemus to rotate the incredibly huge stone and allow his ewes and goats to leave the cavern to graze, to screw, and to shit in the sunshine. The big, hulking, blinded bully sat at the cave's entrance and felt in front, on top, and in between the evacuating animals to ascertain that 'No Man' escaped *his* intensive feeling. My eyes keenly scrutinized the blind giant's careful practice, and my creative brain planned a stratagem to counteract the wounded creep's predictable habit of search and seizure."

"Dear King and Queen; my head pondered and meditated, knowing full-well that a poor decision would cost me my life along with the lives of my remaining bodyguards. Quite ingeniously, the following morning, my keen vision found some leather straps, and I tethered together teams of large sheep in groups of three. Each of the anxious warriors crawled under the body of the center sheep and fastened his legs inside the straps, holding on to the middle animal's fleece with *his* bare hands."

"The hungry, healthy sheep rapidly rushed-out into the sunshine to feed. The vengeful Cyclops meticulously felt the fronts, sides and tops of each set of three sheep passing-by his tactile inspection, but not once ever suspecting that the conniving Greeks had escaped the cave under the belly of the center sheep in the groups of three that passed by."

"As my set of three sheep finally made it to the cave's entrance, the Cyclops reached-down, felt the top of the center animal and declared, "My favorite, most-treasured sheep. Why are you last to leave today? You are usually the leader, the proudest of my flock!"

"Well, dear Phaeacians, my heart was pounding so loudly inside my chest that I feared that the blind Cyclops might detect the abnormally distinct, loud beating. Right when I, being extremely petrified, started pissing myself', the Cyclops delivered some additional sentimental monologue."

"I know kind and faithful animal," the horrible monster verbally proceeded, speaking to his favorite sheep. "You must feel badly because you sense that your master can no longer see. No Man has blinded me, and I must make retribution and kill the dirty son-of-a-bitchin' scumbag. I know that if you could talk, you' pathetic beast," the Cyclops affectionately stated. "You would tell me exactly where my cunning adversary is hiding. I would crush his bones with my bare hands; then collide his head with the walls, and next impact his skull with the solid rock floor, spilling his brains all over the fuckin' cave until there is not an ounce of blood left in his petty, rotten, human arteries!"

"When I finally escaped the cave, I carefully freed myself from the underneath straps, and then assisted my men in being un-tethered from the center sheep in each set of three animals tied together. And with the attitude of genuine plunderers, we ecstatic Greeks led the sheep and goats in a bizarre parade down to the anchored ship, where the remaining crewmen accepted the pilfered animals aboard."

"This is an astounding tale that you've depicted," praised King Alcinous. "Please advance to the conclusion."

"Then, Your Highness; I told my well-disciplined commandos not to weep for their deceased comrades, for their cries of mourning might be discerned by Cyclops's sensitive auditory perception. I still feared that the horrendous freak might be capable of doing significant damage to my ship, despite Polyphemus's most recent blindness handicap."

"When the vessel lifted anchor and quietly sailed a hundred-yards out into the clear-blue harbor, my throat and mouth garnered enough courage to spitefully and scornfully address my blinded enemy. "Cyclops!" I haughtily yelled-up at the top of my lungs. "You have sinned against omnipotent Zeus and against the sacred laws of *Mt. Olympus.* You have rightfully been punished for the evils that you have egregiously committed, and you suffer for the outrageous disrespect you have demonstrated toward guests in your land, and toward *their* gods and customs!"

"The furious giant lividly grabbed hold of a nearby mountain crag and flung the heavy object in the direction from which he believed my explicit taunting had originated. The Cyclops's heave landed and splashed in the shallow harbor, and came within a breadth's length of destroying the ship's rudder. An enormous wave surged, and then propelled the vessel back near the island's desolate beach. I tacitly signaled to my crew to row and not to speak or yell, for then I dreaded that the desperate avenger would become even more provoked, and manage to get lucky with another mountain peak toss, and successfully sink the Bireme with a broadside hit."

"That idiot almost demolished my ship and murdered my crew!" I realized and admitted. "I'm glad we had blinded the savage bastard, and I'm also happy that it is now time to relish the taste of sweet revenge!"

"The oversized asshole has thrown one boulder already and has driven us all the way back to the friggin' shore line," Eurshiddenme accurately protested. "So please, Captain; don't antagonize him any more until we are outside his throwing range!" the first mate implored his sometimes all-too-arrogant captain."

"I hope I will be still-born in my next life because I never want to experience any more fucked-up misadventures like this one!" Eurballsourout told Eurshiddenme and me."

"Cyclops!" I stubbornly bellowed and challenged when the vessel was officially three-hundred-yards or so out into the harbor. "If anyone asks you who had taken your eye out and blinded you, tell that asshole that it was Odysseus, King of Ithaca, son of Laertes!"

"The Cyclops then recalled the essence of an old prophecy told to him by the soothsayer Telemus, son of Eurymus, who had predicted that a man named Odysseus would handily blind the despicable bastard during a major dispute. But Polyphemus was expecting to confront a hundred-foot-tall *Adonis* kicking *his* big fat ass on *his* own turf, and not a little runt like me, the Ithacan King getting the job done under the alias of No Man."

"Come back Odysseus," the Cyclops hollered-out to the deaf sea, "so that I, the son of the vengeful sea god Poseidon, can give you gifts to take back to Ithaca. Come back, and I shall treat you like the royalty you really are!"

"Go fuck yourself', you' big cock-sucking asshole!" I defiantly screamed as loud as I could. "Do you think me half as stupid as yourself! You are just as blind to truth as you are to sight, you dumb, no-eyed fuck!"

"Then, vengeful Polyphemus cupped his hands to his mouth and grievously shouted skyward. "Oh, great Poseidon; hear my plea! If I am indeed your son as everyone on this fucked-up island claims that I am, see to it that Odysseus's shipmates never make it back to Ithaca alive! Let all of his scumbag mariners perish, and let Odysseus return home as a passenger in a foreign ship and discover his house in disarray, and later finds his wife pregnant with another man's triplets!"

"Poseidon heard his distraught son's vile plea, and so the rambunctious sea god yelled-back to his begotten son, "You stupid shit! I am the god of the sea, and I rule all the oceans from underwater with my trident as my royal scepter! Why are you praying up to heaven when that is Zeus's fuckin' domain!" the sea god loudly reprimanded his orphaned offspring. "Now, I know why I no longer visit you and your shit-eating Cyclopes' friends anymore! What a fuckin' waste you', they, and your whole asshole island are! Your land ought to sink into the friggin' sea and be swallowed-up in its eddying maelstrom!"

"Well, men," I announced to my crew of hardy rowers. "Poseidon has now disowned his own blinded son, but the fickle god has promised to kick our vulnerable asses good in future episodes and adventures."

"We're all going to die because of your insolent aggressiveness, and because of your inflexible impudence," Eurballsourout complained to me, his noble-but-imprudent king. "And if we never had sailed to that forbidden island behind us, we would not now be cursed and abused by the ruthless sea-god, nor would we have lost our colleagues to that terrible, blind sore-loser monster, pouting and whimpering up there!"

"You're absolutely right," Eurshiddenme readily agreed with Eurballsourout. "And Captain; thanks for earning us *our* forthcoming execution from Poseidon as retribution for blinding *his* damned ugly freak of a son. And as for you," Eurshiddenme continued. "My King; your punishment will be the greatest of all! You will have to live for at least twenty more years in Ithaca after both Eurballsourout and I are fuckin' luckily dead and gone. Our spirits will be resting in the Elysian daffodil fields planted in the good sector of *Hades,* while you're still alive trying to fuckin' govern your majorly screwed-up kingdom."

"You're absolutely right, Eurshiddenme," my raspy voice glumly acknowledged. "For I am the one who is really cursed at sea, and later fated to be doomed in Ithaca by having to live through the bulk of Poseidon's wicked wrath!"

"Fabulous story; Bravo brave Odysseus," King Alcinous stated. "Admirable tale! Now I definitely believe that you are indeed the legendary hero of the Trojan War, who is rightfully celebrated and heralded throughout the known world!"

Chapter 11

"AEOLUS"

"We next sailed and reached Aeolia, a fucked-up, floating island, where the nature-wizard Aeolus lived, who was the son of Hippotas, whom immortal gods inexplicably hold dear. Around the airborne mass runs an impenetrable bronze wall, and towering cliffs rise-up in a sheer facade of solid rock. Aeolus's twelve children live there in a crystal palace, six talkative daughters as well as six full-grown, blowhard sons. Aeolus, who preferred incest to regular marital tradition, gave the six daughters to the six zealous sons in marriage, and the empty-headed freaks-of-nature are always enjoying gluttony at outrageous and garish banquet feasts."

"Now King Alcinous and Queen Arete. my small fleet reached the splendid palace, and for one whole month, the blow-hard windbag Aeolus entertained me, always asking immaterial questions about every existing academic topic: about Troy; about our Greek Argive ships, and about the great expedition returning back to Greece. I described in detail the entire sequence of events from start to finish. When, for my part, I asked to take my leave and told the pseudo-intellectual Aeolus to send me on my damned way, the flamboyant fuck-head surprisingly denied me nothing and actually helped me get my ass out of there."

"Please review your full visit with Aeolus," Alcinous requested. "I promise that you'll be able to depict your gripping tale with only minor interruptions about certain nuances."

"Well King, the avid prankster gave me a bag made out of thick ox-hide, dense skin flayed from a corpulent plow animal nine years old. And wily Aeolus tied-up the odd gift with ultra-thick hemp. The sealed bag contained all the winds that blow in all directions from every conceivable hemisphere and latitude, for the son of Cronos had made the disreputable clown Aeolus the official Keeper of the Winds, and the dumb-shit could calm or rouse the seasonal elements with real gusto, as his silly, juvenile whims wished."

"Now, listen to this, you Phaeacians. With a bright silver cord, the notorious jester, as a gesture of friend*ship,* tightly lashed that seemingly innocuous bag inside my hollow ship's hull, so as to stop even the smallest breath or breeze from escaping that one-of-a-kind air-tight goatskin container. After receiving the unique windbag from the hoary windbag, my accommodating host provided my twelve ships with a bland West Wind to carry my victorious, stout soldiers on our merry way home to nearby neighboring Ithaca."

"What happened next?" Alcinous asked. "Did you take a crash course in meteorology? Did the goatskin bag look anything like your old bag mother-in-law?"

"For nine consecutive sunny days and cloudless nights, our pilots steered our smooth sailing course, and on the tenth, we all cheered as we glimpsed sight of our native land. Our victorious fleet came in so close to the distant coast that our eyes could see the conscientious workmen who assiduously tend the beacon fires on the shoreline. But then, much to my detriment, sweet Sleep overcame my body and mind, both of which mutually surrendered to incredible exhaustion. All that time, my reliable hands had gripped my lead ship's sail rope."

"Honestly, dear King and Queen; I'd not let go of the gift, or pass the bag on to any muscular shipmate. I didn't want to gamble on him, or any other stressed-out colleague, falling fast asleep before my reputable vigilance would, so that we'd get home more quickly."

"Were Eurshiddenme and Eurballsourout still with you?" Queen Arete wanted to know. "I think that you should've donated the useless services of those two pecker-heads to that weirdo Aeolis."

"I'll get to those two incompetent ninnies soon enough. During my lengthy boredom, and while I was feigning sleep, I deftly eavesdropped on a nearby private conversation. "It's not fair. Everyone adores and honors our ambitious King, no matter where the hell he goes, to any city, barn, or garbage dump," Eurshiddenme softly mentioned in a whisper to equally fucked-up Eurballsourout. "The scuttlebutt circulating on board is that avaricious Odysseus is presently transporting a colossal stash of gold and silver loot, but those of us who've been passengers on the same trip to and from Troy are coming home with empty hands and empty wallets," Eurballsourout answered and then added. "And next, the mutinous conniver stated to his potential colleague-in-mischief the following nonsense: "That impractical joker Aeolus, because he's a valued friend of our money-hungry Captain, I understand that the aged windbag has willfully presented our ignoble monarch with other extravagant gifts as well. Come on, comrade; let's see how much gold and silver Odysseus has stored in yonder bag."

"Now, patient audience; as the jealous subordinates talked like this in confidential tones, in the final analysis, my companions' envious thoughts prevailed. The hateful pair used sharp-bladed knives and managed, after great effort, to untie and open the strongly-knotted bag. All Hades broke loose as the incarcerated winds rushed-out in unrivaled turbulence. Wicked torrential storm gusts seized the mutinous assholes, swept their rebellious torsos off the deck and out to sea, catapulting their mutinous anatomies far away from our temporarily visible native land."

"That's what happens when subordinates go overboard with pursuing their strange ideas," Alcinous inadvertently punned. "Their excessive greed just blew them away!"

"At *that* pivotal point, I instantly woke-up from my deleterious trance. Deep inside my pulsating heart, I was of two alternative minds: I either could jump overboard and drown in the swirling currents, or I could just keep striving to simply exist in unproductive silence, while regrettably remaining among the still-breathing; and while suffering *that* lousy fate, I felt that I was being manipulated like a dumb-ass marionette by the dual adversaries of Poseidon and Zeus. I stayed there onboard and persevered, contemplating the magnitude of my mammoth ordeal. Covering-up my tormented head, I just lay there upon the drenched deck, while our battered twelve ships, loaded with my thousands of jealous, whimpering companions, were driven by those wicked wind blasts and blown all the way back to Aeolus's fucked-up island."

"I see," commented Queen Arete. "Your stormy departure from Aeolus wasn't exactly a breeze. What occurred next?"

"In immense frustration, I disembarked and set-off for Aeolus's splendid home, and my search found the laughing ignoramus feasting like a famished caveman with his dominant wife and obnoxious children also snorting and guffawing. So, I angrily entered the well-constructed estate and sat-down at the threshold, right beside the thick doorposts. In his underdeveloped heart, the weather-control freak was seemingly amazed at recognizing my surprise reappearance. Feigning sincerity, the satirical shit-head busted my balls and asked me:

"Odysseus; why have you returned to my generous hospitality? Can't you live without enjoying my amusing company? I took great care in sending you on your way so that you'd arrive safely back to Ithaca; yes, if I vividly recall, back to your elusive native land."

"That non-digestible, fake horse manure is what the comic jerk-off articulated. Pissed-off to the hilt with a heavy heart and clenched fists, I impolitely answered the dick-head."

"My foolish and about-to-be-pummeled phony comrade; your non-funny antics and semantics, aided by your nefarious ally, malicious Sleep, have greatly harmed my public reputation throughout the civilized and uncivilized world, and I'll be perpetually maligned and ridiculed by goofball bards, poets, politicians, along with numerous cornball philosophers, especially in every part of Mother Greece."

"I'll bet that your serious threats scared the humorous funny-bone right out of the old windbag's arms," laughed Alcinous. "You were going to beat the shit out of the bad humor man."

"But Aeolus," I uttered with a frown. "I'll give you one more chance before I kill you and send your unfunny, black spirit across the River Styx, where the cheerless Charon will take you to see Hades in his dark Kingdom of the Dead. Now then; you must immediately repair the damage that's mocked and insulted me among my talkative shipmates, and I believe that *that* ability is indeed within your air-supply power. If you do not comply with my urgent demand, I'll persist in violently strangling your skinny throat and neck until shit and piss come out of your mouth and nostrils instead of un-comical words, bad breath, and stinking exhaled air!"

"Then, I mercifully released my lethal grip around his seven gulping throats, and after the zany fuck-head choked incessantly for five-minutes, I allowed the trickster another five-minute-period for the professional buffoon to gasp and rectify my faltering reputation among my crewmen."

"So, you administered to Aeolus a rather breathtaking experience," chuckled King Alcinous. "Your bold threat apparently sucked all of the oxygen out of the room!"

"Oh, dear friend, Odysseus," the droll nutcase prefaced. "Of all living mortals, you are the worst example of humility and modesty upon Mother Earth, and your obdurate demeanor is despised and resented by both Poseidon and Zeus, whom you always try mocking and imitating. So, Mr. Hot Shit! You must with dispatch leave this enchanted island with the utmost of speed, and evacuate as if your erratic rectum and testicles are shooting-out poisonous volcanic lava and toxic hyperactive lightning. It would violate all sense of what is morally right if I helped-out, or guided on his way a man of your low-caliber ilk that the blessed gods must absolutely loathe. So, Odysseus, I austerely advise that you promptly leave my luxurious estate before I eliminate your ass from human existence with a powerful northern snow blizzard, along with a series of incredible avalanches, immediately followed by an unearthly blowjob administered by

Medusa the Gorgon, who will then turn you dick, epididymis and balls into solid stone."

"Look here, Aeolis, you A-holeis!" I madly exclaimed. "Just summarize what the fuck you really mean! I don't like the general atmosphere prevalent in this fucked-up dining room!"

"In a nutshell, Odysseus; you're futilely debating with me this minute issue back here in peaceful Aeolia because the deathless gods absolutely despise your trite, human, smelly ass for maliciously blinding Polyphemus, son of Poseidon."

"Well, Aeolis; just remember that my sailors have gotten wind of what the hell you've done, and if we are blown-back here one more time, I will personally cause you, you old-fart windbag, your old bag wife, and your dirtbag kids to all be mercilessly slain and brutally beheaded."

"Then, King Alcinous and Queen Arete, with me being sick at heart, my ships sailed on further, but my rebellious oarsmen on all twelve Biremes were perturbed, weary and worn-down from so much futile rowing, since I had lost many of my mariners to the animalistic cannibals on the isle of the Cicones. Because we'd been such preposterous fools after leaving Troy, there was no breeze evident to facilitate our swift return to Ithaca. Our Biremes kept going in circles for six whole days and nights, operating against Fate, whose mind was in allegiance with both Poseidon and Zeus. But me still being in favor with Athena, and possibly also with Zeus's wife Hera, that vague hope gave my faltering heart moral conviction to persevere and continue onward on my very unenviable odyssey back home."

Chapter 12
"THE LAESTRYGONIANS"

"On the seventh auspicious day at sea, we came to Telepylus, great citadel of mythological Lamus, the important-but-retarded lame King of the Laestrygonians, who as a society, didn't know how to either spell or pronounce the name of their fucked-up people, nor did the illiterate shits care one iota, or give a tiny scintilla of a fuck about learning anything academic. After slowly drifting into a picturesque harbor, featuring sheer high cliffs on both sides, and jutting headlands, all facing one another, extending-out past the seemingly tranquil-but-empty channel. However, the narrow, shallow entrance to the empty dock was quite small and hazardous."

"Sounds like a picturesque paradise for a thriving honeymoon resort?" King Alcinous prematurely noted.

"Dear King; on the contrary; that fucked-up place would be my last resort. The dunces that lived there hadn't yet learned how the wipe their diarrhea asses. All my eleven other Bireme captains brought their curved ships up and moored them as if my inexperienced navigators were trained professional merchant marine pilots. Much to my amazement, everything appeared calm and bright around the scenic vista, despite the apparent evidence of no human activity. But for honoring some alien instinct, I anchored my black Bireme all by itself just outside the haunting harbor, and I had my skeptical crew-members tie and secure my abused warship right against the distant forest land, tethering the battered vessel to a colossal boulder. I climbed the nearest steep cliff on my chaffed knees and just stood there, gazing-about on a rugged outcrop, assessing the general environment, while perceptively looking around, wishing that I owned four eyes. But my poor vision observed no particular evidence of human labor, or any sign of agricultural earth plowing, and my impaired pupils perceived only random puffs of smoke rising and wafting upwards from the distant hills, which at that moment in time, made my weak spirit fume."

"Being somewhat worried, King Alcinous, I assigned and sent four of my intoxicated comrades to learn what the indigenous inhabitants were like. The neurotic scouts left the ship's safety and soon arrived at a smooth road, which wagons were apparently used to haul wood to the town from the prevailing high mountain slopes."

"Outside the antiquated city's gates, the dispatched surveillance contingent encountered a young girl collecting water, a noble daughter of Antiphates, a rather senile asshole Laestrygonian. My vanguard captain asked the preoccupied, disinterested young hussy who ruled the native people, and who the hell the residents were."

"The deaf and dumb, twelve-foot-tall, pre-pubescent future whore, who probably was incapable of screaming-out wonderful cries of pleasure while bring raped by a maniac pedophile during sexual intercourse, quickly pointed out her father's secluded home. My reconnaissance explorers carefully advanced and reached the ramshackle, oversized shanty, and found the hoary gent's whoring wife, who looked more-than-likely to be an immense, mute woman wrestler as her sole occupation, and the wretched, abominable bitch was as humongous as an obese mountain peak, too big for even Polyphemus to throw at me."

"Kind of makes me glad I live in somnolent Phaeacia," Alcinous evaluated and concluded. "But we have more than our share of imbeciles wandering around, talking trash, ambling-around in our garbage-strewn streets and alleys!"

"Naturally, my scouting party was horrified and frightened by the twenty-foot-tall woman, who claimed that she was a mere midget on the island. The wife called her husband, strong and primitive Antiphates, who was attending a cantankerous government assembly, and the forty-foot-tall meathead quickly arranged a dreadful death sentence for all of my designated enemy spies."

"The horrendous-looking monster, displayed shark-like jagged teeth, and the hideous creep viciously seized one of my most-trustful shipmates and prepared to make a meal of him in gross imitation of the lawless Cyclops. The other three trekkers from my ship jumped-up, ran-off through the nearby forest, and frantically scampered back to my anchored vessel. The leader of the group sprinted fast because the other three spies were only dashing young men. Antiphates then raised a huge nerve-shattering cry that loudly reverberated throughout the seemingly abandoned city."

"Your three soldiers were lucky to escape the ogre's greedy clutches," Lord Alcinous determined and declared. "You would think that Lord Zeus would cruelly punish that brazen violator for not honoring the sacred Law of the Suppliants."

"Once the few idiots with decent auditory perception heard his ear-shattering call, the mighty Laestrygonian giants poured-out from all conceivable directions, thronging and shrieking indiscernible syllables in countless numbers, and the only recognizable utterance emanating from their enraged lips was the one-syllable expletive 'Fuck'!"

"I suppose that their simple language communications contained more colloquial vocabulary terms than standard civil vernacular nomenclature," eggheaded Alcinous theorized and commented. "But sometimes, the more words existing in your language, the more stupid everyone sounds!"

"Well, Your Imperial Highness; from high cliffs above the harbor, the lunatic barbarians hurled a flurry of thousand-pound boulders down upon us. The clamor originating from the anchored ships was dreadful. My soldiers were being destroyed, and my other vessels in the fleet were smashing into one another, with those huge imposing monsters spearing my men as if they were helpless fish, and in the process, capturing and stealing new gruesome meals for the giants to consume."

"Naturally, those brave soldiers who remained at my side, attempting to shield their heads and testicles from the tremendous onslaught, all blamed me for being the cause of that disaster, and every other earlier debacle that had occurred."

"Ungrateful, rebellious fools!" Queen Arete decided and said to Odysseus and her husband. "You can't make chicken salad out of chicken shit, that's for damned sure!"

"While the determined and inhuman behemoths were slaughtering the bulk of my besieged sailors, who were trapped and being brutalized in that deep, narrow harbor, I grabbed my sword, pulled it from my thigh's scabbard, and cut the cables on my isolated, dark-prow ship, yelling and ordering to my crew, "Let's get the fuck out of here while we still have a smidgeon of time left to hurriedly get the fuck out of here!"

"The petrified and almost-paralyzed rowers hustled to their separate stations, sat-down quickly like they all had emergency cases of vertigo, and their powerful oars churned the passive water with their hued blades, with everyone aboard excessively afraid of being mauled, maimed, mangled and mutilated. My soul was somewhat-relieved as my ship left the raucous giants, all angrily clamoring atop the high cliffs above, as we thankfully were moving swiftly out to sea. But I was immensely grieving when my brain realized that the other eleven ships, along with their' crews, had been stranded in the perilous harbor, and all had been totally destroyed. My vessel, carrying the remnants of my seditious crew, was the sole Bireme to fortunately escape and survive that rather fucked-up, totally atrocious catastrophe."

Chapter 13
"CIRCE"

L ord Odysseus recited the following comprehensive account to King Alcinous, to Queen Arete and to the spellbound Phaeacian committee, who agreed to allow the Ithacan King to speak without the general assembly asking any further idiotic questions.

"Our remaining ship sailed-away from the assaulting giants, weighing-in with heavy hearts about the great loss of blood and treasure, until our sole Bireme reached the island of Aeaea, home of that dreaded goddess, fair-haired, thick-bushed, magical witch Circe, whom I suspected had brought our only ship, out of twelve, safely to land inside the harbor, which incidentally provided fine anchorage. Some benign god, I speculate that it had been Athena, was guiding us through a perilous ebb tide, and when I find-out who the hell rendered us assistance, I'll pay appropriate homage. Weary and recuperating from our recent wounds and injuries, my warriors disembarked and laid-up in that spot for two days and nights."

"As soon as rose-fingered early Dawn appeared, I quickly organized a meeting and addressed my low-spirited, shabby crew: "Shipmates; let's quickly put our tanned heads together without using glue to see if there's some practical scheme that our inferior brainstorming can devise about obtaining adequate food and shelter."

"I meticulously climbed a rocky crag, which was always my favorite hobby, and from that vantage point scoped-out the verdant landscape. Aeaea was an island with dark blue water surrounding its circumference, and featuring gentle, shallow, aqua-blue water next to the sandy beach."

"The semi-tropical terrain appeared to be low-lying and flat. Through the dense brush and tangled jungle vegetation, I did see some smoke rising in the middle of the island, and that observation prompted me to regretfully remember the fucked-up smoke being emitted from chimneys in the land of the fucked-up maniac giants."

"I considered and evaluated my new environment. Rising smoke meant some sort of human activity, and since this was not a desert setting, the thick vegetation indicated that the island received ample rainfall. I also surmised that there must have been a good variety of fruits and vegetables growing in abundance, but then, I wondered if the resident inhabitants were gay or mental retards."

"That's exactly what I soon stated to my ship's restive sailors, who were pissed-off at me for being responsible for so many deaths and general loss of treasure. But their spirits fell into a greater deep-dive emotional abyss when the aggregate of paranoid idiots remembered what the delirious Laestrygonian king had done to our other eleven Biremes and their now-dead shipmates; not to fully mention the loss of some key warriors at the hands of the mighty brute Polyphemus, that man-eating, blinded, uncivilized, loud-farting, fucked-up Cyclops."

"I split-up my well-armed comrades into two separate groups, each with its own leader. I commanded the first platoon, and godlike Eurylochus I had assigned to lead the second squad."

"When brave Eurylochus's lot fell-out, the scholarly graduate of the Ithaca Military Academy set-off with twenty-two anti-Odysseus companions, all in tears because of my questionable leadership and faulty decision-making, leaving the rest of us behind to grieve about my questionable leadership and my faulty decision-making ever since my battleships had left Troy."

"In an open forest clearing, Eurylochus and his surveillance team found Circe's dwelling of polished stone, an edifice having fabulous views in all four directions. There were mountain wolves and lions roaming around the property, but I suspected that the carnivorous predators had all been bewitched by Circe's wicked pharmaceutical potions. But the ordinarily dangerous animals made no expected attacks against my second squad of encroaching warriors."

"The creatures stood-up upon their hind legs and fawned like domesticated puppies, aggressively wagging their long tails in seeking to be lovingly petted. Just as dogs will beg for scraps and morsels while desiring attention and approval around their master's feet, especially after the pet's owner arrives home from a barbecue feast, that's how the docile wolves and sharp-clawed lions kept purring around my alarmed fellow Greek intruders, who were positively terrified just gazing in astonishment at those rather peculiar-but-tame beasts."

"My suspicious comrades stood-by fair-haired Circe's gate and heard her sweet voice singing about having sex with all of them inside her outhouse crapola, as the entrancing witch spun a pastel fabric back and forth upon her rotating loom, weaving a huge, immortal tapestry, which was the sort of artistic material that gifted Olympian goddesses, along with Queen

Penelope would imagine and create. Circe's intricate pattern-design appeared to be finely woven, quite luminous, and most-beautiful in terms of quality."

"My discourteous exploratory personnel started critically shouting-out, calling the alluring witch 'Bitch', 'Whore', 'Harlot' and 'Hussy'. Circe quickly ceased her weaving and came-out at once from her forest residence, opened the bright doors, and suavely asked her sex-starved critics to eagerly enter. In their juvenile folly, and honoring their throbbing hard-ons, the dumb-shits all anxiously went inside the gleaming mansion."

"Eurylochus was the only member of his scouting patrol to stay outside, since my captain was a homosexual who found heterosexual sex quite anathema to his gay value system. Also, the distrustful son-of-a-bitch believed that sexy Circe might be tricking his porno-lusting subordinates. The gorgeous witch led the twenty-two dick-heads inside and sat their asses and stiff erections down upon comfortable stools and chairs; then, the crafty sorceress made her surprise want-to-get-laid guests drinks of cheese, barley meal and yellow honey stirred into Pramnian wine. But with the tempting food, the scheming whore surreptitiously mixed a potent drug, so that the affected soldiers would lose all fond memories of country, family and home."

"When the stupid-ass trespassers had drunk-down the specially concocted formula, Circe took her magic wand, waved the object at the men's un-magic pulsating wands, and then inexplicably teleported the fools directly into in her outside pig-pens. The twenty-two dumb-shits suddenly had bristles, heads, and snorting voice-boxes, just like oinking hogs, and their bodies now resembled corpulent swine. However, the transformed soldiers' self-oriented minds were just as human as before the dumb-ass fools had entered the witch's premises. Inside their pens, the pigheaded ignoramuses wept like infants suffering from painful colic spasms."

"Circe threw-down some feed in front of them: acorns, beech nuts, and rotten fruit, and the twenty-two deceived dupes greedily ate their lousy meal very voraciously, while simultaneously shitting and wallowing in the pigsty-pigpen's deep mud."

"My Lieutenant, that nitwit Eurylochus immediately sprinted like a scared antelope back to our swift black ship, bringing an incredible report of his companions' pigheaded fate. I slung my large, bronze, silver-studded sword across my bleeding shoulder, grabbed my dependable bow, and hurried-off to confront gorgeous and enchanting Circe."

"Next, dear Phaeacians; as I was rapidly moving through the sacred groves on my route to Circe's abode, I recalled that I had heard from fanciful traveling bards that the bitch was not an amateur charlatan, but rather was a minor goddess and accomplished chemist, highly skilled in formulating many magic potions. I halted my frantic forward hustle when my eyes espied Hermes of the Golden Wand, taking a healthy piss in the dark woods. The startled messenger god looked like a handsome young man experiencing the first growth of hair showing upon his face, under his armpits, and around his tassel-like dangle; that special innocent, adolescent age when youthful charm is at its majestic height. The courier god gripped my hand with his, which was still wet with urine, and then informatively spoke."

"Your fuck-head shipmates, now over there outside Circe's slop-dump, have been penned-up like swine inside narrow, feces-laden stalls. Dumb-ass King of Ithaca; are you intending now to set your lame-brain sailors free? Confidentially, I don't think you'll ever make it back to Ithaca all by yourself; if you trespass and encounter Circe. I assure you, like your crew, that you'll remain there in a stench-filled enclosure, being held captive with your aberrant pig underlings. But come, haughty Odysseus. Heed my sage advice. I'll keep you free from harm and save you from being stored in one of the witch's many hogsheads. Take the remedial medicine I'm now providing you, and continue onward to Circe's house of chaos. The secret ingredient will protect you, and will also keep your penis safe from any venereal diseases this day might bring. The sex-starved witch will not have the power to cast a neutralizing spell that will be able to counteract the medicine I'm offering. The potent herb that I'll provide you with will not allow Circe to challenge the Olympians' superior science."

"After that irrational statement had been communicated, the Killer of Argus pulled a magical plant out of the ground, offered a tablet from one of the thin branches, and explained the pill's exceptional features. Its roots were black, the flower milk-white, and it truly smelled like shit. The gods call it 'Moly'."

"Holy Moly!" I replied, a trifle too disrespectful to all of the vindictive Olympians. "I'll try this preventive protection, even though I abhor taking drugs, either uppers or downers!"

"Then, fleet-footed Hermes amazingly left the forest, and his three-dimensional form almost-instantly vaporized into a fine mist as the god's physical anatomy blended-in with the dense, surrounding, jungle vegetation. I continued on north to Circe's home, which had been somewhat visible from my only ship. As I stridently advanced in my quest, my racing heart was turning-over many gloomy thoughts, and my encumbered mind mulled-over all possible escape scenarios."

"After I had sneakily tiptoed up to the unscrupulous sorceress's gateway, I just stood there and gave a lusty shout. The goddess heard my resonant voice, and at once exited her crystal palace, opened her glimmering portals, thoroughly evaluated my masculine visage, smiled, and invited me inside with a casual hand gesture. Naturally, I had misgivings, but trusting Hermes's intercession, I entered the charming female's opulent mansion, where the conniving witch sat my rear end upon a silver-studded chair, accompanied by a beautiful utilitarian stool to rest my weary feet."

"Now dear King Alcinous and Queen Arete, my captivating hostess mixed her normally effective potion into a golden cup and steadily-handed the preparation to my right hand for me to drink. I conjectured that her heart was bent on enacting mendacious mischief; that the hot-looking bitch wanted to rape me, and perhaps suck me off, and my biological side wished to make my fantasies convert into true reality. The horny hussy used her wand to touch my erect wand and uttered the following words."

"Off now, you human swine, to your assigned pigsty, and lie-down in the muck alongside all the rest of your slimy, stinking, oinking companions."

"The arrogant-but-surprised whore loudly screamed when I methodically drew the sharp sword that had been situated on my thigh, and I charged at her exposed pubic zone, as if the weapon was intent on either murder or unnatural, perverted penetration. Circe's throat emitted a second piercing expletive. The shrieking strumpet ducked to the tile floor, and her sweaty hands were reaching for my strong knees. Through her multiple tears, the viperous destroyer of men spoke to me in a queer sort of pig-Greece, which I shall now endeavor to interpret."

"What sort of superior man, who is immune to my magic, are you? What kind of womb are you from? Human or animal? Where is your native land? Are your' parents mortal, or are they' gods? I'm amazed you drank this drug and then were not bewitched or enchanted. No other shipwrecked sailor who's ever sampled my mixture has ever been able to resist its effect, once the secret compound has passed the barrier of his teeth. Inside that handsome chest of yours, a titanic spirit successfully thwarts against my spell. I assume that you must be fabled Odysseus; that resourceful hero who the reigning gods are both discussing and punishing. The Killer of Argus, Hermes of the Golden Wand, always predicted that the champion Odysseus, arriving in his swift black ship, would stop here on his classic odyssey back from Troy. So, Odysseus; put that nasty sword back in its sheath; put your big boy tunic on, and let the two of us go up into my bed and wildly roll around in the straw. When we've made passionate love, then that is when we can learn to trust each other."

"Once Circe had indicated that proposal, I sagaciously answered her entreaty. "Bitch Circe; how can you ask me to be kind to you? In your own home, I've learned that you've changed half my crew into pigs, and you intend to keep me here because you know that I would never leave your miserable, controlling demeanor without them. You're plotting pernicious mischief as you charmingly-but-erroneously speak in amorous tones, inviting me to go up to your bedroom, into your bed, so when I have no clothes, you can do me harm, and destroy my precious salami with your dagger-like teeth. But I will not agree to screw you with my apparatus and my nuts, unless, slut Circe, you will morally swear a solemn oath that you'll make no more plans to injure my dangling dingle and my testicles with some novel, devious trick."

"When I had stressed those specific, fabricated comments, the irascible witch made the suggested oath at once, promising that she'd not injure my pecker, nor mangle my alternately bouncing, dangling balls. Once the reputed harlot had sworn and finished with the pledge, I escorted Circe to her splendid bed and watched her exotically and erotically remove her sexy, sheer, bedtime apparel in what constituted a magnificent striptease."

"Meanwhile, four women attendants serving Circe's needs were busy gossiping about my incidental arrival inside the female magician's crystal palace. Truthfully, despite my oath of fidelity to Queen Penelope, I would have much-preferred to screw any of the four fat and ugly hussies than to have wild, unbridled sex with a distrustful, voluptuous witch."

"After giving me a bath and a full body massage, Circe's delicate hands rubbed me all over with rich oil, and then the whoring schemer fitted me in a fine cloak and tunic, and led me to a handsome silver chair, actually embossed with expensive silver. An obese maid brought-in a lovely golden jug, and poured-out water into a silver basin, so that I could thoroughly wash, and the accommodating servant set a polished table at my side. Then, the distinguished faggot steward brought-in stale bread and set the loaf before me, probably thinking that I was a vagabond loafer, and not, in the flesh, the famous wanderer Odysseus of Ithaca."

"But in my troubled heart, I had no appetite for either sex or food. So, I just sat there being contemplative and immobile, thinking of other more essential things besides mundane sex and available edibles. But my keen perception was soon sensing something quite ominous, but also very obscure."

"When Circe noticed my apparent lethargy, not reaching for the delicious food, or covetously scrutinizing her thick, brown muffin, the obsessed control freak came-up close and softly whispered in my ear."

"Odysseus, why are you just sitting here, like a deaf and dumb mute, wearing out your heart, and keeping your wonderful sperm juices all to yourself. You've never touched your food or drink? Do you think this is another devious trick? Don't be afraid, brave man. I've already made a solemn promise that I won't injure you. Don't you trust my' genuine words."

"Circe, I want you to listen to this incredulous bullshit I'm about to disclose. What King or Captain with any self-respect would start to gluttonously eat and drink before he had released his shipmates and could reunite with his crew face to face? If you're being sincere in wanting to have the poop pumped out of you on yonder mattress, then I'm demanding that you set my comrades free, so that my own eyes can see my trusty seamen before you receive your special semen. But in essence, Circe; your heart and your mind are so radically depraved that you would probably savor all of my twenty-two incarcerated, grunting hog-men pork the living daylights out of your sexually deprived love tunnel!"

"When I had spoken that hard-hitting remark, Circe angrily rushed through the wide hall with her supernatural wand clutched in her right hand, and the lady tiger, that I was taming, violently opened-up the pigpen's doors. The witch vociferously scolded the herd, and then using a whip from the wall, the lady dictator drove the whole herd out."

"Then, dear King Alcinous; my transformed mariners now looked like full-grown, nine-year-old pigs, oinking and snorting their guts out of their foul mouths. Circe paced through the putrid-smelling group, actively, smearing upon their disgusting backs a uniquely different potion that instantly changed my men back to their normal human appearances, with all of my acquaintances looking much younger, taller, stronger and more handsome than ever before."

"Odysseus!" one called-out, recognizing my illustrious presence. "Why have you caused your crew additional grief and sorrow on this never-ending, fucked-up odyssey? You're a horrible and terrible disgrace to Ithaca, and to all of Greece."

"Circe herself was moved to pity at the soldier's vile testimony, realizing what agony my heart had been suffering, along with the myriad perils, death and devastation that my return from Troy had destructively generated. Standing close to me, the lovely goddess uttered and intimated her sympathy."

"Resourceful Odysseus, son of Laertes and child of Zeus; go now to the seashore to your swift ship, drag it up on land, and stash your goods and all the things you need inside the caves. Then, come back to my crystal palace again, and bring your loyal companions in your second squad with you."

"Because my crewmen now hated my total being, Circe's illogical words easily persuaded my proud heart to comply. I left the premises, and my mind was in a nebulous quandary as I walked in a mental fog back to the anchored Bireme. I found *my* trusty comrades idly standing together, all lamenting sadly and shedding an abundance of genuine tears."

"I immediately sensed that their brains had been tampered with by the unethical witch, and that my sailors didn't need my guidance anymore, because the asshole idiots believed that they were now safely back in Ithaca, and were looking and waiting for impending merchant marine work."

"Meanwhile, Circe had been acting kindly to the rest of my companions still being held hostage as human hogs, against their free will, inside her crystal home. The devious witch had her fat, ugly servants provide the other squad members with soothing, warm baths, rubbed their scrotum sacs with rich olive oil, and had dressed their now-attractive asses in warm cloaks and tunics. All of the converted former pig-men were now feeling jolly in happy spirits, eating crackers and drinking diluted pussy juice mixed with rye whiskey. When my transformed subordinates recognized me again, the selfish dolts completely ignored both my rank and my military presence."

"Resourceful and erudite Odysseus, son of Laertes, come now; enjoy my food, and indulge yourself and drink my special wine. Revive once more the sensational need you once felt for sex and female company. You're weary now, and you have no spirit or appetite for pleasure, which essentially, makes human life both tolerable and satisfying. Your entire fuckin' existence is focused on always brooding about your painful wanderings and the misery that your odyssey has engendered and caused. There's no bland joy or thrill that is residing inside your saddened heart; you have endured so much misery since leaving Troy; crazy 24/7 daily sex with me can magically erase your ever-burgeoning plethora of cruel emotional excruciation."

"My proud ego was affected and further damaged by the irresistible witch's implausible lexicon. I stayed there like a moron for one whole year, feasting on sweet wine, and partaking of huge stores of meat. But as the months and seasons evaporated into eternal time, eventually, the long spring days returned. A full year had passed when my former trusty comrades summoned me to a showdown conference."

"You god-driven, self-centered, non-Cretan cretin!" my old friend Eurassisgras admonished me and my ranking authority. "Now then; you weak-minded dunderhead. The time has come when you must think again about your native land, about your wife Penelope, and about your son, Telawoman, er, I mean Telemachus. If you're really some special jerk-off especially selected by the gods, who's fate is destined or worthy to be saved, you might be able to reach your lofty home and native soil once more. Now is the correct time to act accordionly, er, I meant, 'to act accordingly'."

"My conceited heart was drastically altered by Eurassisgras's irrational argument. So, all day long, until the sun disappeared on the western horizon, I sat there on an improvised picnic table, feasting on huge plates of meat and getting stone-cold drunk on sweet wine. When dusk faded and the pall of darkness settled-in, my pissed-off crewmen staying inside the crystal mansion, and no longer hogs, all lay down to sleep in the shadowy hall. I went to Circe, who was resting in her impressive bed; I clasped her knees, and then gently rubbed her massive, engorged, penis-sized clitoris. The sexually aroused sorceress listened attentively to my entire grief-laden request."

"Beautiful Circe; I plead that you fulfill the promises you had made a year ago to send me home. My spirit's keen to leave your protection, as are the hearts of my envious companions, who now aspire to eliminate my ass, colon and epididymis from this totally insane planet. Oh, strange lady warden; please release me and my destiny at once from your bureaucratic, local government protection program. I humbly seek your blessing for me to depart from your isolated island."

"Crying bona fide tears, the bitch/witch answered in a melancholy tone of voice, saying: "Resourceful and wet-fingered Odysseus, son of Laertes and Zeus's inane, insane child, if it's against your obstinate will, yes; you born with a gigantic stubbed head; you should not now remain in my crystal palace frustrating my sexual needs. But first, I've cleverly manipulated your complicated fate. You must complete another trip and journey-down deep inside the bowels of Mother Earth, and venture to the bleak kingdom of

Hades and Persephone. In that terribly gloomy realm, you are hereby appointed to interact with the shade of blind Teiresias, the deceased Theban prophet. His mind is unimpaired, even though his body has disintegrated into dust decadent decades ago. Even though he's fuckin' dead as a dildo, dreaded Hades, who is the brother of Zeus and Poseidon, has granted the deceased prophet the power to understand your plight, and perhaps absolve your chronic curse, and afford your spirit a viable solution, or perhaps an appropriate remedy. All of the other fucked-up souls trapped down there in that unimaginable hellhole simply flit about, mere shadows and hazy two-dimensional apparitions."

"As Circe finished her brief summary, my desire to live and continue on my arduous odyssey was breaking like a fragile eggshell. I sat weeping upon her bed, for my heart no longer wished to survive, or even glimpse the light of day. But when I'd had enough of shedding tears and rolling around in mental distress, scratching my abominable hemorrhoids and also my crotch-itch, I politely answered her sense of compassion and requested for her to administer benign mercy."

"Circe; who'll be the guide on such a perilous underground trip? No black ship has ever sailed across the River Styx to subterranean Hades. What impossible task are you suggesting?"

"Resourceful Odysseus, son of Laertes and Zeus's illegitimate child who somehow popped out of your father's asshole; do not concern yourself with a competent pilot to adroitly navigate your one remaining ship. Raise the mast, spread-out your peaceful white sail, and just take your seat. And I now oracle that the breath of North Wind Boreas will propel you on your unknown misadventure. But once your Bireme has crossed the flowing Ocean, drag it ashore at Persephone's weeping willow groves; that is, upon the level beach where tall popular poplars grow. The dismal willows shed their fruit, right beside deep swirling Oceanus. Then, dear Odysseus, you must venture directly to disconsolate and dispassionate Hades' murky, sinister throne-chamber, where easy-to-spell Periphlegethon, along with grammatically-correct Cocytus, together form a precarious cascade of grand rapids, which streams and branches-off the dreaded River Styx. Act bolder and you'll locate a boulder precisely where those two foaming rivers have their confluence. Go there, heroic and singular human specimen, and honor my explicit instructions. Dig a deep hole at that place, approximately two-feet-square. Pour libations to the revered dead contributors to Greek Civilization around your shallow pit."

"That's more shit you want me to do than that which overflows a colossal cesspool!" I futilely objected. "Why the hell can't I just set sail for Ithaca?"

"Circe ignored my oral opposition and proceeded to give me more illogical directions. "Then, Odysseus; pray your swollen balls off in earnest to all the hapless, good-hearted Greeks who've died in the past, with a vow that, when you reach Ithaca, you'll solemnly sacrifice a barren heifer, a pregnant cow, and a really fat woman to Zeus and Poseidon. That uncanny promise will grant you a brief conference with the specter of Teiresias."

"When early Dawn appeared, glowing upon her eastern golden throne, Circe dressed me in a splendid cloak and tunic, and as part of her weird farewell ceremony, clothed her body in a long white robe. On her bald head she placed a transparent veil. Next, I dashed through her entire, hundred-room crystal palace, rousing, but not arousing, my pissed-off, rebellious companions. With words of reassurance, I addressed them all as strong warriors and not as dumb-ass pigs."

"No more sleeping now; by that, I mean no sweet slumbering and jerking-off while blissfully imagining hot sex in your fantasy white dreams. Let's go and re-embark on *our* more-than-challenging odyssey back to Ithaca. Lovely Circe has told me exactly what to do along the sacred way. Amazingly, King Alcinous; my remaining crewmembers did not protest and wholeheartedly agreed to comply with my nonsensical request."

Jay Dubya

Chapter 14

"ODYSSEUS JOURNEYS TO HADES"

"Once we had reached our previously damaged Bireme down on the beach, we strenuously dragged the vessel out into the gleaming sea, attached and hoisted-up the sail to the mast in the center of our black ship; led onboard the adequate supply of sheep, and of apples to prevent scurvy, and then embarked ourselves subject to Fate's volatile mercy. All day long, the sail stayed full of a favorable wind. We sped like a smaller version of Hermes across the wine-dark sea, until the sun went-down in the west, and soon the sky grew dark and spookily dreary."

"Yes, King Alcinous and Queen Arete; we gambled on our gambol. Our once-reliable ship then reached the banks of the deep stream Oceanus, a region, according to legend, that always had been wrapped in mist and cloud. We sailed into that fog rather easily, and upon completing our arrival, dragged our ship upon the shore of Oceanus, until we reached on foot the place Circe had graphically described and designated."

"Feeling frightened, Eurassisgras begged and urged me: "Dear Odysseus; please eminent Captain! Let's get the fog out of here!" The non-amusing asshole grieved and pleaded, obviously referring to the intense eerie mist that had spookily enveloped our patrol."

"Perimedes, Eurylochus, Periodontis and Eurassisgras firmly held the necks of the expendable sheep designated to be our sacrificial victims, while I unsheathed the sharp sword upon my thigh and dug the square hole Circe had commanded. I poured-out libations to give honor to all the dead, first with milk and honey, second with wine, and a third with water and semen. Around the sacred pit, I barely sprinkled gluten-free barley meal, oats and imported rice."

"Then, to pay homage to Hades and Persephone, and also to show reverence to the helpless, non-talking heads of the dearly departed, I offered many impromptu prayers, with attached promises that I'd humbly soon sacrifice, and in the future, permanently demonstrate good religious faith, once I returned safely back to Ithaca. And finally, throwing into the overall god-worshipping equation, a cheap, about-to-die, barren heifer would be offered upon an altar of volcanic rock in the center of the city, along with a fat woman. Citing an abundance of prayers and contrite pledges, I, a mere

119

suppliant, called upon the families of the dead to recognize my patriotic allegiance to all Greeks, both living and deceased."

"Next, I held-out the chosen sheep above the hole, slit their throats one by one, and let their dark blood flow into the shallow hollow I had just excavated. Then, out of Erebus came swarming-up shades of the dead: brides; young unmarried men; old farts worn-out from arduous toil; young, tender two-dimensional girls with hairy bushes, and flat-imaged male teenagers with hearts still absorbing new grief. Their sorrowful existence also featured the ghosts of many warriors that had been wounded by bronze spears, who had died in battle at Troy, still wearing their blood-stained two-dimensional armor after being hammered and brutalized. Crowds of them came thronging in from all sides, scaring the living shit out of me, and also out of petrified Eurassisgras."

"Pale fear seized my heart out of hearing scary other-world cries that were emerging out of the pitiless pit. In my great confusion, I called my comrades, ordering them to flay and burn the dead sheep still lying there, and instructed them to pray to the gods like there would be no tomorrow for us mariners, and to especially beg for Pallas Athene's protection from mighty King Hades and pallid-faced Queen Persephone, sitting together in dismal darkness upon their ominous ebony thrones."

"In seconds, King Alcinous; to my expanding apprehension, there suddenly appeared the awesome ghost of my dead mother, Anticleia, Autolycus's deformed child. I had left her still alive when I had enthusiastically departed Ithaca and set-out for Troy in quest of selfish glory and earthly fame. Once I caught sight of her flat ghost swirling about my awed presence, I relentlessly wept and cried like a hungry infant, and I felt pity and remorse in all four chambers of my reprehensible heart. Nonetheless, in spite of my mounting emotional sorrow, I could not allow her nebulous, no-longer-alive specter, get too near the sacred slain sheep blood, until I had interviewed and questioned blind Teiresias, or perhaps first located his maternal ancestor, infamous Mother Teiresias."

"Now King Alcinous, the shade of the prophet Teiresias of Thebes eventually appeared, holding a golden staff that apparently represented his renowned wisdom and sagacity. The eminent savant immediately recognized my identity and began speaking some indiscernible, intellectual gibberish."

"Adventurous and fatuous Odysseus, Laertes' son, and Zeus's bastard child; what now do you seek, you very unlucky man? Why leave the sunlight, come to this horribly joyless place, and see the dead just for your own preposterous folly? Move from the sacred pit you have established, and put-away your lethal sword, so that I may drink the dark sheep blood and speak the truth, as I fathom it, to satisfy your' naïve, dumb-ass inquiries."

"When Teiresias had enunciated that profound rhetoric, I fearfully drew back and stubbornly thrust my studded sword inside its sheath. Once the blameless prophet had swallowed-up the dark blood, the acclaimed shade said these rather pathetic, prophetic words."

"Glorious Odysseus, you ask about your honey-sweet return to Ithaca, if and when it might occur. But an omnipotent and jealous god, who has many grievances and complaints against you, will make your journey absolutely bitter. My gifted vision, which I've somehow retained after death, informs me that as soon as you've escaped the dark blue sea and have reached the sinister island of Thrinacia, you'll find grazing in the resplendent pastures the sacred cattle and rich flocks of Helios Hyperion, who hears and watches over everything in Heaven, and everything occurring on Earth, which includes your plenteous and notorious bullshit activities."

"Now, Odysseus, if you wisely leave the cattle unharmed and keep your mind concentrated on your return home, you may reach Ithaca, though you'll encounter more perplexing, fucked-up difficulties. But if you dare even touch the sacred bovines, then I foresee widespread destruction for your crew, for you, and for your already-damaged Bireme. And even if you yourself miraculously escape, you'll arrive home again later than expected, and grieving your' ass off in someone else's ship; that is, after losing all of your crewmen at sea. And if I may add to your ongoing quandary, there'll be massive trouble waiting for you at home; insolent and reprehensible suitors, worthy of castration, will be parasitically eating-up your livelihood, and wooing your godlike wife by giving courtship gifts with money that had been pilfered from you. But if and when you return from your skein of tragedies, you'll surely take sweet revenge for all their prolific violence and their numerous immoral violations."

"And Mother; what should I be doing in Ithaca in regard to my properties, wife and son?"

"My mother's specter remained silent, so the prophet's shade again spoke. Once you have killed the contemptible suitors, Odysseus, Teiresias's apparition informed; yes, those human worms egregiously dwelling inside your unkempt palace, then I suggest that you cunningly find a well-made oar and go and seek-out a people who know little of the sea, and who don't put salt on any food they eat, and who have no special knowledge of ships painted red, or who know any pertinent shit about well-made oars that serve those ships as ocean-gliding wings. Now great Odysseus, I'll tell you a sure sign you won't forget. When some wayward stranger inadvertently encounters you carrying a fractured oar and asks if you've got a shovel used for winnowing, then immediately fix that broken oar and offer a rich sacrifice to Lord Poseidon with a fattened ram, a bull, a whore, and a neurotic boar that breeds with many sows. Then quickly leave that fucked-up scene and frenetically race home, and in your back weed-infested garden, make sacred offerings to the immortal gods, who hold wide heaven and have jurisdiction over the entire known world. Your death, my senses perceive, will ultimately ascend out of the sea when you are feeble and bent-over at a ripe old age, but with your grateful people prospering around you. In all those futuristic events to come, I'm telling you the inflexible truth."

"The profit's mysterious shade finished speaking. Then, I replied in turn: "Teiresias; no doubt the gods themselves have spun the threads of this future horse-shit, clown show. But come, tell me now, and speak more essential truth. I can see over yonder the shade of my dead mother, sitting near the stench-odor blood saying nothing familiar like 'Fuck you Odysseus', just as she used to yell. I've noticed that her ghost does not dare confront the face of her own son, or even make an effort to speak to me. Tell me, my lord, how she may understand just who I am."

"I'll tell you exactly what the Hades is happening, Odysseus. It's all quite elementary to comprehend. Whichever shadow of the dead you let approach the blood will speak to you and tell the truth, but those you keep away and try to protect from Hades' tremendous wrath, will once again withdraw."

"After articulating those explanatory words, the shade of Lord Teiresias returned to the dark gates of Hades, having made his dramatic prophecy known. I stayed there next to the sacred pit, motionless and undaunted, until my mother's specter flitted around, instantly stopped, and greedily drank the dark sacrificial blood. Then, marvelously, she realized and knew me from our shared past. Full of sorrow, her ghoulish throat spoke: "My disobedient son; how have you come to this black, forsaken, subterranean world while still being alive? For living men, it's both impossible and sinful to discover these arcane things you're presently witnessing! Your occult experience will involve huge rivers, fearful streams, and frightening spirits and goblins. Stand between us, first and foremost, and pray to Oceanus, which no man can cross on foot, unless of course a low I.Q. idiot such as yourself has a death wish to drown. Please Odysseus; pray to Oceanus that you need a sturdy ship to complete your' infamous, fucked-up odyssey. Have you only now voyaged to this condemned territory from Troy? Have you still not reached depleted Ithaca, or seen your wife suffering humiliation and hardship within your own house?"

"Mother, I had to journey and arrive here to Hades', meet and interact with the shade of Teiresias of Thebes, and hear his infallible prophecy. I have not yet approached nor come near Achaea's shores, or disembarked in our ass-backwards native land. I've been aimlessly wandering around this hazardous part of the world in constant misery, ever since I left Ithaca with noble Agamemnon, bound for Troy, to fight against the all-too-fertile small-dicked Trojans. But now, Mother; tell me this unalterable truth! What grievous form of death took you away? Was your' demise a lengthy illness? Did archer Artemis attack and kill you with her sharp arrows? Did you die during a masturbation climax?"

"Obnoxious and incorrigible son; your grandfather had died of extreme heartbreak when you failed to return home after so many years of being absent. Even when you were a difficult toddler, you tried running away from the family palace at every given opportunity. And Odysseus, I gladly kicked the proverbial pottery bowl soon after your grandfather had died from ordinary old age symptoms."

"Mother, before you flit away and vanish, please tell me of my wife, Queen Penelope. What are her thoughts and plans? Is she still there with our son, Telemachus, faithfully keeping watch on everything? Or has my spouse been married to the finest of Achaeans pursuing her ivory-white hand?"

"Odysseus; you can rest assured that loyal Penelope has been both impatiently and patiently waiting for you to return to Ithaca, and is desiring to receive your loving embrace."

"Well, King Alcinous and Queen Arete, in my immortal soul, I thought about how much I yearned to once again hold my mother's shade, for in the past, she had owned many lamps. My spirit urged me to clasp her in my arms, and three times I moved towards her vague image, but on each approach, she slipped-away, like an elusive shadow, or like a hazy summer dream. Then, I mustered the necessary wherewithal to call-out in a disgruntled tone of voice: "Mother, why do you not linger longer with me? I'd like to hold your frail hands, so that even here in bleak Hades, we might throw our loving arms around each other and share our icy lamentation. Or are you a spying phantom, dispatched by royal Queen Persephone, sent to harass my presence and make me groan and grieve still more?"

"My foolish child-man; of all Greek warriors being most unfortunate, no, dreaded Persephone, daughter of Zeus, is not presently deceiving you, nor is the Queen of Death planning to put your breathless corpse on permanent cemetery lay-away. For you see, my son, once mortals die, this phenomenon flashing before your eyes is what's actually ordained for their restive spirits. The ethereal sinews of past heroes no longer hold flesh and bone together. The mighty power of a blazing fire destroys and cremates both temporal flesh and bones; that is, once our spirit flies from its earthly shell, our white bones gradually disintegrate over time. And before that process happens, the everlasting soul slips away like a vapor into time and space, and, like a cloudy dream, the soul flutters around in furious concentric circles, eventually ending-up swirling-around in this horrid, repugnant hellhole known as Hades."

Chapter 15

"ODYSSEUS CONTINUES ADDRESSING THE PHAEACIANS"

Odysseus paused momentarily to clear his raspy throat, and soon resumed describing to the alert and attentive King Alcinous, Queen Arete and their silent, spellbound Phaeacian counselors how he had witnessed in Hades a large number of famous women's shades from olden times, including flat nude specters of strippers, lap-dancers, porno stars and prominent bordello prostitutes. King Alcinous asked his political allies how the incompetent politicians were evaluating Odysseus's stunning testimony.

"Phaeacians, how does this man seem to you in terms of beauty, stature, and honesty? Do you believe that this storyteller possesses a fair, well-balanced mind? Indeed, he is my honored guest, though each of you at this meeting shares in this presumed honor, too. So, don't be quick to send this garrulous fellow away from Phaeacia, and conversely, don't hold back your gifts to one who is in such great need."

Then, old coot warrior Echeneus stood and addressed the others in attendance, both old and young.

"Friends; what our wise Queen, er, I mean King has just stated, as we'd expect, is not wide of the mark. I hereby make a motion that the final decision concerning this odd fellow who claims to be the famed Odysseus rests with Alcinous. As for this Greek Odysseus, here, I'm inclined to tell the itinerant asshole to go to Hades, but by his own words, our prevaricating guest has already been there!"

Once the hoary codger Echeneus finished his opinionated remarks, King Alcinous spoke-out: "I maintain that my wife, Queen Arete, indeed should have the final word in this important matter. But though our guest is longing to return, let him agree to stay in Phaeacia overnight until tomorrow. By then, I'll have collected all our gifts and donations to finance his glorious trip back to Ithaca, wherever the hell that obscure island is located on the flat Earth. Now let our oddball guest resume his story."

"Noble Lord Alcinous; of all the most renowned residents on this island, if you asked me, Odysseus of Ithaca, to stay for one whole year, to arrange my escort and give me splendid gifts, then I would still amiably agree. It's far better to get back to one's own dear native land with more wealth in hand, which I intend and promise to fully repay in the future. I'll win more respect from my subjects and predicates, the city residents, most of whom will be lazy, indolent parasites depending on my generous goodwill to supply the general population with adequate welfare and ample food stamps."

"Odysseus, when we look at you, we do not perceive that you're in any way a lying fraud," King Alcinous stated. "You speak so well, and you have such a noble heart inside your community chest, just like a few carnival barkers who have recently ripped me off, and then the criminal scoundrels fled town in a hurry. You've so far told your story with a minstrel's skill, the painful agonies of the Greek Argives, along with your own singular obstacles and dilemmas, as well. Come then, tell me more of your stranger-than-myth accounting, and speak the honest-to-Zeus truth."

"What else do you want to hear from me?" Odysseus asked Alcinous. "I have a resilient will, and a stubborn disposition, but not a malleable soul."

"Did you see any of your deceased comrades in Hades; those godlike men who went with you to Troy and met their deaths there? This night before us will be lengthy, astonishingly so. It's not yet time to sleep with our favorite fabricated sex dolls; so, Odysseus, tell us more of your marvelous sequence of implausible events."

"Lord Alcinous; once Queen Persephone dispersed those female shadows here and there, wildly swirling-around before my amazed recognition, then the grieving shade of King Agamemnon of Mycenae, son of Atreus, appeared. The frightening ghost knew me at once, and after drinking the sacred dark sheep blood, the leader of the Greek forces against Troy wept aloud, shedding many tears, and stretched-out his cold misty hands to reach my warm grasp. But the dead brother of King Menelaus no longer had any inner power or strength, not like the force his supple limbs had possessed before, when the bad-ass son-of-a-bitch would beat the shit out of me before each ensuing battle. Pity filled my heart at then feeling his overall weakness and demise."

"Then, I called-out to the murdered leader of the Greek forces against Troy: "Lord Agamemnon, son of Atreus, king of Mycenae; what fatal net of grievous death has destroyed you? Did Poseidon stir the winds into a furious storm, and you died from a tremendous blowjob? Or, were you killed by savage enemies on foreign land, while you were confiscating their cattle herds, or purloining their rich flocks of sheep? Or were you fighting to seize their town and carry-off their wives who didn't care who or what screwed them, as long as the kinky whores got screwed up their wet, splashy love tunnels?"

"Ingenious Odysseus, Laertes's son, and Zeus's mentally unstable child; Poseidon did not kill me in my ships by rousing turbulent winds into a vicious storm. Nor was I slain by inspired enemy pyromaniacs performing scorched earth tactics upon the land. No, Odysseus. Scumbag Aegisthus, lover of my unfaithful, adulterous wife Clytemnestra, sister of Helen, contrived my assassination while I was away from Greece ten-years at Troy," Agamemnon's ghost somberly grieved. "That despicable ballbuster Aegisthus was amply assisted by my accursed spouse. The evil pair plotted and succeeded in murdering my ass. Clytemnestra hurled a fish net over me while I was splish-splashing, taking a bath, and then she and Aegisthus repeatedly stabbed me as if I was a common sacrificial tuna fish!"

"That's appalling, dear Agamemnon! Such an ignoble death for such a noble King! Surely, over the years, wide-thundering Zeus has shown a lethal hatred towards the family of Atreus, and also against myself, thanks to the conniving of some evil women behaving worse than Pandora had done with her box. Many Greek champions have died because of Helen, causing the Trojan War fiasco by foolishly eloping with Prince Paris to Troy, and then Clytemnestra arranging an assassination trap for you, while you, Agamemnon, were gallantly fighting alongside me over in Asia Minor."

"Now King Alcinous, poor Agamemnon didn't have a ghost of a chance from escaping his wife's conspiracy against him. I believe that Aegisthus was inspired to reenact the myth of Ares screwing Aphrodite, Hephaestus's wife, while the ugly blacksmith god was away hammering another sex-starved goddess!"

"Did you have any conversation with the spirit of that heel Achilles, who is also dead?"

"Yes, King Alcinous. Achilles, along with his close friend, Ajax, the detergent huckster, were killed at Troy. Ajax was also flitting around in that shadowy entrance to Hades, hysterically behaving as another haunting, uncleansed specter."

"What did Achilles say?" Alcinous wanted to know. "I hope that *that* heel wasn't pulling your leg!"

"Upon being solicited by my quivering voice, the famed hero Achilles addressed me in a creepy, screeching soprano tone:

"Adventurous Odysseus, Laertes's son and Zeus's obdurate child, what a bold and daring dick-head you were and are! What exploit will your vagabond heart ever dream-up to top this imaginative expedition you've undertaken down to doom-and-gloom Hades? How can you dare venture-down-here into this morbid Kingdom of the Dead, the dwelling place for the mindless shades of worn-out warrior assholes? Even the minstrel Orpheus scooted out of here like a bat out of Hades after finding the shade of his beloved sweetheart, Eurydice! Do you realize how mortified I feel being down here with mediocre dumb-shits who accomplished basically nothing of significance in their human existence? What a depressing psychological letdown it is for me, having to share this utterly bleak environment with idle, craven, brain-dead dumb-shits for all fuckin' eternity! Do you now fully understand my great frustration Odysseus, after, while I was still living, achieving such great fame and fortune throughout all of Greece?"

"Mighty Achilles, son of Peleus;" I respectfully replied to the awesome apparition. "I came here to Hades because I had to confer with Teiresias of Thebes, and hear his prophecy of my future return to Ithaca. I've not yet reached Achaean land, where I need to screw my wife Penelope, kill two-dozen suitors, and get laid some more. Ever since my fleet had left Troy, I'm in constant trouble with the mercurial-minded Powers-that-Be. But as for you, Achilles, there's no big or little-dicked man in former days who was more blessed with military success than you, and none will come in the future. Before now, while you were still alive, we Achaeans honored you as we did the gods. And now, the jealous gods have arranged your death, but because of your strong desire, you should rule down here with power among those less-ambitious cowards whirling around you, who have also died. So, Achilles, why the lugubrious expression appearing upon your pallid countenance? You have no cause to grieve, just because you are now stone-cold dead."

"King Alcinous; I then noticed that Hades had given Achilles a very humiliating punishment. The formerly virulent warrior was now stark naked, and the humiliated flat ghost's emaciated body featured a small, hollow weenie hanging between its legs."

"Don't try to comfort me about my unexpected, early death, glorious Odysseus," spoke Achilles' shade. "I'd rather live working as a common wage-laborer in Ithaca than preside-over all the lazy wasted dead-heads here in Hades, who incidentally, were just as lazy and wasted in their earlier earthly lives. Yes, Odysseus; everyone down-here is on the same fucked-up level and privilege, and we have all surrendered our precious free will in order to become lousy, lackluster, dull-minded slaves of apathetic King

Hades and Queen Persephone. Free will is positively everything, Odysseus. Down-here in this wretched Greek hell, there is none at all!"

"With those disconsolate words, King Alcinous, the shade of swift Achilles moved-off and filtered like a vapor into distant meadows filled with faded daffodils. The other macabre shadows stood around me, sobbing in sorrow, all asking an annoying multitude of questions about the ones they knew and loved. The only soul who stood apart from the rest was the shade of Ajax, the detergent entrepreneur, still full of heightened anger for my meritorious victory, when I'd beaten the shit out of his intestines during a minor quarrel that had developed on the shores of Troy beside our ships. In that epic competition between Ajax and me, mutually struggling for dead Achilles's weapons and breastplate, after a lethal arrow had pierced the hero's exposed tendon, which was *his* only vulnerable, unprotected body part, Ajax and I became bitter foes. The Trojan Prince Paris, who Achilles tried to plaster, shot the life-ending arrow, and it was Paris who stole-away King Menelaus's wife Helen from Sparta, and that abduction started the entire fucked-up Trojan War. Menelaus's brother, King Agamemnon of Mycenae, soon organized the major Greek expedition of one thousand ships against Priam, King of Troy, who had approved of his son, playboy Paris, stealing-off with whoring Helen, Menelaus's wife."

"Ajax, worthy son of Telamon, can't you forget our past altercation at the shores of Troy. Even when you're now dead, your vitriolic anger at me over those destructive weapons remains dominant inside your' envious spirit? The gods turned Achilles's armor into a curse against the Argives, and when we regrettably lost you, too, it was worse than visiting a popular brothel only to find gay homosexuals giving bad head to all the dissatisfied patrons. Now that you've been killed, I want you to know that Achaeans mourn your death unceasingly, just as they do that of Achilles, and of Agamemnon. No one is to blame for this ongoing tragedy but Zeus, who in his terrifying rage against the army of our Danaan spearmen regiment, implemented his arbitrary, almighty whims; that's precisely what brought on *your* untimely death. Come over here, my detergent guru, so that you can hear me say that your soul is supposed to be cleansed instead of your unwarranted duration here in Hades being disinfected by fire. Stop being so futilely antagonistic towards me!"

"Grudge-happy Ajax's ghost did not reply, but left, moving away towards Erebus, to join the other rotating shadows chaotically revolving-away in the far distance. For all his colossal rage, the formidable combatant would have talked more verbal garbage to me, or me to him, but at that brief moment, I wished to see and consult more shades of those revered war colleagues who also had died at Troy."

"And King Alcinous, after that session with Ajax, I saw Tityus, son of the glorious Earth, eternally punished for disposing of Leto. Tityus, who when living, looked like a giant female breast, was lying prone upon the ground in Hades, with his suddenly magnified body covering around nine acres or more in width. Two voracious vultures sat there, one on either side of his abdomen, ripping-out his liver and relentlessly biting his one huge nipple; the buzzards' sharp beaks were jabbing deep inside his guts and chest, for his paralyzed hands could not protect his vulnerable body."

"Then, King Alcinous; my astute pupils spotted Tantalus, suffering in perpetual agony. I cautiously advanced through a shadowy cave and entered the spooky area of eternal atonement where the pathetic, grieving ghosts of dead individuals were posthumously punished for violating the capricious gods' supreme laws. Even Sisyphus, who labored for all eternity, pushing a huge rock up a curved hill, only to have it roll down the incline so that the process would have to be repeated over and over again, stopped to greet my' intrusion. Sisyphus was so inspired by my company that the punished victim immediately organized his own underground, ungrateful dead band called 'The Rolling Stones', and instantly began mimicking the musician Orpheus's fine example. Even the crackling dancing flames, that flourished in leaping fences of fire in that atonement section of Hades, soon heated-up the whole damned area."

"Next, I advanced further into the darkened caverns of Hades and again encroached-upon Tantalus, who had been eternally punished by having to stand chained inside a pool that was filled chest-high with delicious water. An abundance of luscious fruits on tree limbs dangled above the hungry and thirsty dead man's head. When Tantalus was 'tantalized' to drink, every minute or so, the manacled figure would bend-over, and the cool water would rapidly drain out of the tank. When frustrated, chained and hungry Tantalus would reach for a ripe peach, or for a savory overhead apple, the desired fruit would either disappear, or be blown-away by a sudden wind gust. The penalized fellow was so enraptured and entranced by my appearance that he momentarily ceased performing his eternal sentence, and Tantalus's rejuvenated spirit fondly recalled, and briefly shared, how wonderful it was once like, just to breathe and be alive."

"And then, King Alcinous, I noticed my mighty idol Hercules's gloomy shade, or at least his flat image. Around the former discus champion, ghouls of the other melancholy dead were making eerie noises, sounding much like an irritated covey of large birds in distress, erratically fluttering their two-dimensional wings in a quite-terrifying manner. And like dark night, the strongest of Greeks was glaring all around him, almost dazed, turning his bothered head back and forth in rapid repetition. The still-muscular specimen, who when alive easily killed, with his bare hands, numerous bears, wild boars, and lions, and indeed, was always-triumphant in his various battles, fights and murders; along with him defeating a catalogue of very daunting evil adversaries. Hercules's saddened eyes alertly noticed my entry into his designated area of atonement, and the disconsolate, eternally sentenced fellow immediately recognized my three-dimensional identity."

"Odysseus, you resourceful warrior, son of Laertes and a disobedient foe of Almighty Zeus; are you now bearing an unhappy fate below the sunlight, as I, too, once did? What the hell are you' doing down here on the wrong side of the grass? I was a son of Zeus, and yet, I had to bear so many troubles, and had been forced by Olympus to perform those twelve demanding labors for a weak, craven king vastly inferior to me, but still, given the authority to keep assigning me the harshest tasks to complete for *his* satisfaction. On one occasion, the feckless royal son-of-a-bitch sent me here to bring away Hades' personal hound back to the surface. There was no other challenge the cowardly bastard could dream-up that would be more difficult for me than *that* superhuman enterprise. But I carried the ferocious three-headed, snarling dog Cerberus off, and bravely brought the fierce canine up from Hades."

"With those incredible words, recollecting one of his most famous exploits, Hercules's specter returned to its preoccupation of constantly searching left and right, which was representative of King Hades' cruel sense of amusement. I sadly stayed at that morbid place a while longer, but then I feared that spiteful Queen Persephone might assign a horrific monster, perhaps grotesque Medusa the Gorgon, to face me by surprise, and instantaneously turn my ass into an inanimate stone statue for all eternity."

"And then, dear Phaeacians; shivering from overwhelming fear, I hastily initiated my recollected path back up to the magnificent sunshine, the purpose of my memorized ascent from Hades being to be reunited with my cherished ship and with my unhappy crew, who habitually blamed me for all of their myriad emotional maladies. My disenchanted sailors reluctantly loosened-off the mooring cables at the Bireme's stern, and my dejected mariners angrily took their seats along each rowing bench. A rising swell gently carried our vessel away, moving along Ocean's swift-moving stream.

The sailors vigorously rowed at first, but then a fair wind blew, and assisted our sea passage onward toward our next unknown, perilous adventure."

Chapter 16

"THE SIRENS, SCYLLA & CHARYBDIS, AND THE CATTLE"

"That second night, our battered ship sentimentally sailed-on along the gentle waves, away from Ocean's tugging stream, across the great wide sea, and in several more days, we reached Aeaea, the island being the presumed home and dancing grounds of Dawn, and the actual bailiwick of the wily witch Circe. Our Bireme sailed into the placid harbor, and soon we hauled our ship up the inclined beach, and then ambled along the serene shoreline. There, waiting for the emergence of bright Dawn, we surrendered to fatigue and fell asleep under a full silvery moon."

"Circe was well-aware of our return from Lord Hades' obscure subterranean realm. Dressed in her finery, the alluring, lonesome bitch quickly came to us with her mechanical-like servants, who were obediently carrying bread, plenty of meat, and flasks of bright red wine. Then, the devious sorceress stood in our midst and immediately criticized our reappearance on her fucked-up island."

"You reckless ninnies; you ludicrous jerk-offs must have toxic worms for brains; you death-wish retards have been down to Hades while still alive, to meet and defy death twice, when other mortals die just once. But come, enjoy this special food and drink this tasty wine. Take all day if you idiots so desire. Then, as soon as Dawn fully arrives, without her boyfriend, Tony, you'll sail-on to your next destination. I'll show you your course, Odysseus, and inform you each sign to look for, although there will be no billboards to view on the oceans. I augur that you'll not suffer any great pain if you adhere to discretion, and not dare to challenge the gods' dictatorial authority."

"Listen, Circe. First of all, close your beautiful legs. Your deep pink hole smells like cheap vinegar. Secondly, even though my crew and I distrust you, horny whore, our proud hearts and peckers agree with the language you've just regurgitated."

"And so, patient King Alcinous, Queen Arete, and all of you other sore-assed, petite Phaeacians sitting there hearing my extended story; all that day, until the sun retired from the sky in the west, we stuffed our stomachs while relaxing on that really weird island, eating rich supplies of delicious meat and drinking-down sweet wine mixed with pig's entrails, until darkness arrived. We slept beside our ship's stern cables, which that night seemed all-too-lenient. But that scheming strumpet Circe, who had the hots for any man's dingle-dangle, large or small, took me by the hand and led me away some distance from my dozing crew. Through her power of suggestion, the kinky doll persuaded me to sit in muck, while she stretched-out beside me upon the muddy, damp ground. I told her every detail of our trip ever since I had left Troy, specifically describing all of the sensational adventures and episodes from start to finish. I never saw anyone yawn as often as Circe did, and I noticed in the moonlight that her dry mouth was almost as wide, but not nearly as wet, as her alluring pink, deep-hole vagina. Then, saddened Circe spoke."

"All these things have thus come to an end, Odysseus, but unlike our imaginary sex life, at least your lengthy skein of troubles has had a definite beginning. But you must listen now to what I say. My gift of prophecy has me comprehending that a god himself will soon be reminding you of something I cannot reveal out of fear of being punished myself. First of all, you'll encounter the Sirens, mermaid chicks of the sea. Like me, the naked, big-breasted beauties seduce all men who come across their powerful beckoning, and no man who unwittingly sails past and hears the Sirens' call ever returns. But unlike my hairy snatch, the Sirens' scaley crotches smell like rotten tuna flesh. Now Odysseus, beware of the Sirens' clear-toned singing, which will captivate your heart and make your manhood erect. They'll be restlessly sitting upon a jetty, near a meadow, surrounded by an immense pile of heaped, rotting, human bones encased in shriveled skin, which stinks even worse than the mermaids' smelly crotches do. Any besides, Odysseus. How the hell do you have sex with mermaids, who are half fish? Believe me. I assure you, Odysseus; the Sirens beaver slits don't taste like chickens of the sea!"

"What will happen next?" I curiously asked Circe. "Now I fully fathom that these Sirens' song should always represent a warning signal, both now, and in the future!"

"Dear Odysseus; I advise that your dumb-fuck crew row-on past the lethal choir with having some sweet wax stuffed inside their ears, so that none of your' mariners can listen, be distracted, and crash your vessel straight into the jutting jetty. But if you're keen on hearing their hypnotic melody, make your crew tie you to the mast, if you enjoy being tantalized like Tantalus down in Hades. When your rebellious sailors have rowed-on past the beckoning Sirens, think about your wife Penelope, because your fragile marriage is also on the rocks. I cannot tell you which alternative to follow on your arduous route; for you yourself will have to trust your instincts to get back to Ithaca, wherever the hell that dump of a city-island happens to be located. You'll be on your own, Odysseus. I can only tell you about the Sirens' danger as your Bireme approaches their jetty!"

"Now King Alcinous, I humbly beg your indulgence. When I was down in morose Hades, the shade of the dead prophet Teiresias informed something important about me passing past a narrow passage having towering rock cliffs on either side. But remarkably, Circe knew about *that* circumstance, too!"

"Odysseus, I do not wish to share the gods' secrets as I like sharing my pussy. All that I can reveal to you are the names Scylla and Charybdis! One will be on the left, and the other on the right of the towering, and sometimes clashing-together cliffs, which will squeeze your vessel flat like the enormous vice belonging to the underground volcano blacksmith, fifty-foot-tall Hephaestus, possessor of the red, two-inch-long penis."

"Circe, the prophet I had consulted down in Hades also mentioned a place called Thrinacia. Do you know anything pertinent about it?"

"Since you have asked me, dear Odysseus, and the source of the inquiry has not originated from my mind or mouth, I can share some vital knowledge with you. Thrinacia, is a secluded, sacred land where Helios Hyperion, the sun god, keeps his quivering cattle to graze safely away from the danger of human arrows kept in quivers. His rich flocks, consisting of seven herds of golden cattle, and just as many lovely flocks of golden sheep, with fifty in each group, are revered by Helios, who believes that silence is golden; so, the sun god never mentions the secret grazing location to anyone! In short, don't dare to even graze the grazing sheep!"

"Will my mariners and I be executed if we trespass on this place Thrinacia, which you've so accurately described?"

"Not exactly, dear Odysseus. The golden cattle and sheep bear no young and never die. Their immortal herders are also divine. Now, if you leave these golden animals unharmed and exclusively focus on your long journey home, I think you may fortunately get back to Ithaca, although you'll meet other misfortunes along the irregular route. But please remember: if you harm the sacred cattle in any way in regard to these cows and sheep grazing, then like Eurassisgras, your ass will be grass! If you dare violate the vindictive sun god's stipulations, then Odysseus, I foresee destruction and ruin for your ship and your crew. Even if you yourself escape the devastating dilemma, a fucked-up debacle that you will have irresponsibly caused, I predict with certainty that you'll get back to Ithaca in great distress, and all alone, after all your shipmates have been killed by factors I cannot now reveal."

"When rosy Dawn finally fully appeared on her golden throne, frustrated Circe left my company to go up-island and search for her magical vibrating dildo. So, I returned back to the ship, where I urged my grumbling comrades to get on board and loosen-off the ropes, not disclosing to them that our mission was destined to be on the ropes, too. The brass-knuckleheads quickly clambered inside the ship, sat-down in proper order at each assigned rowing bench, and struck the gray sea surface with their splintery oars, as a favorable fair wind blew, just like more-than-decent fellatio, behind our damaged, dark-prow vessel."

"Several hours later, the cooperating wind abruptly died-down. Everything was calm, without a hint of gusting. Some interfering sea god had stilled the waves, and our sea passage was no longer a breeze. My comrades, whose dull minds were in the doldrums, stood-up, furled the sail, stowed the material inside the hollow ship's small storage hull, and then sat at their oars, churning the smooth water white with their polished blades carved out of fine pine. Wielding my sharp sword, I methodically sliced a large round chunk of thick wax into smaller bits, and then kneaded the pieces into functional shapes with my strong fingertips. My worried mind carefully considered the whole puzzling situation: my fucked-up sailors have so much grit and grime in their ears that the numbskulls might not really need this wax, but better safe than sorry! I theorized and assessed."

"Once I had sufficiently plugged my comrades' ears with the thick aforementioned wax, the fools, pretending to be rehearsing a mutiny, tied my hands and feet onto and against the ship's central pole, so that I stood upright, hard against the sturdy mast and would not be able to masturbate. The fools next lashed the rope ends to the mast as well, but then returned to their separate work stations, and the rowers sat and struck the gray sea with their dependable oars. But when we were about as far away as a man often discernibly shouts 'Fuck you!', moving forward quickly, our swift Bireme did not slip past the singing Sirens sitting on the jetty. Once we navigated in close without me as the captain barking commands, the very fascinating mermaid bitches began orchestrating their clear-toned cry."

"Odysseus, you' famous, fucked-up, intriguing asshole; yes, great glory of the Achaeans; come over here and wonder at our splendid harmony. Let your sleek ship pause for a while, so that you can hear the marvelous songs we shall sing, like a beauty salon quartet. No man has ever rowed inside his black ship past here without attending his ears to absorb the beauty of our glorious songs; yes, our sweet-voiced melodies, like a Bohemian rhapsody, sung from our own chaffed lips. Our melodic music brings sailors unmatched joy, and mariners depart from here becoming wiser, instant smart alecks, just like you, Odysseus; you dumb-fuck wise-ass. We angelic Sirens, who in the future will be honored by police departments and fire houses, fully understand all the misfortunes your brave men had endured at Troy; yes, hardships faced by Trojans and Achaeans alike, who in truth, did not like each other's body odor. Now Odysseus, order your fucked-up crew to row closer to us, or you'll really make us pissed-off to the point where our entire chorus might be changed by the gods into gay male mermaids, simply because we could not effectively execute Poseidon's vengeful game plan! Thank Zeus that we Sirens are all female altos. We don't' have to have our balls castrated because we already alto-gether sound like high frequency, rap crap, effeminate, eunuch choir boys! We don't need that castration shit!"

"Now King Alcinous, the hypnotizing voice that reached me was so fine and transcendent that my ears could not resist listening any longer to the rhythmic cadence. I shouted at my crew to set me free from my mast tethering, sending the preoccupied rowers vividly clear signals with my eyebrows, which their dedicated activity thankfully ignored. Then, after the crew made a west turn on the eastern ocean, Perimedes and Eurylochus arose, bound me tighter with additional rope, and then being pissed-off, lashed me across my eyelashes. When the highly focused rowers had paddled my boat well beyond the Sirens' sound range, one of the mermaids was still singing solo, so low that I could barely hear her exquisite voice."

"Feeling safe and secure, my elite Phaeacian audience, my loyal sailors quickly removed the wax I had stuffed into each man's ears, and the two main crewmembers obliged by loosening the mast ropes that had wonderfully salvaged my men and me. But once we'd left the island's jetty trap far behind, I viewed giant waves rising, and smoke billowing into the sky not far ahead."

"Then, King Alcinous, my auditory perception discerned a crashing roar. My crew became terrified, fearing a crash of the nearby Titans. I paced through the ship, cheering-up the totally intimidated wimps, standing beside each one as I moved along, and speaking resolute phrases of reassurance."

"Friends, up to this point, we have not been strangers to all kinds of fucked-up misfortune. Surely, the bad omens we're presently hearing and seeing are nothing worse than when the one-eyed Cyclops kept us as trapped prisoners inside his expansive cavern. But even there, thanks to my superb excellence, keen intelligence, and coy planning, we escaped being eaten alive. Seeing no one in my audience being a trifle interested, I felt compelled to continue my superficial prattling."

"I think that someday we'll be remembering these prodigious dangers, too, and relate the tales to our great-grandkids, and emphasize to them how fucked-up mortal life is under the callous dominion of the insane Olympian gods. But come now, ancient mariners; all of us should follow what I say, even though everyone aboard knows that I'm a model asshole not fit to emulate. Stay by your oars, keep striking them against the surging sea, and we'll all sing redundant choruses of 'Row, row, row our boat!' Great Zeus, possibly being distracted by the furry entrance to Hera's entrancing snatcheroo, may somehow allow us all to survive."

"I deliberately did not mention the name Scylla, for I suspected that *that* creature was a monstrous threat for which I could devise no remedy. So, we kept moving-on, up the narrow strait, groaning as we worried about participating in a one-boat demolition derby. On one side of the narrow channel lay Scylla; on the other side, deep below the waves was divine Charybdis, who according to scholars who diligently studied mythology, was a mammoth maelstrom who swallowed-up massive amounts of salt water from the seething and bubbling sea, and then gargled both nearby ships and mariners, and next swallowed the victimized sailors along with the imbibed salt water, and finally, spit their twisted bodies at Scylla, who was standing upon the opposite high rock cliffs."

"When Charybdis began sucking the turbulent salt water-down to the sea bottom, everything in the surrounding environment looked totally hazy and confused; and soon, a dreadful roar arose around the perilous clashing rocks, and in the depths of the maniacal whirlpool, the dark and sandy bottom at the sea's floor was plainly visible. Pale fear gripped my comrades, who all had already shit their tunics at least three times. And when we saw the havoc that Charybdis had been causing, we were afraid we'd be destroyed, mingled with salt water, and then spit-out and propelled onto Scylla's towering crags while involuntarily participating in a real legendary cliff-hanger."

"Captain!" dumb-ass Eurcockisnum loudly shouted in my direction while referring to Charybdis. "I've finally found something that sucks more than you do!"

"During the disgusting encounter, Scylla had snatched-away six of my hysterical companions, right from the recently-swabbed deck; the plucked/fucked mariners being among the strongest and the bravest men I had, including Eurcockisnum, a callow virgin who always wished to be sucked and eaten by a female, but certainly not by the viperous thirty-foot-tall Scylla."

"I instinctively turned to watch as Scylla flipped the screaming sailors high over her head, quickly breaking three warriors' bodies in half with her dagger-like teeth as the awesome monster violently snapped her head back and forth in rapid succession. The doomed victims cried-out and screamed, calling my accursed name. My keen ears heard my ship's fourth mate Eurcockisnum shrieking: "This is not how I fuckin' wanted to be eaten'!""

"Then, King Alcinous, in the entrance to her massive cave, Scylla finished devouring her human quarry, licking her lips as her prey kept on screaming, stretching-out their useless arms in my direction."

"Of all the gruesome and catastrophic experiences that my eyes had witnessed in my hazardous journeying over the turbulent seas, the sight of Scylla gobbling-up my crewmen was without a doubt the most piteous, fuckin' nauseous, distressful adversity I've ever observed. But in the final analysis, it was much safer to drift closer to Scylla and lose a half-dozen sailors than to risk approaching the whirlpool Charybdis, and jeopardizing what was left of my nautical expedition from Troy."

"Once our pummeled vessel had made it past those crashing rocks and escaped the insane vicinity, fleeing from both Scylla and Charybdis, in two days of smooth sailing we reached the lovely island of the sun god, home to those fine herds of broad-faced cattle and plentiful, rich, golden-furred flocks, all belonging to Helios Hyperion, the greedy god of daily sunshine. I recalled the ultra-scary prophecy of the sightless Teiresias of Thebes down in Hades, and the collaborating prediction of Circe regarding the need to not abuse the obsessive sun god's golden cattle herds, or fuck-around with his coveted flocks of golden sheep."

"Shipmates; let all of you now swear this solemn *oath* dictated and offered by this big oaf, your incomparable Captain. If by chance we discover a herd of golden cattle, or a large flock of golden sheep, not one of you potential hoodlums will be so audaciously overcome with foolishness that you will avariciously slaughter a holy cow, or a sacred sheep. Instead, you'll be content to sit upon your scrawny asses and voraciously consume the sufficient food supplies that the witch/bitch Circe had so generously provided us."

"Once I'd emphasized those strict words of condemnation, I compelled the dumb-dicks to swear to Poseidon and Zeus that the sacred animals would not be tampered with, as I had just announced and commanded. When the thick-skulled muttonheads had made their impious promising, I ordered that we navigate our ship inside a nearby shallow harbor, situated by a spring having sweet, fresh water. My hungry companions disembarked and merrily prepared a welcome dinner."

"But later that evening, King Alcinous, when three-quarters of the night had passed, and the zodiac constellations had shifted their predictable positions, cloud-gatherer Zeus, with nothing better to do, stirred-up an extremely hostile wind, accompanied by an amazing storm, and torrential rain poured-down from the dark clouds upon both land and sea alike, and then as if foreshadowing a major calamity, ominous nightfall arrived and rapidly descended."

"Once rose-fingered Dawn arrived the following morning, as was our standard habit, we dragged-up our ship and then secured it inside a deep cave, which was a place that local nymphs used as a fine lap-dancing assembly hall, and also as a group sex therapy location."

"But then the obdurate South Wind kept blowing for one whole month, which seemed like Mother Nature was suffering her four-week period. No other wind had sprung-up, except those few times when the East or South Wind occasionally blew mild squalls. Now, while the partying crewmen still enjoyed their sweet red wine and soft bread, the undisciplined jerks obeyed certain orders and did not touch the sacred cattle or sheep. The temporary gentlemen were keenly focused on basically staying alive. But once the food and drink we had stored inside our ship was gone, the crap-brained cretins had to roam the island, scouring around for game, fish, and birds to swallow-down for supper. The inventive boneheads made bent hooks with which to fish, as sudden starvation gnawed-away inside their growling stomachs."

"At that point, I ventured inland, and then up-island, to the plateau's highest summit, to pray to the gods, hoping that one of the 'don't give a shit' tyrants would show me a viable way back to Ithaca. One time, I had moved across the island, far from my companions. I washed my hands in a protected spot, a shelter from the wind, and said my solemn prayers to all the eccentric gods who resided atop Mount Olympus, who mercifully poured sweet sleep across my weary eyelids."

"Meanwhile, doltish Eurylochus began lecturing truly bad advice to his hard-headed, low-mentality companions."

"Shipmates; although you're suffering diarrhea and distress, hear me out. For us wretched human beings, all forms of demise are hateful, including shitting ourselves to death because of dehydration. But to die from lack of food, to meet one's fate in such a hostile manner, *that* is the worst sort of death of all. So come; let's drive away the best of Helios's golden herds, and then we'll sacrifice several of the animals to the immortal gods, who hold dominion over wide Heaven and Earth. And if we ever get home to Mother Ithaca, we'll construct for Helios Hyperion a resplendent temple, and inside the impressive marble edifice we'll include many expensive gifts of thanksgiving, although we presently have no such national holiday. If spiteful Helios becomes enraged about his straight-horned cattle being killed for food, and desires to wreck our warship, and the other equally-powerful gods agree, I'd rather lose my life once and for all by choking on a wave, than starving to death on this miserable, abandoned wasteland."

"Eurylochus spoke very dangerous rhetoric, but his fellow comrades, valuing biological needs over rational thought, agreed with the jabberwocky-type polemics the knuckleheaded dunce had stated. The imbeciles quickly and eagerly rounded-up the finest beasts from Helios's herd, and also from the sun god's golden corral, which was situated close-by. The crazed fanatics stole sleek, broad-faced rams with curved horns, the animals being found grazing near our dark-ship's-prow. My lame-brained sailors stood around the selected rams and cows, their throats all praying to the gods for approval."

"Once the obsessed mob had falsely prayed to Olympus, the sinners cut the creatures' throats, flayed their flesh, and severed-out portions of the thighs. These slices the violators then hid in double layers of fat, and laid old raw meat on top to conceal their egregious misdeed. All of this evil action had transpired as I soundly slept inside a cove, lazily dreaming and fantasizing about my two favorite Greek tailors, Euripides and Eumenides."

"The noodle-brained sailors had no wine to pour-down upon the flaming sacrifice, so the lunkheads used some salt water for libations, and being asinine ignoramuses, the heretics roasted all the ram and cow entrails inside the blazing fire. Once the thighs were completely broiled, and the phony gourmets had a taste of delectable inner organs, the aberrant fools skewered the various portions upon burning spits."

"Now, dear Phaeacians; I meandered from the higher elevation and ambled-down by the shore to the vicinity of our swift ship. As I drew closer, the sweet smell of hot fat floated around and wafted into my sensitive nostrils. I immediately felt obligated to groan and apologize to the offended immortals, particularly Lord Poseidon and Lord Zeus."

"Father Zeus, Lord Poseidon, and revered members of your sacred family. You've forced this perilous travesty upon me in the form of that cruel sleep I just had, and your grand design was to bring about my impending doom. For my goonish companions who remained behind have planned and initiated something terribly disastrous."

"A messenger, presumably fleet-footed, sandal-winged Hermes, quickly came to Helios Hyperion, with the distraught herald bringing the regrettable news that a military contingent from Ithaca, leaving Troy, had brutally killed the fit-to-be-tied sun god's sacred cattle and holy sheep."

"Without delay, King Alcinous and Queen Arete; Father Zeus heard Helios's plea and contemplated taking his notorious vengeance-out on those pagan-behaving crewmen, whom the erratic Olympian King regarded as all being indolent, renegade companions of mischievous, diabolical Odysseus, Laertes's disobedient son."

"If those punk sailors don't pay me proper restitution for those marvelous beasts that the Greek nutcases have indiscriminately butchered, then I'll go down to Hades and aggravate your macabre brother by shining brilliant sunshine among the dead."

"Friend Hyperion; I think you should keep on shining sunlight for us immortals, and also for mortal beings polluting and contaminating fertile Earth. With a dazzling thunderbolt, I myself will quickly strike at that swift ship of theirs and, in the middle of the wine-dark sea, smash the Bireme into tiny toothpicks. But first, I will take my anger out against one of the more flagrant violators."

"Zeus peered-down to Earth and witnessed horny Eurdicisin screwing, up the ass, one of Helios's sacred golden sheep. The king of gods raised his right hand and sent a wicked lightning bolt straight up Eurdicisin's anus hole, instantly killing both shocked Eurdicisin and the recipient sheep, in what amounted to a rather electrifying climax."

"Now King Alcinous; I soon learned of all this bizarre excitement from the fair Nymph Calypso, who informed me in a vivid dream that she herself had heard the report directly from the lips of Hermes the Messenger."

"For six monotonous days, those delinquent comrades I had idiotically trusted, feasted there, eating the golden cattle that the dumb-fucks had rounded-up, indeed the finest beasts in Helios's herd. But when Zeus, son of Cronos, brought to us the seventh blustery day, the fierce stormy winds had died-down to a mere bland breeze. We climbed-aboard our warship at once, put-up the mast, hoisted the white sail, and promptly left the wholly dysfunctional island behind."

"Zeus was not satisfied with simply electrifying Eurdicisin up the ass with the powerful lightning blast, so the king god, with the assistance of his demented brother, Poseidon, produced a severe tempest that snapped the mast of my once-stellar vessel. The heavy pole landed squarely on my helmsman's skull, shattering the sailor's bones into tiny white fragments."

"On the tenth night thereafter, I was again guided to Ogygia by the influence of the gods; yes, we landed upon the fucked-up island which fair-haired Calypso called home. Still hot for my hurting body, the horny nymph welcomed and treated me with delicate care. But why should I redundantly tell you Phaeacians *that* same story again, now from which I had originally started? If you recall, King Alcinous and Queen Arete, it was only yesterday, in your palatial home, that I had told both of you the strange interaction I had experienced with the captivating nymph, Calypso. And quite frankly, it's an irritating disservice, I think, to re-tell a fantastic story that's been clearly narrated once before."

Jay Dubya

Chapter 17

"ODYSSEUS LEAVES PHAEACIA"

Odysseus paused to gauge the total impact that his narrative had had upon his seemingly mesmerized audience. All Phaeacians present sat in silence, motionless, and evidently spellbound inside the vast shadowy hall.

"So, you see, kind Phaeacians. I've tried to describe my crazy adventures to you noble residents in true chronological order, but one thing is certain. I've sadly lost all my sailors, and all twelve of my fifty-man Biremes. I've arrived to your admirable land alone, after my self-made raft had been demolished by Poseidon's cruel wrath, presumably caused by me blinding his inhuman son, the all-too-primitive Cyclops, Polyphemus."

"Odysseus; since you're visiting my meeting hall, with its brass floors and high-pitched roof, I think you won't leave here and go back to your Ithaca disappointed, although you've truly suffered much bad luck along the way. Clothing for you, our distinguished guest, is packed already, and stored in a polished chest inlaid with gold, as well as all the other gifts brought here by designated Phaeacian government counselors."

King Alcinous dispatched a staccato voiced herald to conduct his counselors to the dock where the fast Phaeacian ship had been moored. Once the farewell party had walked-onboard to inspect the sleek vessel, the dockworkers immediately carried the food and drink items, and stowed the abundant supplies inside the ship's hull. The assembled "departure entourage" spread a rug and a linen sheet upon the deck at the stern, so that Odysseus could relax and enjoy a peaceful sleep during his imminent sea passage.

The fatigued-from-speaking Trojan War hero ambled aboard, and lay down in silence. Each rower then sat in proper order at his assigned oarlock. The conscientious port laborers loosened the cable from the perforated stone. Once the muscular rowers leaned-back and stirred the water with their oars, a calming sleep fell upon Odysseus's eyelids, undisturbed and very soothing.

Not even reeling hawks zooming in flight, or the swiftest of all flying species, could match the beautiful vessel's speed, as the rugged sea conqueror raced ahead, slicing through the splashing ocean waves, bearing on board a special passenger whose mind was like a god's distinguished cerebrum. The main passenger's heart, in earlier days, had undergone much pain and duress, as the renowned warrior, known for his strength and guile, had maneuvered through conflictive wars and had suffered much hardship upon the formidable sea waves. Now, Odysseus slept in peace, forgetting all his troubles, and dreaming of how his return to Ithaca should be coordinated and executed.

The Phaeacian ship, named "Piece of Ass", was usually utilized as a floating whorehouse, but this current voyage was its first legitimate charter. The one-eyed navigator, had once visited Ithaca, and had a rough idea where the remote island was located, somewhere far from historic Lesbos, the very popular lesbian resort and spa destination.

When the most splendid of the morning stars appeared, which always comes to herald light from early Dawn, the fast sea-faring "Piece of Ass" was nearing Ithaca like a speeding piece of hanging antelope shit. Those athletic rowers' arms had so much strength that half the boat, which was moving quickly, was driven-up on shore and immediately created a burrow six-foot-deep upon the sandy beach. Once the crew had clambered from that well-built merchant ship onto dry land, first the mariners carried-off Odysseus, lifting him out of the hallowed hollowed hull on that isolated section of the ghetto island Known as Ithaca.

Odysseus was still wrapped-up in the linen sheet and splendid blanket, looking much like an ancient Greco frankfurter. The mariners next placed snoozing Odysseus down upon the shore, which was loaded with sandfleas and other bothersome, biting insects, but the hero was still fast asleep.

The sailors then brought ashore the fabulous gifts which the Phaeacian noblemen had given their illustrious guest; all thanks to the goodwill of powerful Athena, who had stimulated their donations, and who had subconsciously promised the junior stevedores good individual and group sex for the remainder of their mortal lives.

The workmen placed the extravagant golden chests containing silver and porcelain gifts, expensive jewelry, and versatile adult sex toys against the trunk of a decaying olive tree, and quickly, neatly stacked the rare metal containers in a conspicuous pile, situated some distance from a path, in case some staggering drunk or mendicant came-by and stumbled-upon the magnificent goods, before Odysseus could wake-up from his extended slumber. Then, the motivated Phaeacians climbed aboard their sleek vessel and set-off for home, ready to indulge in obtaining eager-beaver sex from the whores that Athena had cleverly suggested to their subconscious libidos.

In the interim, livid Poseidon complained to Brother Zeus about what the naïve, humanitarian Phaeacians were doing to assist Odysseus, and sympathetic Zeus immediately granted permission to his equally vengeful sibling to "severely punish the fucked-up do-gooders". So, Poseidon, using an accurate mask facsimile of Medusa the Gorgon, turned the Phaeacian ship and crew to stone, just as the "Piece of Ass" identification logo then remarkably read in etched stone, "Piece of Shit".

Meanwhile, brave Odysseus, asleep in his own land, finally woke-up. But the napper did not recognize just exactly where he was. And so, all things seemed unfamiliar to the returning king; the long straight paths; the majestic harbor with safe anchorage; the sheer-faced stony cliffs, and the deciduous trees in rich full bloom. So, feeling spry and energized, the returning king jumped-up and looked-out at his barren native land. Odysseus groaned aloud and struck his thighs with both his palms, and then cried out in sorrow:

"Where the hell am I now? Whose strange country have I come to this time? Are the inhabitants violent, unjust, and cruel? Do the natives of this dump welcome lost strangers? Do their minds respect the fucked-up Olympian gods? And all this treasure here; where do I take the extravagant gifts without getting robbed? What the fuck do I have to do to safeguard these priceless valuables?"

Then, overwhelmed with a severe longing for his native land, the new arrival weakly wandered upon the shore dunes beside the crashing surf. But then his Olympus patron, Pallas Athene, floated-in on a low cloud, and soon the talented goddess shape-shifted into the form of a handsome young man.

Odysseus, happy to catch sight of what he thought was another human, came-up and spoke to him/her.

"My friend; since you're the first one I've encountered here on this thorny, desolate beach, tell me the honest truth; where the hell are all the sun bathers? What country is this land? Are you also marooned on this island, even though your skin color is not lavender? Is this nightmare place some sunny island, or is this merely a small cape jutting from the mainland out to sea?"

Athena, goddess with the gleaming eyes, replied: "Disoriented Stranger, far from either China or Japan; you must be a full-fledged, wacky fool, or else you've come here from somewhere far away like Hades or the Moon. If you must ask about this land's identity, its name is not unknown. Many men have heard of it, either gay, straight or transgender. Ithaca is well-known, even to paupers in Sparta, in Mycenae, and also in Troy; all three cities being a long way from this accursed Achaean land."

Lord Odysseus instantly felt great joy, being happy to learn of his ancestral land firmly beneath his feet. Bright-eyed Athena smiled and stroked him with her hand. Then, the versatile deity changed herself into a lovely, sexy, tall woman, because the caring Daughter of Zeus was very adept at creating and projecting splendid and adorable visions.

"Odysseus, of all Greek warriors, you're the best at making plans and giving persuasive speeches, and among all gods, I'm well-known for my gentle subtlety, and my divine wisdom. Still, you failed to recognize in your midst Athena, daughter of Zeus, who's always at your side, whether the hell you can see me or not. Whether your diminutive pea-brain realizes it or not, I'm looking-out for you in every novel crisis. Yes, noble hero; it was I who had compelled all those feckless Phaeacians to love your worthy ass. Now, I've come to weave a looming scheme with you, and help you hide those luxurious goods you've stupidly placed behind that decaying olive tree."

"What is to happen to me upon my weary entrance into my own palace? Will my wife Penelope and my son Telemachus even recognize me?"

"I'll generally tell you what unchangeable Fate has in store for you, oh great adventurer. You'll find harsh troubles abounding within your now-dilapidated palace. Be patient, impulsive Odysseus; for you must endure all challenges to achieve desired success. Be vigilant. Don't tell anyone, man, woman or neuter, that you've just returned from wandering aimlessly around the known world. Instead, against your garrulous nature, keep silent as night. Bear the many pains as if you're giving birth to sextuplets. When grown men act like savages in your house, do nothing. By nothing, I mean 'no thing'. Now, brave Odysseus; let's not wait another second, but put away these treasures you've obtained from the idealistic, very gullible Phaeacians. We'll hide the precious gifts in some dark recess of yonder sacred cave, where the goods will stay safely stored inside. And then, let's think about how all these things may turn-out for the best. Like turnips, one never knows what will turn up!"

"After Athena and I hid the magnificent gifts inside the nearby cave, we sat-down by the sacred olive tree's gnarled trunk to seriously think of ways to eliminate the insolent suitors who had been courting and harassing Penelope."

"Listen-up, intrepid Odysseus. Think how your mighty hands may catch those unethical charlatans, who for three-years now, have been lording-over and cavorting inside your palace, shamelessly wooing your godlike wife, and offering Penelope their cheap marriage gifts. Most honestly, Odysseus; your faithful spouse longs for your return and your caress."

"Patron Goddess; if you had not told me all this contemporary insanity, I would've gladly shared the fate of Agamemnon, Achilles, and Ajax, and suffer and repeat endless redundancy down in Hades. Come, and weave a viable plan so I can pay those parasitic suitor bastards back for their brazen, evil greed. Stand in person by my side, beautiful Athena, and fill me with indomitable courage, as you had done when we loosened the bright diadem of Troy. Many think I am brave, but in my faltering soul, I feel both wimpy and craven."

"You can be certain I will stand by you, and I won't forget your myriad sacrifices when the real trouble starts. I predict that the blood of many suitors, who have consumed your livelihood, will be splattered, and their brains scattered, all over your palace's tawdry hall. But come now, Odysseus; I shall magically transform your appearance, so that no one on Ithaca, not even Penelope, will recognize your identity. You must first go to see the swineherd, who tends your scrawny, underfed pigs. He's well-disposed to you and loves your son, and also advocates for wise Penelope. If you have some pertinent questions, ask the loyal swineherd for guidance, for he has had some experience working with disruptive juveniles as a quack child psychologist. In the meantime, I'll speed-off to Sparta, and there, Odysseus, I'll summon back your dear son, Telemachus, who has gone to spacious Laconia, to the home of laconic Menelaus, to hear news if you are still alive, or if you are dead."

The benign goddess touched Odysseus's staff with her staff as a mild token of indirect affection. The Daughter of Zeus then mystically wrinkled the smooth skin on Odysseus's supple limbs, and transformed the dark hair upon the king's head and made it totally gray. The cunning goddess covered his arms and legs with an old man's dark-spotted skin, and next dimmed his handsome blue eyes. Odysseus next was amazed to find himself dressed in a beggar's ragged cloak, and a dirty tunic, both garments tattered, disheveled, and stained with stinking soot and stench-laden smoke.

When the two ancient schemers had finished reviewing their unique plans, Pallas Athene vanished, heading to Lacedaemon to locate and bring back Odysseus's nomadic son to Ithaca.

The returning king, disguised as a worthless tramp, left the secluded harbor, taking the rough path into the woods, and soon pacing across the rolling hills, ambled to the place where Athena had told the wanderer he would meet the uneducated-but-sagacious swineherd, who was, of all the servants that Lord Odysseus had, the one who faithfully took the greatest care of his master's hogs and pigs.

The returning warrior found the hoary gent squatting-down and taking a lengthy crap into a deep rabbit hole. But with the appearance of Odysseus, the swineherd's constipation ended when the silent intruder scared the shit out of him.

All of a sudden, the swineherds ferocious dogs observed Odysseus, and the canines howled and darted toward him, barking furiously. The returning King of Ithaca was alert enough to drop his staff and sit to show the attacking animals that he was of a friendly disposition. But the loyal swineherd hobbled-up as fast as his feeble legs could muster, hurrying and rushing forward, vociferously shouting a series of unpleasant expletives at his vicious dogs, and scattering the irritated canines by hurling a hail of stones in their' direction.

"Old Man; those dogs would've ripped you apart in no time, and then, like any lying vagrant-pedestrian, you would've heaped the blame on me. Well, I've got other troubles from the gods, for as I stay here on my master's estate, raising fat pigs for other sinful men to eat, I'm full of sorrow, for my noble master, who has been away for twenty-years, and I fully regret that countless miseries haunt and contaminate his family; all caused by a gaggle of fucked-up suitors. But come Stranger; enter into my ramshackle hut, and I shall provide you with adequate food and drink, because I pity your plight as an indigent seeking vital nourishment."

"Thank you, kind swineherd; your generosity is quite exemplary! May the gods reward you!"

"When you have had enough to eat and drink and your heart's content is satisfied, you can tell me where you come from, and what hardships and obstacles you've endured."

With those sympathetic words, the loyal swineherd entered the hut, waved Odysseus inside, and invited his new-found guest to sit and eat five-day-old leftovers. Odysseus was glad to receive that meager hospitality, so the master of the estate politely addressed the swineherd.

"Kind Swineherd; may Zeus give you whatever wishes you desire; I appreciate that your magnanimous heart has welcomed me into your troubled life."

"It would be wrong, Stranger, for me to disrespect a less fortunate guest," swineherd Eumaeus answered. "Even if one worse-off than you arrived, for every guest and beggar comes from Zeus, rich or poor, under the protection of the Olympian's Suppliant Law. Now where did you come from?" Eumaeus asked. "And please don't tell me from your mother's vagina!"

"I'm a traveler from Crete, but I got lost on my journey back home. I didn't have enough coins to pay my entire fare, so the captain ordered that I be dispensed with at the next island stop, which is this weird place, Ithaca, I believe," Odysseus lied.

"Well, if you're from Crete as you say, you must know all about Minos!" Eumaeus asked.

"What the hell is wrong with your nose?" Odysseus answered. "Do you have three nostrils?"

"Well now, mild-mannered, dirtbag Stranger. I'd like to know everything about the famous Minotaur."

"Most tours in Crete last much longer than an hour," the itinerant Beggar cleverly replied.

"Okay, anonymous Visitor," Eumaeus declared. "Please tell me about the advanced civilization on Crete."

"The Cretans are a very smart people. The Cretans definitely are not cretins!" Odysseus coyly and confidently stated.

As those two mental cases were sillily conversing, the younger estate herdsmen came-up, bringing home the property's twenty-two remaining hogs. The sows were shut-up and contained inside their customary pens, and the emaciated pigs gave-out weak squeals, as the animals were herded inside for sleep time.

"Bring a boar in here, the best there is, so I can butcher it for this peaceful Stranger, who has arrived from another country," Eumaeus ordered his young associate.

"Thanks again for your courteous hospitality," the shrewdly disguised beggar indicated to his sympathetic host. "You are most accommodating!"

"We too will get some benefit from pigging-out," the head swineherd joked. "We can't afford lamb chops, but pork chops are definitely on the menu. But Stranger; my mundane existence is quite boring, watching these slimy, stench-laden hogs porking each other all day long; that is, when I'm not actively slaughtering the squealing bastards. I've even learned and mastered their simple piggy language. One oink means 'Let's eat'; two quick oinks mean 'Let's sleep'; three fast oinks mean 'Get out of my damned way'; four consecutive oinks mean 'I gotta' take a shit', and five rapid-in-succession oinks succinctly mean 'Let's fuck'!"

Once Eumaeus uttered that informative declaration, the elderly swineherd used his sharp bronze axe to chop wood for kindling, while his protege led-into the hut a large tusked boar, five years old, and stood the snorter by the humble hearth. The kind-hearted pig-keeper solemnly prayed to the zany gods that his master Odysseus would return and reclaim his rightful, entitled estate.

The junior hog attendant proceeded to raise his arm, and holding a huge oak club, struck the boar's head, and life instantly left the beast. The subordinate herdsmen skillfully slit the dead creature's throat, singed its bristles, and, working quickly with both hands, deftly carved-up the carcass.

"Eumaeus, may father Zeus treat you as well as you are treating me with this abundant boar's flesh, and if I may add, the very finest cut of meat, even though I'm just an impoverished beggar sitting inside your modest hut."

"Eat plenty, god-guided Stranger, and enjoy the only kind of food I have to offer. A deity capriciously gives some favors and holds others back, as his or her fickle heart prompts, for the inimitable Olympians can do all oddball things."

According to tradition, Eumaeus prayed again and offered to the eternal gods the first and best pieces he had cut. The pig-master poured gleaming wine as a libation, handed another cup to Odysseus, fearless sacker of cities, and then sat-down to eat his portion.

Twilight soon converted to night, bringing stormy winds and inhospitable rain, with no moon visible in the black sky. Showing compassion for his frail guest, Eumaeus covered the sleeping Odysseus with his only blanket, as heavy rains penetrated the leaky, thatched roof, saturating both humans inside the dilapidated hut. The sleeping king appreciated the wonderful kindness of his old faithful servant, and Odysseus, realizing that he had knowledge of one dedicated ally on his side, was quite tempted to reveal his true identity to loyal Eumaeus, whose troubled mind only ever thought about his oinking hogs and his missing master.

Chapter 18

"TELEMACHUS RETURNS TO ITHACA"

In less than a blink of an eye, Pallas Athene zoomed-down to Sparta and visited Telemachus, telling the lethargic dreamer to return home and communicate with the swineherd Eumaeus. Meanwhile, back in Ithaca, Odysseus and Eumaeus continued to thoroughly discuss the treacherous situation prevailing inside the Ithacan royal palace.

After receiving his final full-body massage from seventeen spa attendants, Telemachus departed Sparta for equally-depressing Pylos, and next reluctantly set sail for his raunchy homeland. A week later, the assigned lesbian and transgender crew spotted the Ithacan coast and tossed the son of Odysseus into the raging surf, making the callow punk swim to shore after the adolescent refused to have wild sex with a homosexual male gorilla that had been stowed on board.

The feckless teen finally got his bearings straight, even though he was nowhere near fictional Alaska, and the soaking-wet trekker soon miraculously reached the farmyard and the herds of oinking pigs, among whom the loyal swineherd still lay asleep, always-contemplating nice gentle thoughts about his assumed-dead master and owner.

At dawn, Odysseus and the loyal pig custodian, Eumaeus, without any formal arson education, lit a fire inside the dingy hut and prepared their smelly breakfast of hog entrails and raunchy piggy-sausage.

As Telemachus approached the ramshackle hut, the yelping dogs stopped barking and fawned after recognizing the familiar human. Perceptive Lord Odysseus peered-out the only window, noticed what the vicious dogs weren't doing, and quickly relayed that irrelevant information to the half-asleep swineherd.

"Eumaeus, I believe that some friend of yours is either encroaching or approaching your hut. Your ferocious dogs aren't barking and are acting peculiar and friendly."

Soon, Telemachus was standing inside the unlocked entry portal, still dazed from being tossed into the surf and landing upon a surprised sand-shark, that had been eating a large crab. Recognizing the drenched kid's face, the amazed swineherd jumped-up to enthusiastically greet his current master, before addressing the seventy-five-pound weakling.

"You've come back to this sour land, Telemachus, you sweet light. I thought I'd never see your ass around here anymore. You know, I did study to be a proctologist when I myself was an ambitious youth. But now, once you had sped-off to Pylos in that ship paid for by the parasite suitors, and with your own money, I thought you had run-away from home, seeking a better life as a reckless recluse. Come in here now, dear boy, so that my heart can feel the joy of seeing you inside my humble pigsty, now that you've returned from experiencing your' experiment as an isolated, crabby itinerant playboy."

Immediately, hearing Eumaeus say his son's name, Odysseus stood and offered Telemachus his rickety stool.

"Stay put, Stranger. We'll find a stool somewhere, perhaps inside Eumaeus's potty outhouse. I'm surprised that the swineherd has taken you in. Usually, Eumaeus doesn't give a crap about a stool."

Odysseus went back and sat down again, thinking about his next bowel movement. Then, after a brief silence, Eumaeus heaped a pile of green brushwood upon the dirt floor, and spread a fleece on top where Odysseus's sore-assed son sat-down to soothe his burgeoning hemorrhoids. "Telemachus, let the three of us break our fast and have breakfast together. Then, you can review for my guest and me your dumb-fuck travels to Pylos and to distant Sparta."

Being filled with nostalgia and sentimentality, Telemachus felt compelled to speak the truth amongst the chorus of three growling stomachs. "Old friend, Eumaeus; you must go quickly and report to wise Penelope that I've returned," the wimpy adolescent related. "I felt most wanted and welcome in Pylos, where everyone there had piles and nasty hemorrhoids, just like myself. I'll stay here inside your hut, until you've told the news to my mother that I've returned with accomplishing absolutely nothing at all. No other Achaean must learn about my being back here in Ithaca, for I think that I'm too young to be violently castrated and beheaded. I suspect that the evil suitors are hatching a tailor-made, dangerous plot against me, and I fear being brutally executed for the first time. After you've informed my mother of the news that I'm safely back, then rush here to this shanty right away. Don't go roaming around the fields looking for senile Grandpop Laertes. Instead, tell my mother to send her maid, the housekeeper whose name I can't remember, but she should send the bitch quickly, and in secret. The housekeeper can report the news to the old man, not to my Old Man, but to forgetful Pop-pop Laertes, who erroneously thinks that Mother Penelope has become a nun working as the head priestess inside the downtown Metropolitan Holy Olympian Apostate Temple."

After Eumaeus scurried-out of the pathetic shack to report to Penelope that Telemachus had returned, Pallas Athene appeared upon the scene, only visible to Odysseus and the barking dogs, but not to Telemachus, who was itching to scratch his pimpled rear end.

"Son of Laertes, adventurous Odysseus, sprung from Zeus," Athena prefaced her declaration. "Now is the time to speak and address your only son, who after being evicted from your palace, will have no street address in which to call home. Make yourself known to the potential juvenile delinquent, and don't conceal the vital facts, so that together, you two awkward simpletons, along with Eumaeus, can plan the suitors' lethal fate. Then together, trek to your infamous city, and enter your palace with a pure heart, so stay-away from all the local bordellos and brothels until your vital revenge mission has fully transpired. I won't be absent from you for very long, Odysseus; for I'm an avid, vicarious battle witness, and I'm eager to view your upcoming fight against the leeching suitors."

After the enchanting goddess enunciated those cryptic words, Athena touched Odysseus with her golden wand, and immediately, an unblemished cloak appeared around his now-youthful body, which was much taller, and had been marvelously restored to a much younger age. The hero's skin grew dark once more; his countenance filled-out, and the beard covering his chin turned black-as-pitch again. Once the miracle-worker had initiated those dramatic changes, even before the days of plastic surgery, Athena vanished in a puff, and Odysseus stepped-back into the hut, thinking about what wild and crazy sex with a goddess would be like. His dear son was amazed at the sensational transformation of the former feeble mendicant. The timid lad turned his eyes away, afraid that his father was a god, ready to beat the shit and piss out of him.

"Stranger; now you look quite different than you did before. You're wearing different clothes, and the *pig*mentation of your skin has changed. Your new skin changes the complexion of everything! In this phenomenon I'm seeing, I'm noticing what actually happens when someone rubs the disgusting skin of filthy hogs all day long? I suspect that you're one of the fickle gods who rule over wide heaven. If so, be gracious, so that I can give you pleasing offerings, and well-crafted gifts, as soon as my irresponsible father returns home to reclaim his ass-backwards, bankrupt kingdom."

Long-suffering, regal-looking Lord Odysseus then answered young, still-shocked Telemachus. "Don't insult my intelligence, Foolish Fellow.

I'm not one of the fucked-up gods arriving here to break your' tiny stones. Why do you compare me to immortals? But indeed, and truthfully, Telemachus; I am your itinerant father, on whose account you are grieving and are suffering such tremendous distress, having to bear ambitious fools' committing acts of insolence, while still not being old enough to be a skilled mariner or warrior; I believe that you're now awkwardly navigating through the wimpy phase of your pre-adult life."

Telemachus reflexively embraced his noble father, whom the idiot still thought was a prankster Olympian god deliberately frustrating his emotions with a lousy impersonation of the Ithacan King. Both father and son lamented, and cried like irritated babies bawling for more breast milk. That's exactly how those two groaning grown assholes let tears of sorrow fall from underneath their melancholy eyes. And at that precise moment, light from the brilliant sun almost-disappeared, as the reunited pair incessantly wept. Telemachus soon found a greasy rag to clear his wet face, and then asked his rejuvenated father about *his* hanky-panky activities while being AWOL from Ithaca for two decadent decades.

"Father, in what kind of advanced ship did drunken sailors carry you here to Ithaca? Where did the stupid-shit fools say they were from? For I don't think you made it back here on foot, wading your way through the wine-dark Mediterranean."

"All right, my sperm-less child. I shall tell you the uncouth truth. Phaeacians, those famous sailors of yore that bards and retards often sing about, brought me safely back home. The bored idiots have nothing better to do than to escort lost castaways to their native lands and take them all over creation, as is *their* quixotic habit and reputation. But now, it's time to tell me the approximate number of leeching suitors there are, so that I may know exactly how many obnoxious fuck-heads are hanging-out like dirty laundry inside my palace, and what the human vermin are truly like. Then, once my noble heart has thought-over all possible and impossible contingencies, I'll make-up my disheveled mind, whether we two dreamers are powerful enough to take them on alone, without assistance, or whether we should seek-out and employ the fighting services of other stout-hearted, mercenary, Ithacan warriors."

"Father, I've often heard about your great renown, you being a mighty warrior in search of your destiny. Your hands are strong, and I'm sure that your plans will be intelligent enough for any low-level moron to fathom. But what you've now contemplating is far too big a task to initiate. I'm astonished that you believe that you and me alone could fight against at least two-dozen arrogant-and-powerful bellicose fucks, who prey upon your dwindling estate, all having fixations of marrying Mother Penelope, and then humping and pumping the poop out of your wife on your own hard mattress, or atop your tin palace roof, or on top of your pet camel, er, I meant to say, on top of your favorite dromedary!"

"All right, I'll tell you straight-up, Telemachus. Pay attention now, and listen with all three of your ears. Do you believe that Athena, along with Father Zeus, and possibly also legendary Mother Goose, will be enough support for the two of us inspired fools to combat the crazy suitors, or should I think about who else might help us? Perhaps if we prudently pray hard enough, we can obtain the aid of Hephaestus, the deformed blacksmith god, to hammer some volcanic lava up the freeloaders' colons and semi-colons!"

"Father, those Olympian allies you've mention are quite excellent. They sit high in the clouds, ruling others, immortal gods, demigods and men," Telemachus naively agreed. "We'd better include the easily-slighted, chariot-riding sun god, too, so that we don't have to apologize to Apollo for leaving Helios Hyperion out of our capricious strategy alliance."

"Yes, pathetic dumb-shit!" Odysseus agreeably boomed. "Only empathetic Athena cares a scintilla about what the hell happens to me. All of the other gods have amnesia about constructively helping us defeat this ravenous, diabolical horde of licentious vultures. But for now, Telemachus; when Dawn arrives with her hairless crack, go to the palace, join company with those haughty suitors, and cordially mingle with the demented scoundrels. The swineherd Eumaeus will accompany me to the city later on. I'll be disguised like a pretentious beggar, old and wretched with arthritis all over my body, except in my incomparable fadorkenbender. If the obnoxious dregs are abusive towards me, let that dear heart within your chest endure the cursing and derision of the nasty dirtballs, while I'm being badly mistreated and scorned, even if the diabolical scumbags drag me by my testicles all throughout the house, attempting to hold my feet and scrotum sac to the fire, and then meanly throwing my ass out the door, and then begin hurling sharp objects and weapons in my direction."

"How will I know when all the exciting drama and the trauma will commence?" Telemachus asked. "I want to get directly involved and not become a useless part of the Mr. Olympus protection program!"

"Keep looking forward with anticipation, vernal Telemachus, and hold yourself in check, until the appropriate time is ripe. When wise Athena plants the exact 'go signal' inside my mind, I'll give you the nod to participate in the melee by bobbing my head up and down like a neurotic mental patient. Once you see that symbolic gyration, remove all of the weapons of war ornamented upon the external hall walls, and stow the spears, bows and arrows in a safe place, perhaps in the lofty upstairs storage room, modeled after the one I had once seen in Attica."

"Any other directions, father?"

"Be sure to leave behind a pair of swords, two spears, and two ox-hide shields for the two of us to grab when we make a wild rush at the surprised, partying bastards; I'm confident that our colleague, Pallas Athene, will keep the son-of-a-bitches' minds preoccupied with visions of perverted and gay pornographic images. I'll tell you something else of a meritorious nature; if you are my son, truly of our family blood, let no one in Ithaca hear that Odysseus is back home."

"Can't I even tell grandfather? He won't remember anything I say, anyway!"

"Don't even let Laertes know, even if *my* senile old man has amnesia and has developed six brain tumors. And keep our secret away from the swineherd Eumaeus, and the remaining vigilant slaves, or even Queen Penelope herself must not know of my reappearance and planned insurgency. The goddess Athena, my son, had just told me in a vision that King Menelaus has sent a ship with additional gifts for me to the house of Clytius, the brother of Clitoris, for safe-keeping until our vengeance has been fully enacted and consummated!"

Meanwhile, back at the palace, Antinous, the chief suitor, was addressing his inebriated and apathetic colleagues. "My friends; to tell you tiny-pricks the blessed truth, in his great fantasy, Telemachus has carried-out his preposterous trip, and remarkably, the silly dumb-shit prince has had great success. We never thought he would complete his fruitless mission, but against all odds, the lucky oddball has been successful. So, fellow rogues; let's do something terrible and gruesome to him."

No sooner had vile Antinous uttered his devious plot that ambiguous Amphinomus, turning in his seat beside a dirty broken window, observed an alien ship anchored in the deep harbor. Mariners were bringing down the sail, while others were holding their oars. With a hardy laugh, Amphinomus lustily addressed his nefarious comrades, thinking that the foreign ship was carrying Telemachus and his ample supply of gifts from Pylos and Sparta.

"Well, this is certainly the worst news ever since all-too-curious Pandora opened her box, not the one between her legs, mind you, but the one sent by Zeus to distract humanity, since the god was afraid that mortal intelligence could eventually rival and conquer the Olympians, just as the foul Olympians had risen-up, rebelled against, and defeated their ancestor Titans," Antinous lectured. "And as we all know, all of the evils contained inside Pandora's chest, not the one under her neck, but the one that was a gift from deceitful Zeus, curses flew-out of the container to plague and bewilder mankind forever. This time, the devious gods have made sure that Telemachus has been kept safe from our plot to kill him, being entertained first in Pylos, and later by King Menelaus in Sparta. Our attempt at ambushing that little squirt Telemundo, er, I mean Telemachus, is much more resilient than I had originally imagined that annoying punk to be!"

"So, once that pesky pest Telemachus is satisfactorily eliminated, we can all fairly compete at wooing and courting Queen Penelope," snidely Amphinomus, wicked brother of Iamanignoramus maintained.

'Ludicrous Fool!' Antinous selfishly conjectured. 'Penelope will consent to marrying me, because I have the most wealth, and at three-inches in length, I own the biggest erect penis amongst all of us!'

Jay Dubya

Chapter 19

"ODYSSEUS AS A BEGGAR"

As soon as rose-fingered early Dawn appeared upon the eastern horizon, Telemachus, dear son of godlike Odysseus, tied dirty sandals upon his feet and ankles, grabbed a powerful spear that was well-suited for the scumball suitors' chests, and soon gathered enough courage to articulate a firm message to Eumaeus, the pig-herder.

"Old brain-dead friend; I'm now leaving for the city, so that I can see and possibly commiserate with my saddened mother. I don't believe that the Queen's dreadful grieving, along with her sorrowed sobbing, will cease tears from cascading down-her cheeks until Penelope, not through commonplace hearsay, but through actual and true interaction, gets to communicate with me face-to-face. So, I'm telling you, Eumaeus; although I'm not a medical doctor, I prescribe that you do this particular event in the exact order which I'm now commanding. Take this vagrant Stranger now dozing in *my* bed into the city. Once there, the Vagabond can beg for food and charity from any well-bred person who'll offer him moldy bread and cups of stagnant water. I can't take on the weight of everyone, not when I have these myriad sorrows inhabiting my heart. As for the stranger-than-fiction Stranger, if he's especially upset at this plan, things will turn-out worse for him."

Odysseus, who was eavesdropping on the oddball monologue, rose from the hut's only bed and stated to the swine-keeper. "Friend; I myself am not all that hot-to-trot to be held back here in suburban Ithaca. For a beggar, it's better to ask mealy-mouthed people for a meal inside the city instead of asking for bullshit from the cows and steers in yonder grazing fields, that ironically, the pastures themselves never graze. Whoever's willing to give me alms from their palms should voluntarily contribute to the sustenance of my general welfare. I still possess a zest for living, despite my ragged, disheveled appearance."

"Oh, marvelous Beggar," Eumaeus commended. "You seem to possess artificial intelligence coming directly to you from the clouds! May Almighty Zeus be praised for the mental telepathy your brain is receiving from Olympus's supreme transmissions!"

Telemachus walked-away, moving at a rapid pace, and making sure the hut's squeaky door didn't hit his skinny ass on the way out. The lad's only thought was his strong desire to sow seeds of trouble for the covetous suitors, while Penelope was preoccupied upstairs, sewing and unsewing her huge tapestry.

When the sole son of Odysseus entered the deteriorating palace, Telemachus stepped through the main hall, tightly gripping his sharp spear which he had never used. Two swift-but-ferocious dogs accompanied him into the edifice, to be commanded to attack pond-scum villains if necessary. The arrogant suitors thronged around the newly-arrived youth, making phony, courteous conversation to awkwardly conceal their deep, vitriolic hatred dwelling within their minds and inside their dark souls.

Telemachus' marvelous mother had abandoned her upstairs sewing pursuit and sat across from her son, by the doorpost of the hall, leaning from her seat to spin fine threads of delicate fabric and to tell family yarns. The pair reached-out with their hands to partake of the meager crumbs and scraps prepared and set before them. When the twosome had satisfied their stomachs with rancid-tasting food and drink, the first to speak was the son.

"Mother, since this poor-diet meal, which consisted mostly of meat morsels and tasteless vegetables, I say that this low-budget dinner could only be described as being totally fruitless!"

"Telemachus, get serious for a moment! Once I've gone upstairs to my quarters, I'll lie in bed, which has become for me a place of despair, always damp with tears, ever since Odysseus sailed-off to Troy with Atreus's vengeful sons Agamemnon and Menelaus. Yet you don't now dare to tell me clearly of your father's twenty-years' absence, before the haughty suitors come back here and again shame my home and your father's legacy; in short, you've provided no substantial word of what the hell you have recently learned fucking-around down south in Pylos and in Sparta."

"All right then, Mother. I'll tell you the meaningless truth as I know it. First, my entourage and I had sailed to Pylos and reached Nestor, shepherd of his flock. The older elder welcomed us into his home with hospitality and kindness, like a genuine father-substitute would do; that's how Lord Nestor looked after providing for my stomach, but-not-after-my-great sexual needs. But as for brave Odysseus, alive or dead, Nestor had nothing worthwhile to offer that his defective ears had heard from any visiting horse's ass living on Earth. The old coot sent me off, providing me with a primitive chariot with wobbly wheels, to visit that famous spearman Menelaus, son of Atreus. In Sparta, I met Argive Helen, for whom countless Achaeans had desperately struggled hard to liberate from Prince Paris's sexy charm. Menelaus, skilled at yelling war shouts, at once questioned me, asking: Why had I come to Sparta? Was I looking to lose my virginity to the million whores humping and pumping their diseased genitals all over the city, even in the public streets? I'm telling you the honest-to-Zeus truth, Mother, describing every minute detail as I recollect them."

"Did Menelaus give you any new information concerning my husband?" the Queen wondered and asked. "That's why the hell you traveled there in the first place!"

"That travesty over in Ithaca that you're inquiring about is disgraceful and sinful!" Menelaus impulsively replied to me and my earnest plea. "The good-for-nothing two-dozen predators wasting your inheritance inside your' father's house all now-desire to lie-down in the bed of a courageous warrior and pork his faithful wife, when they themselves are cowardly jerk-offs. I predict that intrepid Odysseus will soon arrive and bring those avaricious shit-heads to their disastrous end."

"That can't be all you learned!" Queen Penelope exclaimed. "You could learn more going to a teachers' college!"

"That's exactly what great spearman Menelaus said, Mother, and in plain Greek, that's about all she wrote."

Meanwhile, indomitable Odysseus and the loyal swineherd were hastening to leave the stenchy pig-fields behind and start walking toward the city, striding past veteran battle-weary warriors in trances, and passing by the historic Ithacan National Shrine, the Sacred Country Cunt-tree. Eumaeus amiably offered Odysseus his smelly staff that he himself often used to shove-up the asses of uncooperative hogs, instantly sending the giant pigs down to swine hell as newly snorting hog-goblins.

Then, the clumsy pair approached the city center, while barking dogs and apathetic herdsmen remained two miles behind to guard the farmyard, and to spend their time pissing and shitting into rabbit, snake, chipmunk and rat holes.

The faithful swineherd casually led his anonymous master deeper into the inner city, himself also appearing much like a beggar; yes, another old-and-wretched vagrant, with his filthy body covered by shabby, threadbare rags. But as the dirty duo made their way along the cobblestone path, finally leaving the odor-laden outskirts, the twosome reached a well-made spring, with a steady flow, where townsfolk drew their daily water with pails, and not crayons.

At that crossroads, Melanthius, son of doleful Dolius, approached, driving a herd of unshaven goats, all sporting exaggerated goatees beneath thin chins; the finest ones in all the flocks, designated to serve as delicious dinner for the demanding palace suitors. When Melanthius started yelling shameful insults at his goats and at his servant underlings, Odysseus became enraged at such abuse being vocalized in public.

"Now, Eumaeus; here we have a truly filthy man vehemently cursing at another filthy scoundrel. As always, a god matches like personality with like character. Buzzards of a feather, generally always flock together! The wretched, self-important goatherder!" Odysseus the Beggar explained to Eumaeus, the don't-give-a-shit pig-master.

"Where are you off to with this disgusting beggar asshole, a tedious bore who'll most-certainly interrupt our palace feast?" Melanthius screamed at Eumaeus. "Beggars can't be choosey, but *you* certainly can!" the suitor's favored servant criticized.

Melanthius, the unethical goatherd buffoon, soon entered the decaying palace, and at once sat among the never-satisfied suitors, directly opposite Eurymachus, who was fond of the nasty dumb-shit more so than the other garrulous grubbers were.

Meanwhile, Odysseus and the wifty swineherd paused as the two came closer to the former gleaming fortress. Around them rang the music of the hollow lyre, for minstrel Phemius was about to sing another gay tune. But then a hunting dog, Argus, Odysseus's favorite, raised its head and pricked-up its ears. But before the master could enjoy being reunited with the gray-hound, the King of Ithaca's heart sadly regretted leaving the comforts of his dog and palace to venture-off to distant Troy on his twenty-year odyssey.

Odysseus looked away and brushed aside a tear he wished to hide from the swine-herder's scrutiny. "Eumaeus, it's strange that this seemingly familiar dog is lying prone here, resting in the dung without his costumed canvas dungarees that I've heard Queen Penelope had sewn for him," the master observed and commented. "Indeed, according to scuttlebutt all around the Mediterranean, the once-formidable boar-hunter had a handsome body twenty years ago. I'm not sure right now if his speed once matched his awesome looks, or if Argus is presently like those table-mooching canines that weak men perpetually pet, the extremely-spoiled pooches that their masters raise and keep for show and tell."

"Yes, clever Stranger. This muscular dog belongs to a courageous man who probably has died somewhere far away. If the gray-hound had the form and acted as he did when Odysseus had left him, and voyaged to Troy, you'd quickly see his speed and strength, and then you'd be amazed at the animal's incomparable dexterity. No wild animal that Argus had vigorously chased into the forest ever escaped his pursuit in the deep, thick woods, for that tenacious gray dog could track a scent; especially nasty ones emanating from between a horny woman's legs. But poor Argus is in a bad way now. His master's more-than-likely dead in some foreign land, and careless older women don't look after him because the elderly hags no longer enjoy having their dried-up pussies smelled. For when self-centered masters can no longer exercise their assumed power, observant slaves no longer demonstrate any desire to do their work properly."

Eumaeus carefully led the Stranger deeper inside the formerly stately mansion, walking straight into the main hall to join the ignoble, always-protesting, confiscators. But once he'd seen and recognized the odor originating from his master's crotch, after twenty years of separation, Argus's legs collapsed, and his remaining dog spirit was suddenly gripped by the fatal clutches of ever-stalking Death.

Ignoring the demise of Argus, Telemachus was the first to notice Eumaeus making the palace scene. The alert Prince, in essence, a royal pain in the ass, quickly summoned the pig-herder by nodding his head like a neurotic parrot. Eumaeus cautiously looked-around, and then picked-up a stool, placed it where a servant usually would sit, and proceeded to carve massive cuts of meat to serve the unruly, rowdy, vitriolic, fucked-up suitors.

Odysseus, looking like an old, miserable, impotent beggar, had entered unnoticed into the huge chamber directly behind Eumaeus. The returning King, with his curved back bent-over, was leaning upon his staff, with his totally covered body dressed in putrid-smelling rags. The pathetic-looking beggar sat upon the ash-wood threshold situated inside the termite-infested doorway, and the lit fireplace embers burned his sensitive ass, and nearly set his entire attire ablaze. Then, like a Greek theater actor, Melanthius, the cynical goatherder, called-out to the gathering, and imperatively yelled derogatory remarks at the newcomer to the daily feasts.

"Listen to me, those of you courting the glorious queen, about this impudent Stranger who has just entered. I've seen him before, and I've also noticed that the lowly swineherd was the one who had brought him here. I don't know the intruder's identity, or the family he might claim to have come from, but I have *bad vibrations* about this stinking trespasser, and the feeling I'm receiving doesn't exactly send me to any fucked-up, idyllic blossom world, either."

Then, Antinous turned on Eumaeus, to reprimand, embarrass, and scold the pig-keeper, and also mock and ridicule *his* apparent association with his peculiar Stranger-Beggar-acquaintance.

"You really are a nuisance scum-wagon. Yes, Eumaeus; you who cares for wallowing pigs without demonstrating any cultural esteem for your' sophisticated superiors. Why are you' so intent on bringing this scruffy fellow here into the center of town without giving the dirty piece of shit a decent ten-hour bath? As far as drifters and vagrants go, do we not already have too many of these dependent freeloaders indiscreetly panhandling around this city and inside this palace; yes, worthless bloodsuckers who cavort with impunity around the local straight, the gay, and the tri-gender communities; obviously being troublesome, greedy tramps who recklessly disrupt our elite banquets, simply to ask for our benign mercy?"

"Antinous," Eumaeus audaciously addressed the detestable head glutton. "You may be an aristocrat of sorts, but what you've just articulated, insulting this humble guest to the House of Odysseus, is indeed not a commendable and honorable speech. You are sinfully abusive, and a poison to my master's slaves, more so than any of the other detestable suitors in your company; and your harsh tongue and stinging language are especially offensive to me. But honestly, I don't give a flying fart; not while suffering Queen Penelope lives here in this once noble edifice, reigning with brave Telemachus."

Noticing Odysseus moving around the vast room begging for food, Antinous spoke-out against "lowlife from outside entering the great hall".

"What insane god sent this filthy dirt-bag into our midst to interrupt our festive feast? You're basically an insolent and shameless beggar, with no respect for educated, august noblemen. You confidently and presumptively approach each of us without conscience, one by one, and we generously give you scraps and tiny edibles, with no holding back, for we prestigious fellows religiously obey the laws of the gods without exhibiting sinful deviation."

"Well now, repugnant and pugnacious Antinous," Odysseus the Beggar defiantly challenged. "It seems as if that phony, conniving mind of yours does not match your ugly looks. You'd refuse to give even a grain of salt from your own house to a disciple of yours, and now you sit in someone else's home and do not even offer me a half-cup of diluted wine. And yet, there's plenty of sour vino in that jug sitting right in front of you."

The chief suitor glared at the stubborn mendicant and, with a wide scowl upon his countenance, gave his derisive response.

"I no longer think you'll leave this hall unharmed, decrepit Stranger; now that you've begun babbling lowlife insults in my direction. I believe that you're begging for elimination besides asking for charity!"

After perturbed Antinous screamed those derisive words, the incensed blowhard grabbed a stool and threw the heavy piece of furniture, which in seconds impacted Odysseus at the base of his right shoulder. But the brazen recipient of the toss stood firm, like a rock, and the Beggar did not stagger or buckle one iota, while Antinous became somewhat befuddled and astounded.

At the time of the ensuing argument, Queen Penelope was conversing with her chief servant women, while later, Lord Odysseus sat quietly and munched on paltry scraps and petty morsels. But then, Odysseus's dignified wife slowly stood and calmly called-out to the steadfast swineherd.

"Good Eumaeus," Penelope affably beckoned. "Go and ask the extraordinary Stranger you've brought here to come meet me, so that I can greet him warmly, and ask if he perhaps has heard any news about my brave Odysseus; or perhaps our guest might have somehow caught sight of my husband with his own aged eyes. For indeed; our unexpected, withered visitor looks like a weary man who's spent a very long time wandering all over the scientifically-proven Flat Earth."

"Honored Stranger," Eumaeus calmly said. "Wise Penelope is summoning you and your alien ideas to have a parley. For her heart, in spite of bearing much anxiety, is urging her to inquire about her husband's travails since Troy."

"Eumaeus," Beggar Odysseus sternly answered. "I'll tell the honest-to-Athena truth, along with all the significant details, and reveal the facts to discreet Penelope, daughter of Icarius, and I'll accurately describe everything pertinent rather quickly. Frankly, Eumaeus; I happen to know King Odysseus fairly well. Please tell Queen Penelope, for all her restless eagerness, to patiently wait until the predictable sun goes down in the west. Let the Queen ask me at that time about her husband's itinerant drudgery; and about the day of his wonderful return, and about everything else that the audacious adventurer has both endured and survived. But right now, let me sit close by the warm fire, for the clothes that I'm wearing are rather thin and pitiful, and my garb stinks-to-High-Olympus, like a putrid gallon of skunk piss, and as you well-know from your own offered hospitality, and from your dreadful occupational experience, I directly came to your hut first for help, smelling and reeking like a lousy, dirty, rabid rat. In the sense of existing parallel odors, Pig-master Eumaeus, you and I are indeed kindred brothers."

Chapter 20
"EURYCLEIA RECOGNIZES ODYSSEUS"

Irus, a frequent beggar to the palace, came inside and started abusing Beggar Odysseus, whom the wise-ass regular suspected had been representing new competition for food and charity. The pair fought, and Odysseus easily knocked-out Irus, hitting the bully double-crosser with a flurry of left hooks that beat the brown feces and the yellow urine out of the aggravating son-of-a-bitch. Penelope, very impressed with the Beggar's pugilistic ability, encouraged the parsimonious suitors to bring presents for her, and the want-to-get-laid, in-heat idiots did so with dispatch. Meanwhile, Beggar Odysseus admonished the female servants, criticizing them for being too sympathetic to, and too friendly with, the belligerent suitors. Eurymachus decided to ridicule Odysseus in return, and in imitation of Antinous, threw a stool at the disguised King, but missed his target and hit the wine steward, knocking the servant unconscious. Being amused, the inebriated gluttons continued feasting, and then the contented moochers departed thereafter to their separate residences.

The wimpy Prince and the camouflaged King quickly and surreptitiously removed the weapons on display from the empty hall and stealthily concealed them in a remote storage room.

Telemachus, becoming fidgety, paced through the main hall, moved below the flaming wall torches, out into the room where he used to rest when sweet Sleep trespassed into his troubled mind. Lord Odysseus also stayed, lingering and pensively contemplating how to kill the contemptible culprits; of course, with Pallas Athene's guidance and inspiration.

After unraveling her daily tapestry enterprise upstairs, wise Penelope emerged out of her quarters, looking like a combination of huntress Artemis and golden Aphrodite. Beside the fire where the Queen used to sit, an alert servant placed an elaborate chair for her, inlaid with ivory and silver. Penelope sat, and then spoke to Eurynome, her often-preferred housekeeper.

"Fetch a comfortable chair over here with a thick golden fleece, so that the visiting Stranger can sit and share sincere conservation, er, I mean 'sincere conversation' with me. Although I know nothing about police work, I want to thoroughly interrogate the Beggar."

Obedient Eurynome quickly brought-in a polished chair, placed the object by her Queen, and as instructed, threw a clean sheep fleece over it. Lord Odysseus, who had endured so much hardship, sat-down next to his grieving wife, who found interest in specialized in conversing with lowlife guests.

"Stranger; you appear to be a cultural moron! Who are you among men? What is your' nationality? From what city, town, land, or village do you originate? And where the hell are your negligent parents who have not adequately provided for your prosperous development?"

"Noble lady; wife of gallant Odysseus, all right, I'll tell you everything, even though it's impossible for anyone who is mortal to know everything. I've been wandering all over flat Earth, traveling through many towns of men, and suffering great distress. Still, there's a place in the middle of the wine-dark sea called Crete, where I had been born, son of Deucalion and his wife Decalian, who liked to draw logos and glue the artistic renditions onto babies' asses for identification. I am a grandson of Minos, and please don't ask me if I was born out of one of his nostrils. In regard to your absent husband, I had seen Odysseus in Crete, where the fickle wind's whims had forced his warships to land, as his twelve Biremes were sailing for Troy. So, I invited your spouse into my house, and I entertained him well with a warm welcome."

As Odysseus spoke and fibbed, the disguised tramp made his many falsehoods sound just like truth without consequences. But he held his pupils steady between his eyelids, and the prevaricating King adroitly kept-up his verbal deceit and deftly concealed his tears. But then, when Penelope had had her fill of shedding tears and sobbing her laments, the curious Queen austerely spoke to the cunning visitor once more.

"Now, marvelous Stranger. I think I'd really like to test you out, to see if you did, in fact, entertain my husband in Crete, along with his fine companions as you've just claimed. So, describe the style of clothing Odysseus was wearing then, and the kind of man he was. And also, tell me all about his principal comrades who had loyally accompanied him."

"My Fair Lady; it's difficult for an aged beggar such as myself to recall exactly what I had observed twenty long years ago, but I'll do a mental deep-dive and delve-down into my hazy memory. In contempt of the gods, Lord Odysseus wore a double woolen, purple cloak. The brooch on it was made of gold, and it had a pair of clasps along with a fine engraving on the front. The first clasp featured an angry dog, and the second one a dappled fawn. Everyone standing and observing him at the dock was astonished at viewing those magnificent gold animal representations; the dog held-down the fawn, as the canine throttled the weaker animal, and the fawn was apparently struggling with its feet, trying to flee the predator's powerful grasp. I noticed the transparent tunic on your husband's body glistening like a dried-out onion skin. I mean, what is the purpose of clothing? Why would a man wear a see-through tunic and show his pubic area in public?"

As Odysseus spoke his wily rhetoric, Penelope sobbed and wept more, because the Queen had recognized signs of truth in what the unique beggar had just revealed.

"Stranger-than mythology, Stranger; though I had pitied you upon first impression, you'll now find from me genuine welcome and respect. I was the one who had dressed my husband in those exact clothes you've just so eloquently described. I brought them from the room, smoothed them out, and pinned on the shining brooch to be an ornament, a unique conversation piece."

"Wife of famous and infamous Odysseus, don't mar your lovely skin or waste your heart by weeping for your careless husband," the Beggar insisted. "Dry your tears, and listen to my factual words that will sound like absolute fiction. I've already heard gossip and discussions around Ithaca about Odysseus's recent return. He's close by, hanging-out in the wealthy land of Thesprotians, still barely alive in the Thespian and Lesbian Colony, and in quest of additional exploration and adventure."

"Oh, Stranger with the smelly clothes; I wish what you've just divulged is true. But my injured heart has a sense of what will certainly materialize in reality. Odysseus won't be coming home again, and you'll not find an escort out of this decaying palace, because there are no leaders of Odysseus's prowess and pure character in this enemy-occupied fortress. Despite these tremendous adversities, I'll command my servant women, to wash your stinky feet, that emit a foul odor even worse that my husband's had emitted two decades ago."

"Honored wife of great Odysseus, it's now time for me to be completely honest, and not facetious. I've hated cloaks and shining coverlets since I first left the snow-draped mountains of Crete, when I departed on my long-oared ship a full week after your husband's sandal scandal you have failed to mention. So, I'll resolve to lie-down, as I have done before through hundreds of sleepless nights. And having my feet washed brings me no afternoon delight, nor sky meteors in flight, into my heart, because in truth, I love the odor of grimy toes and heels. No woman serving in this house will ever touch my feet, unless there is an old one, who reveres true devotion, and who has suffered in her heart as many emotional pains as I have hurtfully endured in my many frustrating travels."

"Are you explicitly saying that you don't wish to have your smelly feet washed with stagnant water?"

"I'd not resent it if the old bag touched my feet, because in the end, everything comes-out in the wash," replied Odysseus, imaginatively inventing a novel cliché.

"Dear Stranger; no visitor from far-off lands who has come into my house has ever been as wise at spewing magnificent profundity as you have by inventing crazy and fantastic idiomatic expressions. Now, I have in my service a wrinkled old hag who possesses an understanding heart. She had often provided my helpless husband her fine care, ever since the day his mother gave birth to him. Although she's presently quite weak and feeble, she'll wash and clean your feet and rub sandpaper cloth between your' grimy toes. So come now; stand up, wise Eurycleia. Bathe this man's walking arrangements the same as if he's your former master."

The old woman clasped her hands and then spoke with certainty to the warrior having the gross athlete's feet condition.

"And I'm willing, For Queen Penelope's sake, to bathe and wipe your stinky feet as if they were your smelly asshole."

The old servant used a bright bowl to commence with her washing assignment, but then realized that she needed water to continue her task. Eurycleia slowly poured-in plenty of cold liquid, and soon added warmer water to rub-off the inch-thick crud and excess dead skin. Odysseus then turned and sat some distance from the hearth, and quickly turned around towards the central darkness. The disguised beggar was afraid that the old hussy would notice a prominent scar shown upon his left ankle, and also a red birthmark upon his right heel, and then the Beggar's actual identity would be readily discovered.

When Eurycleia (a former Ithacan national spelling bee champion) began her specialized cleansing, the hoary, foot-cleaning specialist immediately recognized the inimitable scar, a wound that Odysseus had suffered at Mt. Parnassus, years before Troy, that had been obtained from the razor-sharp, white tusks of a ferocious, wild, hungry boar.

After recognizing the scar along with the associated red birthmark, the scrubwoman dropped the heavy foot, worrying that she had rubbed the beggar the wrong way.

"Either this is a remarkable coincidence, or it's positively genuine truth. Queen Penelope; I've seen ugly clodhoppers similar to those belonging to this old goat, and I can attest that this ancient codger is indeed your husband Odysseus. Nobody has body odor to this horrendous extreme than your husband does. The stench is enough to exterminate every fly, mosquito, ant, cockroach and spider in the entire palace."

While Penelope was preoccupied swatting disturbing flies and mosquitoes landing upon her legs and crotch, Odysseus's arms quickly reached-out for Eurycleia's throat.

"Stay silent, old bitch, so that no one roaming the hall finds-out what you have just identified. For I'll tell you something, and it will soon happen. For the time being, shut the fuck up, and don't utter either a vowel or a consonant."

Frightened to death and aware of Odysseus's notorious temper, Eurycleia frantically left the room and sprinted like an athletic teenager down the adjacent hallway. After swatting a bevy of flies and mosquitoes, Penelope again addressed the stench-laden Beggar.

"Stranger, my body requires sleep and masturbation. So now, I'll ascend the rickety steps up to my chambers and lie on the bed, where I sometimes think and mumble to myself the truth."

Jay Dubya

Chapter 21
"THE BOW CONTEST"

When twilight in the form of Dawn arrived inside Odysseus's former fine home, the women servants were already up kindling the fire. Then, the male attendants who fearfully served the despicable Achaean lords arrived inside to perform their duties. Behind them came the swineherd, leading the three chosen corpulent hogs, the best oinkers of all he currently had in his pens. The hog guardian turned the squealers loose to feed inside the butchering room, and while multi-tasking, the versatile fellow exchanged assuring lingo with Beggar Odysseus.

"Stranger; these fucked-up, voracious Achaeans have no regard or deference for your plight. The vain assholes are mocking and insulting you the same way that the privileged scum-wagons had meanly done yesterday."

"Well, Eumaeus. I hope the gods pay back the injuries that the egocentric, fucked-up leeches so recklessly have planned in another's home; yes, and the disgusting pond scum are obviously showing no evident sense of guilt, shame, or remorse for their transgressions."

A few seconds later, Melanthius, the antagonistic goatherder, came-up close to the pair of conferees. The coy, ill-tempered fellow was leading the very finest she-goats in his flocks, designated to be the major part of the suitors' feast.

"Stranger; are you still bothering us here, inside this confiscated house, begging food and copper coins from the kind Achaeans?" Melanthius prefaced his nasty derogation. "Why don't you get the fuck-out while you still have an ass from which to shit? I think it's obvious that you and I will not say goodbye until after we've had a taste of one another's fists. The way you contemptuously beg is not ethically correct. Achaeans, particularly well-mannered suitors, are valid authorities on practicing proper etiquette at feasts, you know."

Shrewd Odysseus recognized Melanthius's bravado as being sheer braggadocio, and the Ithacan King remained reticent and said nothing in return, shaking his oversized head in disgust.

Then, a third more civil servant Phuloshitus, an outstanding man when he wasn't standing inside the palace, brought-in a sterile heifer for the

175

suitors' banquet. Phuloshitus tied-up the noisy beast with care, approached Odysseus, and spoke to the laconic Beggar.

"Greetings, honored Stranger. Though you're facing many troubles now, may you find pleasant happiness in future days. When I recall Odysseus and think of his illustrious presence in this once-magnificent house, I start to perspire, even though my wife tells me, 'Don't sweat the small stuff'. My eyes fill-up with abundant tears. For wandering Odysseus, I think, if still alive, would be dressed in tawdry rags just like yours, roaming around this flat Earth, and admiring the sunlight while drinking plenty of moonshine."

"Herdsman; you don't appear to be a fellow who's bad in character, or one who lacks common intelligence, for I can plainly sense that your sympathetic heart is functioning well-above the moron level of meditation," the cleverly disguised King replied. "And so, I'll swear a mighty oath to you. I predict that your mentor Odysseus will soon come home. With your own eyes, you'll see the evil suitors slaughtered like oinking pigs and squealing goats, if that's your secret wish."

"Ah, philosophical Stranger," Phuloshitus acknowledged and muttered. "How I wish Cronos's erratic son might bring about what you've just told me. Then, with Zeus's awesome assistance, you would find-out how strong I truly am, and what my hands can do during Odysseus's battle, should my master ever triumphantly return to retake Ithaca."

Eumaeus also prayed a similar plea in a low tone to all the Greek gods, the pig-keeper's theme hoping for Odysseus to return to his own home and reclaim his righteous jurisdiction over the island.

The ball-busting degenerates continued to feast and verbally abuse Odysseus, still-masquerading as a common, dependent panhandler. Bright-eyed Athena then placed inside the heart of Penelope, the creative idea that Telemachus' mother should set-up inside Odysseus's main hall the lord's incomparable bow, along with a series of a dozen gray iron axes for the suitors to engage in a friendly competition for the Queen's hand in marriage; but in reality, the unique bow was a secret prelude to the vile fiends' impending deaths.

Graceful Penelope stepped cautiously and furtively into the storage chamber and collected Odysseus's bow and his favorite axes. Once the lovely lady returned to the great hall and reached the suitors, the elegant and eloquent Queen stood beside the door-post of the deteriorating chamber, and a bright thin veil covered her still-beautiful face. On either side stood loyal women attendants, wishing that they would soon die and speed directly down to dismal Hades, and lead more normal existences as flitting spirits.

"Listen to me, emboldened, sex-driven suitors, who've been ravaging this home with your incessant need for food and drink. Now, my husband's been away so long that I could never recognize him if he were present standing or sitting next to me in this great room. The only story you fools could offer-up as an excuse to acquire the wealth of my husband's estate is that you all desire to marry me and take me as your wife. So, since I want to marry only one of you, come now, suitors; and since I seem to be the prize you falsely seek, I'll place this great bow right here; the favored weapon that once belonged to brave Odysseus. Whichever one of you clumsy goons who can grip this incomparable bow and string it with the greatest ease, then shoot an arrow straight as a dart through the dozen carved openings inside the positioned twelve axes, all of them lined-up in a row one, after the other, I'll promise to go with him to the altar and then to the bed where I'll make the lucky winner the Principal at my Beaver Academy."

When Penelope declared her vowed intention, the Queen told Eumaeus, the swineherd, to set the twelve iron axes for the suitors' imminent contest. But to the suitors' alarm and surprise, Telemachus spoke-out with new-found royal authority.

"Well now, Zeus, son of Cronos; your power of suggestion must have made me foolish and frivolous. My dear Mother; although quite sensible in her offer, says she'll shack-up with one of you professional jerk-offs. But now, it's prime time for you amateur archers to axe-tually get started!"

As Telemachus uttered that ludicrous nonsense, the impulsive lad quickly threw-off the purple cloak covering his back, and then impetuously jumped-up and removed the sharp sword hanging and dangling from his wimpy shoulders.

Fortunately, the greenhorn fool didn't have to carefully set-up the axes in a straight line, which had already been deftly accomplished by Eumaeus and Phuloshitus, the pig-master's occasional animal-tending confederate.

Amazement gripped the suitors' souls as the cruel critics looked at Telemachus and watched how the youth had directed Eumaeus and Phuloshitus to properly align the axes, though before then, the neophyte archer had never even seen those particular weapons.

Then Antinous, who had graduated Magna Come Loud from the Ithacan Orgasm Institute, nervously addressed the assembled rabble. "All you intrepid suitors; get-up in order of strength now, two lines from left to right, in order of height, beginning from the place where the steward pours and spills the wine."

Antinous spoke, and what he had proposed, the rest of his ilk found agreeable. The first suitor to stand was Leiodes, who often bragged about having three-and-a-half large testicles, along with an enlarged clitoris bulb situated at the top of his hairy asshole.

Leiodes, was the first contestant who picked-up Odysseus's bow and the accompanying arrow. After moving to the threshold and standing there, the famed archer tried pulling and bending the bow, but unbelievably, the strongest among the suitors could not string the weapon. Much to his embarrassment and chagrin, the nutcase's powerful hands and arms soon grew weary, before the contestant could ever succeed in hooking-up the string, which was a rather simple process that Leiodes had performed thousands of times before with ordinary bows.

"My friends and colleagues in practicing mass palace mooching; despite my unrivaled hunting reputation, I'm not the man capable of stringing this trick bow. So now, let someone else take hold of it who perhaps has the savvy to figure-out the damned, confounded device. As for me, this fuckin' bow is a puzzling conundrum! And I'm not being arrow-gant when I humbly state those wimpy words of surrender."

Chief suitor Antinous felt obligated to denounce the champion archer's concession. "Leiodes; what wretched, sorry words filter from your' fat lips! As I listened, your craven remarks made me extremely angry. Your royal mother did not produce a feckless coward who lacks sufficient strength to draw an ordinary bow and shoot a regular arrow. But I'm convinced that some other motivated man among these noble suitors will succeed in his endeavor. Come now, Melanthius, you uncouth goatherder," Antinous prodded. "Light a fire in the hall and next set a large chair in front of it; and after doing those simple procedures, spread a fleece all across. Then, if your raisin-sized brain can remember, I want you, lard-ass, to fetch a hefty piece of fat so that these young competitors here can warm the bow and rub heavy grease onto it, making the bow more flexible. That precautionary measure should easily eliminate any particular margarine for error!"

Feeling threatened by the disreputable bully, Melanthius soon lit a tireless fire. Then, the volatile-tempered goat-herder carried a large chair next to the hearth, draped a fleece upon it, moved and set the seat-down beside the roaring flames, and then a minute later, from inside the kitchen, fetched a large piece of fat to respect and butter-up Antinous.

So, then the young servants in attendance followed directions and warmed the bow and tested it, but even the strongest among the palace security guards could not string the hunting mechanism. Antinous and Eurymachus, the lead suitors, still remained as scheduled participants slated to test their bow-stringing ability.

Melanthius, the moody goat-herder, and Eumaeus, the benign keeper of the swineherd, both aged servants to Beggar Odysseus, soon left the palace to monotonously shovel pig and goat manure onto a crap-corroded donkey cart, the animal dung to be later used for crop fertilizer.

So, harried Lord Odysseus moved and slinked away to also silently leave the palace unnoticed. The costumed King walked through the weed-infested backyard, and swiftly followed *their'* irregular path. When the pig and goat custodians had passed beyond the rear courtyard, and then sauntered past the classic-designed gates, Odysseus called to the preoccupied laborers, and uttered certain reassuring words.

"You there, yonder goat-herder and swine-keeper. Shall I tell you something, or should I keep my secret all to myself? My Athena-stimulated spirit tells me I should not speak goat or pig-shit; not horse-shit; not dog-shit, but instead, important bullshit to you two paragons of virtue. Now then; if Lord Odysseus were to come back suddenly, brought by a god from somewhere like the moon, perhaps as a fucked-up, disoriented space alien, would you two degenerates be the sort of loyal underlings who would volunteer to defend his legitimate return? Would you support the exploitive suitors, or would you actively fight with, and for, noble King Odysseus?"

"Oh, by virtue of Father Goose, er, I mean Father Zeus," Melanthius the goatherder yelled-back. "May that virtuous King return, and may his actions be led by some fickle, mercurial-minded god. Then, if that impossibility ever happens, you would know the kind of strength I have, and how my hands can easily demonstrate my strangling power. Instead of choking goats, I'll just transfer my knowledge to strangling a suitor or two."

And then, Eumaeus, too, made the same sort of commentary to all the apathetic gods, wishing that wise and insightful Odysseus would return to his own home and "royally kick ass".

Once the Beggar King had clearly realized how resolute the dual animal attenders were in their cited testimonies, the King spoke to the common dregs again, in an authoritarian voice.

"Well, kind servants; here I am in person, after suffering much hardship and distress for two decades. I've managed to finally return to Ithaca in the twentieth year to righteously reclaim my own wife and property. Of those who had worked for me, I recognize that you're the only two males who want me back as the main decision-maker. Among the rest, I've heard no one praying that my return would bring harmony, and also melody, to my seized palace. I'll tell you both how this is going to go-down, and I'll speak the truth, if, on my puny behalf, some empathetic god will assist me in overcoming and vanquishing those illegitimate scoundrels."

"What's in it for me?" the very interested goat-keeper and pig-herder simultaneously hollered to the astonished Beggar, whom the pair believed was being facetious in making his extraordinary, unorthodox statements.

"And furthermore, I promise that if our ultimate battle is victorious, both of you lackluster dimwits will be amply rewarded with expensive gifts, elite homes, and either wall-to-wall heterosexual or homosexual activity for the remainder of your happy life' tenures."

"Count me in!" both Melanthius and Eumaeus screamed in unison. "Count me in!" the dumb-dick assholes reiterated.

Odysseus pulled aside his rags, exposing the great scar that verified his true identity. Once the two animal-herders had recognized the identification mark and noted every unique detail, the bisexuals both threw their arms around the wise Odysseus, and the wimpy snowflakes burst into tears. Melanthius and Eumaeus kissed their master's head, shoulders, left nipple, scrotum sac, and finally, both nutjobs kissed his kisser.

"Okay; stop these dumb-ass laments immediately, you stupid-shit faggots," Odysseus chastised the two all-too-affectionate idiots. "Let's have no more crying, or homo' kissing. Someone might come-out from the hall, see us, and tell people in the house that we're three active members of the anti-conservative LBGTQRMSV community. Let's go into my palace, one by one, at one-minute intervals. I'll go first. And let's make this our sign for us to initiate action. Eumaeus, as you carry that massive bow of mine around the hall, put it first into my hands, and tell the women servants that they must lock and bar the hall doors from the outside to keep all of our prospective victims trapped inside."

Odysseus paced back into the hall and nonchalantly sat-down upon the stool where he had been sitting before. The two animal keepers, godlike Odysseus's servants, went in after him, farting and crapping their dirty tunics out of amplified anticipation and general excrement excitement.

Eurymachus already had the challenging bow in hand, warming the sturdy weapon here and there in light and heat from the blazing fire. But even doing that, the frustrated fuck-head could not competently string the bow after several failing tries.

"It's too bad. I'm disappointed for myself and for all of you," humiliated Eurymachus apologized. "I'm not that unhappy about losing the marriage with Penelope, although I'm upset about losing these nightly feasts and our merry camaraderie. There are many more convivial Achaean women with serious abdominal maladies to pump the poop and intestinal gas out of, some here in sea-girt Ithaca itself, and other harlots screwing-around in various neighboring towns and villages. But if we distinguished noblemen are so weak compared to godlike Odysseus, so puny that we can't even string his favorite bow, then our failure is a disgraceful embarrassment which future generations will learn about from their history lessons in years to come."

Antinous, desiring to delay his turn at stringing the bow, then felt compelled to offer his evaluation of recent events. "Eurymachus, that's not going to happen, as you yourself well-know," the chief suitor maintained. "At this moment, in the country, there's a special feast day, sacred to the gods, but I can't recall which one. So, who would bend the irrelevant bow? It really doesn't matter. Set the trick item aside without mentioning any more gossip about it. Come now; let the steward begin pouring fresh wine in our size D cups, so we can make libations and get plastered like Paris had done over in Troy. In honor of the anonymous religious feast day, let's put the curved bow-down, and in the morning, we'll test the weapon again when one of us remaining rivals will abruptly end this moronic contest."

Antinous finished his self-serving recommendations, and once the compliant stewards had poured the libations, and the already-intoxicated suitors had drunk wine to their hearts and stomachs' content, Odysseus, a very crafty and scheming fellow, thought it was time to gain the attention of the pursuers of Penelope's hand.

"Suitors of the most splendid Queen," Odysseus began his response to Antinous. "Listen to me, so that I can assess what the heart beating inside my chest is prompting me to state and do. It's a request, a plea, especially to you Eurymachus, and to you Antinous, since what the Chief Suitor had just suggested was most appropriate. I do believe for the moment that you should postpone this business involving the bow contest until another date and time. Give me the polished bow, Eumaeus, so in this hall I can test these hands of mine and determine if my supple limbs still possess the strength and the dexterity I used to have, or if my wandering, and my lack of nutrition have quite destroyed my muscular potency."

Hearing the intense bravado originating from the already-despised Beggar, the freeloading drones instantly became extremely agitated, but in their black hearts, the human parasites were fearing that a lowly beggar might capably string the polished bow.

"You wretched, warp-headed Stranger," Antinous rebuked the bold Beggar. "Your mind lacks any sense of decent respect for Ithacan culture and advanced Greek civilization. You possess no academic education, and have little rudimentary knowledge of laws, religion, ethics, morality and traditions, whatsoever. Aren't you content to feed your grimy face and share a feast with us, such eminent men, and to have the privilege of listening to the sagacious word exchanges that we philosophically speak to one another?"

"Antinous," Penelope vehemently chimed-in. "It's neither good nor proper to deny guests of Telemachus a chance to democratically participate in discussions and debates, no matter who it is who comes as a welcomed guest to this house. And if, trusting in his strength and power, the ragged Stranger in our midst manages to successfully string Odysseus's great bow, do you believe that this Beggar will take me home and make me his valued wife? I'm sure he himself bears no such hope inside that tanned chest of his. So, none of you prospective husbands should grimace and criticize this flesh and blood Beggar at our daily dinner hour. It is your nasty derision, along with your harsh brow-beating that dishonors this house, and not this unfortunate Beggar's rather insane comments."

"Among Achaeans, especially those present too weak and afraid to go to Troy, *no man* has a right stronger than my own to offer this bow to anyone I wish, or withhold," Telemachus asserted and contributed. "Among these same assembled crooks and hoodlums, no one will deny my will by force, if I wish to give the bow to this feeble, frail Stranger as an outright gift, it is my explicit privilege to do so, for in terms of character, none of you swine are as straight-as-an-arrow. But Mother; you should go to your own rooms and keep busy with your proper duties, weaving the complex tapestry upon the loom and spindle. The bow-stringing will be a matter for the men to decide, especially me, since power in this house is justly mine," Telemachus chauvinistically indicated.

Penelope, astonished at witnessing her formerly wimpy son's stellar oration, went-back up to her rooms, taking to heart the prudent words recently uttered.

The worthy swineherd, as instructed, had picked-up the curved bow and was carrying it in the direction of the disguised King. Eumaeus came to the chair of shrewd Odysseus and placed the device into the Beggar's worthy hands. Then, the often-forgetful pig-herder summoned the nurse, Eurycleia, and said to her, "Wise servant; listen carefully. Telemachus is telling you to lock the closely-fitted doorway to this dining hall. If any valet hears groans and death screams coming from inside this room, or detects any noise emanating from the throats of scared men within these walls, he or she is to remain busy with work responsibilities, and is to ignore any shouts or shrieks, or yells of 'What the fuck'!"

Without any hesitation, Eurycleia rapidly departed the huge room, and the anxious nurse frantically raced to bolt all the doors to that enormous hall. And the old woman's female colleagues, without ever even whispering a word, slipped-out of the large chamber and soon obediently also locked the courtyard gates.

Odysseus already was holding the awesome bow, turning it this way and that, and testing it in different ways to see if, while its lord had been away, still had the same feel and flexibility. The shrewd archer, getting used to the string-resistance of the shooting device, in five seconds easily strung the difficult bow. Then, the champion marksman picked-up the arrow lying by itself upon the nearby table, and set it against the bow, right upon the bridge. Next, he pulled the notched arrow and the bowstring back, and still casually sitting inside his chair, and with the sure aim of Cupid, let the old arrow fly. Amazingly, the projectile sped through every single hole near the top of all twelve axe heads. The projectile, weighted-down with bronze, emerged unscathed, exiting out of the last opening.

"Telemachus," the Stranger-turned-archer summoned his amazed son's attention. "I have not disgraced you. I did not miss my aim, or work too long to string my cherished bow. Now it's time to get a dinner ready for these lecherous Achaeans, while there's still some daylight, we'll entertain ourselves with your minstrel singing diriges, and playing the various lyre lyrics."

Telemachus, recognizing his father's repetitious head-nodding signal, cinched his sword belt tight, closed his fist around a bronze spear, and moved-in close beside his father.

Jay Dubya

Chapter 22

"THE KILLING OF THE SUITORS"

Ingenious Odysseus stripped-off his tattered rags, grabbed-up the nearby bow and accompanying quiver full of arrows, and sprang-up from his chair. The returning King then loudly shouted at the suddenly alarmed suitors.

"This contest to determine who is best bow-stringer is now over. But there's another target in which to aim; one that *no man* has ever struck. I'll soon find-out if my past ability can hit the mark. May Apollo grant that I receive the desired glory I seek."

As Odysseus spoke his astonishing words, which were both cryptic and obscure to the appalled moochers, the returning King aimed an arrow straight at Antinous, who was just about to raise-up to his lips a fine double-handled goblet. Among those feasting, who would have ever thought that a lowly Beggar would or could also be a formidable assassin? Odysseus had taken steady aim, and his lethal arrow hit Antinous right in the neck, with its honed point passing directly through the victim's tender throat. Thick spurts of blood came flowing quickly from the targeted creep's nose and mouth. When the other suitors had observed Antinous falling to the slate floor, the frightened rogues raised an uproar and profusely shouted and cursed expletives at the keen-eyed Beggar.

"Vile Stranger; you'll pay for luckily shooting an arrow at that innocent nobleman. You'll pay heavily for your malicious violation. It's certain you'll be killed, and now vultures are going to feast upon your evil flesh and blood," Eurymachus shouted above the rest.

The drunken freeloaders did not realize that Odysseus had deftly killed Antinous on purpose. In their folly, the fools did not imagine that they, the onerous villains, were now tightly enmeshed in destruction's unfailing net. Shrewd Odysseus scowled at his bitter enemies, and sternly communicated his vengeful intent.

"You mangy dogs; because you had fallaciously speculated that I was never coming back to Ithaca from Troy, you've been wildly ravaging my house, incessantly raping innocent women, bullying my son, and, in devious ways, evilly wooing my faithful wife, while I was still alive defending Greece's honor. You exhibit no fear of gods who hold reign over wide heaven, or of any mortal who might take his revenge in days to come. And now venomous assholes, a shrewdly planned fatal snare has caught you all."

As Odysseus articulated his great animosity, pale fear seized his adversaries' hearts and minds. Each craven egomaniac looked-around to see how he might flee the imminent administration of complete destruction. Only loquacious Eurymachus mustered sufficient gumption to answer.

"If, in fact, it is true that you are the invincible Odysseus of Ithaca, arriving back home again, you're absolutely right in what you say about the actions of us Achaeans' demonstrating reckless conduct inside your home. Our many foolish behaviors in the fields and in your' palace have been reprehensible. But the instigator who had been responsible for all that mayhem is repulsive Antinous, who has just been killed. Now that the misfit is dead, and deservedly so, his warped mind taken out of commission, you should spare the rest of us because the snake's head has already been severed. Later on, we'll contribute adequate compensation to pay for what food and drink we've abundantly consumed over the years, and I hereby promise that you'll be reimbursed annually with large amounts of oxen, with bronze objects, and with gold and silver coins."

"Eurymachus; I believe that you're trying to save your own ass from death while attempting to place the entire blame for your enumerable felonies on dead Antinous. Even if you offered me all the goods you' retards have inherited from your own fathers, everything which you now own, and offered that total sum to me as retribution, I would decline out of pure principle; for from my point of view, none of you dumb-fucks deserve to be safe from slaughter. Now you miscreants have a distinct choice: you can either fight me here in my palace face to face, or you can run away. But I think that there's not one of you slimy bastards who will luckily escape being utterly destroyed, since all of the palace doors have been locked tight; so therefore, your simple choice is either to fight, or to fight!"

"Friends, this unsavory bum claiming to be Odysseus won't dare box all of us with those all-conquering hands of his," Eurymachus yelled to his suitor associates. "Instead, now he's got the polished bow and quiver, and the lunatic bastard will just keep on shooting arrows and insults at us, until the crazed fanatic has killed us all. So, colleagues; let's think now about how we should fight this unethical renegade. Pull out your swords, and set-up turned tables to block his wicked arrows, and then let's charge the son-of-a-bitch, going directly at the pestilence all together in an unstoppable assault."

Showing what the gifted orator considered a good example of resistance, Eurymachus pulled-out his double-edged bronze sword, and then recklessly charged forward, rushing at Odysseus with a blood-curdling shout. As the attacking fool did so, Lord Odysseus shot a sharp arrow, piercing the hostile bloodsucker directly in the lower chest, and penetrating right through his spine. Eurymachus's sword slipped-down from his bloody hand onto the slate floor. The fatally wounded braggart bent-over, writhing upon a blood-laden table, and soon collapsed into death's throes. The antagonist's forehead kept hammering upon the now-crimson floor, and with his heart writhing in agony, and with both of the knave's feet futilely kicking at the nearby chair's legs, making it shake and shimmy twice, the vile suitor's heavy breathing quickly expired. Soon, a hazy veil fell over both of Eurymachus's non-blinking eyes.

Another possessed, nutjob, marital candidate Amphinomus, brother of snake-like Amphibius, charged straight at glorious Odysseus, the attacker wielding his raised sword, but Telemachus aimed and threw a bronze-tipped spear, hitting the aggressor from behind in his behind, although the youth had as his target the blade landing between the assaulter's shoulder-blades. With a loud crash, Amphinomus fell forward upon a turned table, his dazed forehead then striking hard against the slate floor. Telemachus quickly sped across the supper chamber to his arrow-shooting father, whose reliable quiver never quivered.

"Father; now I'll bring you a shield, two spears, a helmet made of bronze; one that fits your exposed temples. I'll also hand weapons to the petrified swineherd and to the paranoid goat-keeper, both of them now lying on the floor, pretending to be dead! It's better if we fully arm ourselves, just in case we lose a wrist or an elbow."

"Hurry son! Get those battle weapons to me fast, while I still can shoot arrows to protect my humorous funny bone and my shoulders," Odysseus yelled. "If I am disarmed, I'll have no appendages left to hold and swing my sword!"

Telemachus obeyed the explicit orders and hurried to the house's storeroom area. From a cabinet, the harried youth removed four shields, eight spears, and four helmets with horsehair plumes, and clumsily rushed across the chamber and tripped over a table, thus inadvertently supplying the suitors with additional weapons and battle equipment with his clumsy fall.

"It would be easier for chickens to fly the coop, than to have you cooped-up trash-mongers escape your imminent doom!" the abused Prince awkwardly stood and illogically hollered.

The two apprehensive servants arose from playing possum and grabbed available dropped spears and helmets, audaciously joining the bloody imbroglio. But skilled Odysseus needed no new weapons or armor, using the bow and arrows he already had to kill his scared-shitless adversaries, one by one. As the suitors' bodies began piling-up, the remaining combatants finally realized that they, the illicit scoundrels, were soon to also be in a heap of trouble.

But once Odysseus shot and used his last arrow from his quiver, the incensed King could not again shoot his *bow* towards any other prospective marital *beau* in pursuit of Penelope's hand. So, the creative archer then propped his hunting weapon against the dim room's massive doorpost, and let the weapon lean beside the massive entrance.

Suddenly, ageless Agelaus yelled-out, calling to all his frantic colleagues scurrying around, but before the old geezer could finish his death sentence, or even his death phrase, Odysseus picked-up the loudmouth curmudgeon, and despite the fact that the King had no undertaker training, the husband of Queen Penelope easily lifted and tossed Agelaus's wrinkled ass above the hearth, and flung the elderly coot directly into the raging fire, in what amounted to an instant ancient cremation."

"That elimination of Agelaus felt better than making a killing in the city livestock market," Odysseus screamed across the room to Telemachus' ears. "The old asshole's hopes and dreams have all gone up in smoke!"

Goatherder Melanthius, demonstrating his true traitor nature, picked-up several shields, spears, and bronze helmets that had been accidentally dropped upon the floor by Telemachus, and the deceitful turncoat began distributing the items to various suitors that were still scurrying around the vast room, still searching for a means of escaping Odysseus's intense wrath.

"Telemachus, it seems that one of the women residing in this house has stirred-up a nasty fight against us, or perhaps the suspect goat-herder Melanthius is a stupid-ass transgender who has somehow impressively grown concave tits and a quite useless, very dry cunt."

"Father, I'm an inexperienced cub cadet, and I bear the entire blame for inadvertently arming the enemy! But now I intend to mow them all down!"

Melanthius, the dastardly goatherd, jealously shouted a coarse insult at his master. "Guileful Odysseus; you indeed are a clever ass-wiper! You've penned-up the suitors like I daily pen-up my goats!"

"Fuck you, Melanthius! If you had eight brawny suitors standing behind you, you'd still be asinine! I'm not a cowardly scapegoat standing here to suffer from your false allegiance! You're on your way to goat heaven, that's for damned sure!" Odysseus shouted as the proud king flung a sharp-tipped bronze spear at the two-faced scumbag, whose skull immediately shattered in half.

Since Odysseus's bow and his swift arrows had brought-down and executed the principal suitors, the remaining rabble of insurgents were all in a panic-stricken, hysterical mode, being picked-off one by one.

Led by spiteful Amphimedon, brother of Trachodon, who generally looked-like a gigantic prehistoric lizard, the terrified suitors that were still standing kept on throwing spears, tables, lamps and porno' paintings at their good-guy opponents with frantic haste, but benign Athena appeared upon the battle scene, and the biased goddess made their in-flight projectiles amazingly veer in opposite directions, killing their comrades instead of impacting Odysseus, Telemachus and Eumaeus. But dastardly Amphimedon, flailing-away with a lengthy knife, got lucky and managed to cut Telemachus' left hand with a glancing blow across the wrist. However, the minor injury proved to be a badge of honor to the inspired youth.

Being stimulated at receiving his first battle wound, Telemachus managed to hit the bronze metallurgist Leocritus, striking the brass-balled, tin-headed combatant squarely in the groin. Leocritus lurched forward, his entire face and forehead quickly smashing against the slate floor, coincidentally earning valorous Telemachus the lad's future title, "Expert Ballbreaker Son of Odysseus!"

And then the minstrel Phemius, who had been compelled to sing against his will while standing before the suitors, attempted to evade his own disastrous fate. The gay entertainer set-down his hollow lyre, left the musical instrument upon the slate floor, awkwardly placing it between the mixing bowl and the silver-studded chair. The scared musician rushed-forward and quickly knelt-down to clasp Odysseus's knee, and then addressed the monarch with a desperate plea.

"I implore you, King Odysseus; show me respect and pity. Show me mercy! I was forced to sing for the abominable suitors, but I will gladly praise you in my songs!"

"Hold-on, Father. Don't allow your sword to injure this innocent minstrel. We should save Medon the Herald, too, who faithfully delivers news all over your square square. Please spare those two cowardly gay guys from your tempestuous rampage!"

Medon the Herald, was also pouting and acting like a crying baby, cowering beneath a high-chair, but then the fool jumped-up and pleaded to young Telemachus.

"Here I am, my friend! Tell your father to restrain himself, in case, as he exults in his great strength, he accidentally, in his fury, strikes my' should blades with hist sharp bronze blade. If I fortunately live through this crisis, I promise that I'll stop sleeping and having unnatural sex with Phemius the Minstrel. I now realize that both mine and his assholes are exits and not entrances. And I also pledge to forget all this homosexual gay stuff, too. I promise to marry a plump, ugly female who is a fine cook, and I also promise to go straight, thrusting my diminutive dingle right into the sex-starved whore's wet, pink love tunnel!"

"Don't worry, Medon!" Telemachus exclaimed. "My Father will spare your life, even though he despises all of your bullshit lyrics and your perverted homo' life style! But I believe you'll luckily be making the right choice. Never make a pretty woman your wife! Instead, marry an ugly whore who can cook!"

Satisfied that all of the suitors had been killed, Odysseus, Telemachus and Eumaeus dragged all twenty-four enemy combatants, and Melanthius too, out of the great hall, sliced-off their testicles and limp peckers from their abdomens, and left the severed reproductive organs in a small, putrid mound for the hungry hounds to eat and savor. The rest of the suitors' bodies were then heaped into a putrid pile. Thus was the demise of Antinous and his wicked confederates, along with the emancipation of Penelope; all wonderfully accomplished by the incomparable and persistent Odysseus, who had salvaged his land from utter destruction.

"Now Telemachus, I believe that the famished canines can have a temporary food source from their everyday dog-eat-dog existence! The eager hounds can now relish the suitors' severed wieners without consuming their buns!"

"But Father, where did you ever get the idea to dress like a beggar and isolate the two-dozen suitors into a closed hall, and then systematically execute the bastards one by one."

"Well, Telemachus," Odysseus objectively explained. "When I had visited the fantastic palace at Knossos, and conferred with King Minos, and also with my fellow hero Theseus, slayer of the frightful Minotaur, the dual geniuses gave me some very excellent abstract and con-Crete military strategies to seriously consider!"

Chapter 23

"ODYSSEUS AND PENELOPE"

Old wart-faced Eurycleia climbed-the steep steps to an upstairs room, laughing to herself, so the old dame could merrily tell her Mistress Penelope that Odysseus was again triumphantly present in the house. The exuberant nurse stood beside her lady's head, happily bent-down and spoke into her ear.

"Wake-up now, Penelope, my dear child, so you yourself can see with your own eyes what you've been wanting and desiring each and every day. Odysseus has arrived home. Better late than never, but he's back and has been kicking ass downstairs. And he's just killed those screwball-haughty suitors who have maligned and upset this home, used-up his possessions, and also his financial resources, and victimized his only son."

After twenty-years of mounting disappointment, Penelope held her emotions in check and did not immediately rejoice. The Queen, who had been deep asleep, tossing and turning while dreaming about wild fighting in Troy in regard to the loud noises occurring downstairs, hastily jumped-up out of bed, hugged the old woman, and soon an abundance of' tears fell from her eyelids and cascaded down her cheeks.

"Come now, fanciful Eurycleia, my dear nurse. Tell me the truth and cease with all of this fictional mythology nonsense you profess. If Odysseus is truly here, back in lackluster Ithaca as you've maintained, then how could he ever contend with and defeat those shameless suitors? He was alone, and in this house, and those scurrilous harebrains were always causing havoc when together in a large two-dozen group."

"I didn't overtly see any actual violence or massive massacre occurring," the nurse admitted. "I only heard the haunting groans of grown men being methodically killed. I slinked myself downstairs and took a brief glimpse of the aftermath. My disbelieving eyes found King Odysseus standing victoriously with the bodies of numerous dead crackpots laying upon the slate floor; yes, lying all around him. The carcasses of the loathsome assholes were heaped-up together, which indeed was a heart-warming sight for my' eyes to witness. And your valorous husband was standing there, covered with blood and gore, just like a successful lion after a great hunting pursuit. Come along with me, my Queen, so that you too can be reunited and build content within your heart. You've been through so much misfortune, and now the joyful occasion you've both been anticipating for so long has finally arrived. He's come by himself; home without any observable entourage; home to his own hearth, ready to be warmly welcomed by Telemachus and you. After enduring countless trials and tribulations, and gaining his sweet revenge upon all the insufferable suitors, our King has finally liberated his home; and Odysseus must feel wonderfully vindicated in eliminating the two-dozen leeching crazies, while freeing his property and family from their horrific exploitation. I can't wait to hear your husband's proclamation of emancipation!"

"But quixotic Eurycleia. This fantasy story you're telling me can't possibly be true. It totally defies reality! I prefer to believe that one of the immortal gods has killed the sinister suitors out of sheer unhinged rage, reacting to the dirt-bags' heartless pride and shameless deeds. The impostors have met disaster through their foolishness, and their fate had been enacted by Zeus's imperial decree. But in some place far-away, I still fear that Odysseus has given-up his journey to Achaea, and that he himself is lost forever from my sincere embrace. It is exceedingly hard to fathom the complex plans of the eternal gods, even though, my aide, you're truly wiser than most straight and homo sapiens. But let's go to my son, so that I can praise Zeus, and witness the vile crackpots all dead, and closely view the special man whom you claim had killed the odious purveyors of repugnant evil."

"But Mistress; I've heard from fairly dependable palace-intrigue gossipers that the suitors' bodies are now stacked-outside in the courtyard with their tiny dingles and testicles sliced-off! Your hungry hounds are now feasting off their piled wieners and buns!"

Penelope rose and soon left her upper room, descended the rickety steps; slowly crossed the stone threshold; entered into the virtually empty hall, and gently sat-down near the blazing fire-crematory, positioning herself opposite shabbily-clothed Odysseus the Beggar.

The fatigued King was just sitting stationary, resting by a tall marble column, symbolizing the monarch being a definite pillar of the community. And while staring at the bloody slate floor, the exhausted king was waiting disconsolately to find-out if his elegant wife would speak to him. But Penelope quietly sat-down and stayed silent for a long time, trying to manage the mounting wonder and apprehension residing inside her charitable heart. Sometimes, the Queen's eyes peered straight at the grimy visitor, fully gazing at his heavily-bearded face, but at other times, Penelope turned her head in the opposite direction, disbelieving the silent, shabbily-clothed Beggar's claimed identity.

Telemachus then spoke-up, addressing a stinging rebuke directly at his mother.

"Saddened Woman; you're a cruel and conceited female displaying an unfeeling, dispassionate marital heart," Penelope's son criticized. "Why turn aside from my father in this unnatural and peculiar way? Why not sit over there, close to him, and ask relevant and irrelevant questions? No other woman's heart would be so hard as to make her so distant from a husband who has miraculously come home to his native land in the twentieth year, after surviving so many harsh ordeals. That heart of yours is sometimes harder than the stone columns that support the palace roof."

"My impetuous, idealistic child; inside my head and inside my chest, my mind and heart are quite astounded. I feel alienated from reality, and cannot speak with confidence, or ask applicable questions, or even look this mute Beggar in the eye. If indeed it's true that our visitor is Odysseus, and he is home again, surely the two of us have more certain ways to know each other that both of us stubbornly giving each other the silent treatment. But we do have uncanny signs which only the two of us can understand; a sort of mental telepathy, and other observing people are not able to recognize the established pattern."

As the abashed Queen spoke her mind, Lord Odysseus, who for two decades had borne so much travail, smiled and immediately addressed his son's perceptive inquiry.

"Telemachus; let your mother thoroughly test me in this all-too-familiar, bloody hall. Soon, the Queen will possess more certain knowledge of my personality and character. Right now, I'm filthy, but twenty years ago, I was filthy rich, with disgusting expensive clothing worn upon my body. Your mother has always preferred the finest and most costly attire, and I believe that she presently rejects me because I look grossly pathetic, and appear as a derelict pauper in her blurred eyes; all because of superficial external appearances. Why she repels me and will not admit so is because of her greed for materialism, and in that monetary aspect, your materialistic mother is much like the dead suitors. Even when your mother was a hot-to-trot teenager, she was without a doubt a material girl, living in a material world. But as you are obviously convinced, Telemachus. I am your authentic father and patriarch, Odysseus, King of Ithaca. Thank Zeus that

I've been guided by good-hearted Pallas Athene on my arduous ten-year odyssey, despite my infatuation with me wearing the color purple!"

Once Odysseus had articulated those pertinent remarks, Eurynome, the veteran tri-sexual housekeeper, gave the great-hearted king a comprehensive bath; thoroughly rubbed him all over with rich oil; administered to the Ithacan monarch a full King-sized body massage, and finally placed a purple tunic upon his body, along with a resplendent purple cloak. In an invisible state, Athena interceded, and poured magnificent handsomeness upon her favorite hero, providing Odysseus with an abundance of blond hair; a much taller stature, and much more robust arm and leg muscles.

"Strange Lady, to you, those simpletons who live in marble temples atop Mount Olympus have given to you more than to any other wife, a two-valve half-heart. No other woman would harden herself and keep her distance, if her husband, in the twentieth year, came back to his spouse in his own native land, after going through so much agony with so little ecstasy to remember. So, come now, Nurse; you old ill-tempered hag; spread-out a bed and blankets meant solely for me, so that I can lie-down by myself and dream about my incredible wanderings, and not about this cold-crotched bitch sitting across from my aching ass. The cold heart beating inside her frigid breast must most-definitely be made of futuristic iron, even in this obsolete Bronze Age."

Wise Penelope then answered her perturbed husband: "Strange Man," Penelope retorted. "I'm not making too much of my lack of passion at this moment, or ignoring your somewhat familiar voice. Nor is it the case that you've offended me in any way, sounding much like the petulant jerk-off I had once known, whose identity I cannot presently recall. I understand the sort of narcissistic hardhead Odysseus was when he had left Ithaca in his long-oared ship. So come, Eurycleia; set-up for this guest outside my well-constructed bedroom, that strong bed my husband had carefully made for himself in anticipation of marriage. Put that sturdy bed out-there in the corridor, and throw some random blankets upon it, consisting of itchy fleeces and unclean cloaks taken from the palace cloak room."

"Small City Woman," perturbed Odysseus rankled. "Those sharp words you have just uttered are each one a painful dagger. Who has ordered my bed shifted to somewhere else, other than it staying inside the master bedroom? That task would be difficult, even for someone truly skilled, unless an ambitious god like fucked-up Hephaestus came-down from Olympus in person to strenuously perform that complicated maneuver.

Quite frankly, Woman; your sarcastic, negative attitude sounds like penis envy to me!"

Hearing no oral response, Odysseus stubbornly continued his melancholy oratory. "But among men, there is no such adept asshole living, no matter how much energy the mortal fellow possesses, who would find it easy labor to shift that bed into the nearby hallway. In fact, if I were a carpenter, and you were my lady, I still wouldn't do that difficult bullshit at your command. For built into the alluded-to, well-constructed bedstead is a great symbol, which I had made myself, with no one else's assistance. A long-leaved olive tree was growing in the yard. It was in full bloom and flourishing, and the fluffy thing reminded me of my pretty girlfriend's hairy bush when I was a mere carpenter's apprentice, and she was a young lady studying to be a beautician at the now-defunct Ithacan Trades and Cosmetology School."

"Tell me more, anonymous Beggar," Penelope demanded.

"In woodshop class, I had built my palace bedroom around that fluffy olive tree, until I had finished the project with well-set stones. I had constructed a fine roof upon the growth, and added closely-fitted jointed doors, one leading to the adjacent cloak room. After that enterprise had been completed, I cut-back the excess foliage, all-the-while imagining that I was getting turned-on by meticulously trimming Lady Penelope's bush gardens. I carefully carved-off the tree's trunk, upward from the root, trimming it skillfully and honing it true with bronze sides, so that my enormous endeavor followed a straight line. Once I'd made the bedpost, with an auger, I bored-out the entire structure. Then, I cut-out my bed, until I was done my project, and my colossal effort received an A-Plus grade from the woodshop teacher. And that's the romantic symbol I now describe for you. Now Lady; I honestly don't know if that bed of mine is still in place and usable, or if some other man has cut that wonderful olive tree down at its base, and set the tree-mendous bed up in a different spot."

Haggard Lady Penelope felt a weakness in her knees, and her heart grew softer than her aroused clitoris button. For her hard-to-persuade mind finally recognized that the Strange Beggar-turned-King-Charming's stirring words were truer-than-fact. The Queen's blue eyes filled with tears; her cataracts almost as large as the Nile's; the Queen rose from her chair, and rushed across the room to the male whom Athena had now wonderfully and magically transformed into a handsome, strong, virile young warrior. Penelope instinctively threw her arms around Odysseus's neck, kissed his head, and suddenly, her crotch lips became wetter than those around her mouth.

"Don't be angry or sad, dear Odysseus; not with me and my characteristic cold nature upon our original contact. In every other matter to date, you've been the cleverest of men I've ever known. The fickle gods have brought us a plethora of sorrows that weren't exactly pleasant bestowments. The jealous deities atop Mt. Olympus were not willing to decide that we two should stay merrily married, and to happily enjoy the recollection of our shared youth, and now we have reached together with dignity the threshold of old age. It is not the time to rage at me, resenting what misery I've caused you upon your return to this decaying palace, first dedicated to Pallas Athene."

"I feel likewise, my dear wife and Queen!"

"There are many avaricious men such as deceased Antinous, who dream-up terribly wicked schemes. Argive Helen of Sparta, reputed to be a child of Zeus, would never have had sex with a man who came from somewhere foreign, if she had known Achaea's warrior sons would ally and bring her back to her native Greek land, after temporarily experimenting with being Helen of Troy. But now Odysseus, you have accurately described that clear symbol meticulously carved into *our* bed's headboard, which no one else of elite status has ever seen, other than the two of us romantic lovebirds. Odysseus, you once took my virginity; now you can take my twenty-year frigidity!"

While the reunited couple kept reminiscing shared memories with each other, Eurynome prepared the bed with soft coverlets, with the master bedroom being illuminated, the light originating from flaming torches. Once the servants had hurriedly arranged the soft bed sheets, the chief servant, Eurynome, led the couple on their way to their mattress, with a flaming torch gripped in her right hand. Once the servant had solemnly escorted the King and Queen, horny Eurynome went-away nearby to eavesdrop on the expected humping and pumping that the nosy whore anticipated were about to be heard. Odysseus and Penelope approached with joy the place where their bed still stood from earlier days.

After Odysseus and Penelope had enjoyed making love together for the first time in over two decadent decades, the pair entertained themselves by telling family stories, and also by playing games of 'Pin the Asshole on the Asshole'. and then the more popular afterglow sport of 'Spin the Dildo'. The rejuvenated Queen talked of all she had to bear in her own home, dealing with that destructive group of greedy parasites, who, because of her royal title, kept butchering so many cattle and fat sheep, and shamelessly draining so many large jars of vintage wine. Odysseus, told his attentive wife of all the troubles he had brought and wrought upon men, and of all the grief the famed wanderer had stubbornly caused for himself; the many troubles occurring because of the itinerant's obstinate defiance of vengeful Lord Poseidon.

"Let's have some good, old-fashioned *Bed*lam," the zany King suggested as Odysseus used his favorite word for 'crazy sex'.

"Oh, Odysseus; now I know for sure that you are indeed my long-lost husband! A tiger never changes its stripes; a leopard never changes its spots, and true to your past disgusting habit, you never change your smelly undergarments!"

Penelope was extremely happy listening and reviewing the many fond memories from the nostalgic past, and Sleep did not zoom-down and close her eyes until her spouse's complete story had been thoroughly told, and when her sex appetite had also been fully satisfied.

Then Pallas Athene, radiant goddess with the extraordinary glittering eyes, came-up with something rather special. When Zeus's daughter thought that Odysseus and his wife had strengthened their hearts with pleasure and with sleep, the prankster-goddess stirred-up Dawn, enthroned in gold, to rouse unaroused Odysseus from his soft bed.

"Now that we've come back to the bed we love, you should seriously tend to our remaining wealth inside this once-opulent palace," the King lectured the Queen. "As for the flocks that those haughty-naughty suitors had stolen and consumed, I'll seize many area beasts as acquired plunder on my own pursuit; and Achaeans will gladly pay more taxes to merrily finance our numerous bad habits. Now, obedient Wife. I'm going to wander outside the city to check my forest lands, and there I'll see my noble father, Laertes, who, on my accursed behalf, has suffered so much worry and grief. So, dear Wife; since I know how wonderfully intelligent you are, I'm asking you to closely follow my sage advice. Once sunrise comes, the story will be out in the city about the suitors being viciously slaughtered inside our home. So, you should go now to your upstairs room with your female attendants and stay there. Do not visit or question anyone. As you can plainly fathom as I head for the hills, my attitude towards life has not made any significant adjustment in over twenty years."

"Wow, Father!" Telemachus exclaimed as the jolly pair left the palace to explore and hunt wild boar inside the forest. "Like father; like son! But

Pop. I can't wait for you to tell me all about your fantastic adventure with the heinous Cyclops!"

"Well, my dear son," Odysseus explained. "The Cyclops was indeed a ferocious monster, and besides, the awesome brute also was a very dangerous enemy. So naturally, to protect my delicate ass, I had to always keep an eye out for the formidable bastard!"

Chapter 24

"ZEUS AND ATHENA END THE FIGHTING"

Once Odysseus and his son had left the city, the pair soon reached his father's once fertile, well-managed farm, which Laertes had won by his own efforts, after many earlier years of unsuccessful dice gambling. Laertes's crumbling estate was still there, with numerous sheds surrounding the formerly stately mansion, where the old codger's servants, having no other means of subsistence, still worked diligently to carry-out the old coot's austere wishes.

An ancient Sicilian woman, imported from Syracuse, lived inside the codger's house; looking after the about-to-die asshole; carelessly caring for aged Laertes, and baking large brick-oven tomato and cheese pizzas for the constipated old fart to swallow-down every single day.

"You hungry men should now go into the poorly-built home and quickly kill the finest pig they have, so that we can eat and greedily pig-out," Odysseus commanded several of his father's lethargic slaves. "Now Telemachus; I'll follow the snoring sounds and try to locate the field where my Old Man is napping. I'll awaken the neurotic nutcase, who was already-sleeping twenty-three hours a day twenty-years ago when I had embarked with my twelve ships to Troy."

"Why the hell have we come here to this horrible dump?" Telemachus wanted to know. "I thought you desired to bond with me by taking me hunting and hiking in the forest?"

"I want to see if my blind father still recognizes me," Odysseus answered. "I'm assuming that your grandfather Laertes is now totally blind, because when I had departed for Troy, the then almost-blind idiot thought that I was a kinky female prostitute standing at his door to whom he owed money."

Odysseus roamed the vast, run-down estate with Telemachus and eventually located Laertes, assiduously digging his own grave in a not-so-well-tended vineyard. The old man's Old Man was garbed in a disgusting, shabby, patched-up tunic, with laced-up, ox-hide shin pads upon his lower legs, stitched to protect his bony knees and ankles from abrasive scratches and painful insect bites.

On his aged, wrinkled hands, daft Laertes wore gloves to protect both his palms and fingers from needles and thistles that grew all over the entire farmland. On his head the senile fellow wore a tattered goatskin cap. In those tawdry clothes, Laertes was dealing with failing health, with esteemless self-confidence, and with an obvious lack of wealth.

As Odysseus gazed and sniffed at his decrepit and miserable-looking father, the sorrowed King could feel sharp pains shooting-up his nostrils. The Ithacan King jumped over, embraced Laertes, and kissed the grunting fogey's farting asshole twenty times, once for every single year the famed warrior had been away.

"Father; I'm here, back home in the twentieth year, sauntering around on my own native island. Stop your grieving, and producing all these tearful sighs. I'll tell you everything, although my' lips have to move at triple speed, since I don't think that neither you nor I will live for all twenty years of my exciting oration. I've killed the parasitic suitors who had been traducing my palace, and I've avenged their malignant evil, along with their heartless insolence."

"If what you're now relating is true, self-proclaimed Odysseus," Laertes remarked, "this estate is still my damned land; and Telemachus, you are not down on junior's farm."

"But Father; I am indeed your son Odysseus returning home from Troy! Don't your ears recognize my voice?"

"Well, if you are indeed my lame-brained son and have come back to salvage your property, then show me some clear evidence of your identity," Laertes demanded. "I wish to see something tangible so that I can be quite certain of who the fuck you are, and who the fuck I'm talking to."

"First, let your eyes inspect this scar that an insane wild boar had inflicted upon me with its sharp white tusks when I had visited Mt. Parnassus to commiserate with the family of Autolycus, Queen Penelope's father. My real purpose in visiting the asses in Parnassus was to obtain the dowry gifts that the stubborn bastards had previously promised me."

As Odysseus spoke and complained, his skinflint father's fond heart fluttered with an irregular rhythm, and the old fart's feeble knees buckled. Unaware of his father's short aortic valve spasm, Odysseus proudly showed Laertes his foot-long limp fadorkenbender, and the hoary curmudgeon was finally totally convinced that Odysseus was truly his boner-fide offspring.

Being overwhelmed by excessive emotion, Laertes threw his frail arms around the son he so loved, and the aged coot's lungs struggled hard to breathe. Lord Odysseus, who had endured so much hardship and duress during his ten-year odyssey, held Laertes upright, hoping that he didn't have to administer CPR to a faltering geezer having a really bad case of halitosis.

After Laertes revived from his brief seizure episode, and the half-assed nutcase's spirit and will to live were miraculously restored inside his scrawny chest, Odysseus's father addressed his companions.

"Father Zeus, it appears that your gods are still interfering with human affairs from atop high Olympus," Laertes enigmatically hollered-up to the sky. "If it's really true that those intrusive suitors have paid the ultimate price for their deplorable arrogance, I am exceedingly grateful to you and your majestic family, for Odysseus will be staying inside his palace and not bothering the hell out of me here on my country farm. But now my alert heart contains a dreadful fear that all the vengeful men of Ithaca will soon rush here like barbarians onto my worthless estate and then rebel against the three of us. And they'll send-out messengers for reinforcements to every town in Cephallenia, wherever the hell that dumb-shit place is!"

"Take courage, Father, and do not allow these ass-backward ideas weigh-down your all-too-weak heart. Let's go into your three-seat outhouse, the one close by the fruit orchard, so that you, Telemachus and I can take triple dumps and review the past twenty-years in a delightful, aroma-filled atmosphere."

Meanwhile, several of Laertes's more conscientious servants had finished working the fields, pastures, and orchards, and dinner was being prepared. After leaving the three-seater outhouse without moving their clogged-up bowels, Odysseus, Laertes and Telemachus sat-down at the supper table, parking their rear ends upon wooden chairs that sounded like flimsy objects that were about to collapse. As the three diners were reaching for table-food, old Dolius appeared, carrying a large greasy tomato pie with anchovies, pepperoni and sausage. The bitchy Sicilian hag, thinking that she had recognized King Odysseus, dropped the hot pizza upon Laertes's head, and soon ran over to kiss Telemachus, whom the woman's poor vision had mistaken for his father, King Odysseus.

"My friend and most excellent King," Dolius began with thick cataracts evident in her eyes as her active lips were still kissing and caressing Telemachus' astonished face. "You're finally back here in Ithaca with us coinless paupers. I've longed for your wonderful return, but my eyes never thought I'd either see your head, or your ass again! Gods themselves must have been leading you at every step of your challenging journey. Joyful greetings, my Lord! May the gods grant you continued success and many years of enjoying prolific, volcanic-type ejaculations!"

While that annoying bullshit was going on at Laertes's kitchen table, rumors, gossip and scuttlebutt abounded and sped swiftly throughout the entire island, spreading distorted, false news about the suitors' appalling deaths.

Relatives of Antinous heard about the great palace massacre and sprinted all over the city in all directions, gathering with mournful sighs before Odysseus's run-down mansion. Each demonstrator vehemently protested, shouting a chorus of expletives outside the king's neglected mansion. The agitated mourners then found and carried the corpses of the deceased suitors off the ruinous property, vociferously cursing Odysseus for committing his grave revenge, and eventually tossing their dead relatives onto awaiting donkey carts. Antinous and his lifeless companions were soon to be put on permanent lay-away inside the local, weed-infested cemetery.

Up on Mt. Olympus's dazzling summit, adorable Pallas Athene, perceiving a massive insurrection developing against Odysseus, Penelope and Telemachus, respectfully approached Almighty Zeus, sitting in purple attire upon his majestic throne. And the apprehensive virgin goddess earnestly pleaded that all future violence performed against her earthly champion should be prevented from occurring.

"Father of us all, and son of Titan Cronos," Athena prefaced. "Answer and grant me my fondest wish. In regard to wandering Odysseus, who has suffered unbearable calamities for two decades now, issued mostly by your vindictive brother Poseidon, can you please inform me exactly what fate you are concealing inside that erratic mind of yours? Will you now foster further savage wars and fearful battles among the Greeks and their neighboring mortals?"

"My favorite child, why are you asking this petty human nonsense of me?" Zeus annoyingly replied. "Why do all these meaningless, unimportant questions about one dumb-ass, insignificant human down on Earth concern you so much? Were you not the one who put this last plan in motion all by yourself, so that your hero Odysseus could take-out his revenge against those avaricious Ithacan suitors, after he got back from Troy? Do as you wish, Daughter. But to appease you, I'll devise an appropriate solution that I think might be right. Since your Lord Odysseus has now accomplished his sweet revenge upon his bitter enemies, I decree to let the remaining Achaeans living in Ithaca swear a binding oath that your' hero shall remain their king for life, and let us make them all forget the way their brothers and their sons had been killed, and the population should learn to love one other as the dumb-fucks had done before the start of that petty Trojan War. And let there be wealth and peace to satisfy all the puny assholes living now, and also in the future, in deplorable Ithaca."

Being allotted the appropriate divine authority to act, Athena anxiously swooped-down from lofty Mount Olympus to implement erratic-minded Zeus's favorable command.

Meanwhile, back at the dysfunctional suburban ranch, after Telemachus and the returned King had satisfied their appetites for pizza, and while Laertes was blasting quantities of methane gas out of his dual exhaust assholes from suffering massive intestinal *fart*itude, Lord Odysseus, who had borne so much adversity, was the first to speak.

"Father," the wandering hero commenced. "I haven't said a word all-meal-long because I remembered that you had taught me from when I was a toddler to never speak with my mouth full. But now, someone should go outside, pretending that he is a weather vane, looking around the vicinity in all directions, and seeing if the livid relatives of the killed suitors are getting close to our vicinity."

Telemachus rose from his seat and paced to the termite-infested doorway, and his vision detected a loud crowd of armed men rapidly advancing toward Laertes's decaying domicile.

"Father, our enraged enemy from the city is here and closing-in already! Let's gather all available weapons! We'd better hurry, as if we both had the runs!"

The inspired twosome moved quickly to Laertes's storeroom, and Odysseus put-on tarnished, bronze armor. Laertes, although he had sparse gray hair upon his head, but no semen inside his withered testicles, donned his thin tin breastplate, and was then artificially ready to join the imminent battle.

Odysseus led the two nitwits out of the humble dwelling, but then Athena, with the shape and voice of Mentor, appeared before the three idiots, and soon stood by totally senile Laertes, instructing the old coot in a forceful tone: "Child of Arcesius, by far the dearest of those old farts I cherish; pray to Father Zeus and to me, Pallas Athene. Then, without delay, brandish that long spear that you're holding, and when you have the chance, hurl the weapon at Antinous's cousin Eupeithes's scrotum."

Pallas Athena spoke those dramatic words, and then breathed into Laerte's limp fadorkenbender enormous power, making the old codger have his first significant erection in twenty-years. Laertes offered a short prayer to great Zeus, and another to the god's benign Daughter, and then, the old fuck slowly lifted-up his long-narrow spear. The uncoordinated old geezer awkwardly threw the ancient projectile at flabbergasted Eupeithes, piercing the aggressor's vulnerable scrotum sac, and permanently incapacitating and busting the bellicose asshole's balls.

Next, before Antinous's insolent cousin could collapse to the wet turf, Telemachus also tossed his sharp spear that hit Eupeithes upon the attacker's bronze helmet, finishing-off and decapitating the uncouth loudmouth for good.

"My Son!" Odysseus proudly shouted. "You're learning and discovering correct combat methods quickly! You've just demonstrated the best way to get a head in this world!"

Odysseus and his splendid son together boldly charged at the opposing combatants standing in the front line, attacking them with their remaining swords and double-edged spears. The King and his livid son would have killed all of the crazed aggressors; but then, Pallas Athene intervened in the conflict, and cried-out in a bellowing, loud-soprano voice:

"Men of Ithaca; you must stop this disastrous, low I.Q. warfare at once, so that you mortal fools can quickly go your separate ways without spilling any more blood, and without pissing and shitting your tunics from experiencing overpowering lightning attacks from my father Zeus, reigning atop Mt. Olympus."

Athena, in skilled imitation of Almighty Zeus, spoke thunderously. And instantly, a pale fear gripped the combatants' minds and throats. The avenging assaulters were so terrified at the booming sound of the goddess's earsplitting voice that the intimidated retards dropped their weapons to the damp ground and dizzily spun around like toy tops. The terrified mob hustled like prostitutes soliciting quickies, frenetically scurrying back in the direction of the inner city.

Then, much-enduring Lord Odysseus's larynx emitted a most-distinct, blood-curdling shriek. Startled because his voice-box had been operating independent of his addled brain, King Odyssey soon gathered his normally confident composure. But at that particular moment, unpredictable Almighty Zeus shot-down from Mt. Olympus a flaming thunderbolt that struck between the sandaled feet of bright-eyed Athena, who in the process, had suffered a mild hotfoot.

"Intrepid Odysseus," the goddess addressed her most-admired hero, as Pallas Athene wobbled while holding her slightly-scorched right foot with both hands. "You have certainly encountered much sorrow during your wild odd sea odyssey. Please now, Laertes's son. I insist that you stop this senseless feuding and fighting, for unlike non-compassionate Poseidon, my father, Great Zeus, who sees far and wide, grows angry with your misbehavior, and will decide to give you two nutcases shocking lethal hotfoots instead of just one."

When the famed Ithacan King had heard Athena's electrifying words, Odysseus, fearing the nuts and bolts of his predicament with his testicles possibly being scorched by hot lightning bolts, the returned ruler then respectfully obeyed his patron goddess's command, and the Greek champion suddenly found a small amount of peace developing inside his vengeful heart.

And then, Pallas Athene, beloved daughter of aegis-bearing Zeus, both in shape and form, appeared as a judicious instigator in the image of famed sage Mentor. The talented shape-shifter compelled both Odysseus and Telemachus to swear dual solemn oaths professing community tranquility, with their pledge of allegiance specifically designed to put a cessation to all hostility against the belligerent, pugnacious relatives of deceased Antinous, and equally dead Eurylochus.

"As my future heir, Telemachus," Odysseus explained and emphasized on the mile-long trek back to Ithaca City. "I've learned from my lengthy twenty-year ordeal that eternal life would be unbearably monotonous and boring, and I now fathom that it's the challenges and problems in human existence that make our lives interesting. If you don't like challenges and problems, then you won't enjoy living!"

"Father; philosophically speaking, do you have any other relevant advice for me to consider?"

"First and foremost, Telemachus; never kiss ass, but always kick ass! Someday, dear son; you will proudly become a royal pain-in-the-ass, just like your stubborn Mother and your' obstinate father have always been, and just as we will continue to be until the bitter end!"

About the Author

Jay Dubya is author John Wiessner's pen name and also his initials (J.W.) John is a retired New Jersey public school English teacher and he had taught the subject for thirty-four years. John lives in southern New Jersey with wife Joanne and the couple has three grown sons. John is the creator of sixty books.

Jay Dubya has written adult satires *Fractured Frazzled Folk Fables and Fairy Farces* and *FFFF and FF, Part II. Black Leather and Blue Denim, A '50s Novel* and its sequel, *The Great Teen Fruit War, A 1960' Novel* and *Frat' Brats, A '60s Novel* are adult-oriented literary endeavors constituting a trilogy.

Pieces of Eight, Pieces of Eight, Part II, Pieces of Eight Part III and *Pieces of Eight, Part IV* are' short story/novella collections featuring science fiction, paranormal and humorous plots and themes. *Nine New Novellas* is the companion book to *Nine New Novellas, Part II, Nine New Novellas, Part III* and *Nine New Novellas, Part IV.* And *So Ya' Wanna' Be A Teacher* is a satirical autobiography describing the author's thirty-four-year educational career in American public schools.

Ron Coyote, Man of La Mangia is adult humor and the work is an imaginative satire/parody on Miguel Cervantes' Don Quixote, published in 1605. *Mauled Maimed Mangled Mutilated Mythology* is a work that satires twenty-one famous ancient tales. *The Wholly Book of Genesis* and *The Wholly Book of Exodus* are also adult satirical *humor. Thirteen Sick Tasteless Classics, Thirteen Sick Tasteless Classics, Part II, Thirteen Sick Tasteless Classics, Part III* and *Thirteen Sick Tasteless Classics, Part IV* are adult satirical rewrites of famous short fiction.

John has also authored a trilogy of young adult fantasy novels, *Enchanta, Pot of Gold* and *Space Bugs, Earth Invasion. The Eighteen Story Gingerbread House* is a new collection of eighteen diverse and creative children's stories.

Jay Dubya likes '50s rock and roll music and he also enjoys pop' songs by the Beach Boys, Fleetwood Mac, the Eagles, the Rolling Stones, ELO, John Mellencamp and by John Fogerty.

Author Biography

Born in Hammonton, NJ in 1942, John Wiessner had attended St. Joseph School up to and including Grade 5. After his family moved from Hammonton to Levittown, Pa in 1954, John attended St. Mark School in Bristol, Pa. for Grade 6, St. Michael the Archangel School in Levittown for Grades 7 and 8 and then Immaculate Conception School, Levittown, Pa. for Grade 9. Bishop Egan High School, Levittown Pa was John's educational base for Grades 10 and 11, and later in 1960, the aspiring author graduated from Edgewood Regional High, Tansboro, NJ. John then next attended Glassboro State College, where the future author was an announcer for the school's baseball games and also read the nightly news and sports over WGLS, GSC's radio station.

John Wiessner had been primarily an English teacher in the Hammonton Public School System for 34 years, specializing in the instruction of middle school language arts. Mr. Wiessner was quite active in the Hammonton Education Association, serving in the capacities of Vice-President, building representative and finally, teachers' head negotiator for 7 years. During his lengthy teaching career, John had been nominated into "Who's Who Among American Teachers" three times. He also was quite active giving professional workshops at schools around South Jersey on the subjects of creative writing and the use of movie videos to motivate students to organize their classroom theme compositions.

John Wiessner was very active in community service, being a past President of the Hammonton Lions Club, where he also functioned for many years as the club's Tail-Twister, Vice-President and also Liontamer. John had been named Hammonton Lion of the Year in 1979, and in 2009, the community helper earned the prestigious Melvin Jones Fellow Award, which is the highest honor that a Lion can receive from Lions International.

John also was a successful businessman, starting with being a Philadelphia Bulletin newspaper delivery boy for two years in the late 1950s in Levittown, Pennsylvania. After his family moved back to New Jersey in 1959, John worked at his grandparents and his parents' farm markets, Square Deal Farm (now Ron's Gardens in Hammonton) and Pete's Farm Market in Elm, respectively. He later managed his wife's parents' farm market, White Horse Farms in Elm for three summers.

Also, in a business capacity, for 16 summers starting in 1966 John Wiessner had co-owned Dealers Choice Amusement Arcade on the Ocean City, Maryland boardwalk and also co-owned the New Horizon Tee-Shirt Store for eight summers (1973-'81) on the Rehoboth Beach, Delaware boardwalk. In addition, "Jay Dubya" was a co-owner of Wheel and Deal Amusement Arcade, Missouri Avenue and Boardwalk, Atlantic City. And then, for 18 summers beginning in 1986, John had been the Field Manager in charge of crew-leaders for Atlantic Blueberry Company (the world's largest cultivated blueberry farm), both the Weymouth and Mays Landing Divisions.

After retiring from teaching in 1999, writing under the pen name Jay Dubya (his initials), John Wiessner became the author of 60 books in the genre Action/Adventure Novels, Sci-Fi/Paranormal Story Collections, Adult Satire, Young Adult Fantasy Novels and Non-Fiction Books. His books exist in hardcover, in paperback and in popular Kindle and Nook e-book formats.

In January of 2022, Jay Dubya was nominated into Marquis Who's Who in America for his 34-year career in teaching public school English; for his community volunteer work for the Hammonton Lions Club; for his business enterprises in Ocean City, MD, in Rehoboth Beach Delaware and Atlantic City, and for his publishing of 60 hardcover and paperback books. And in April of that same year, Mr. Wiessner was one of nine distinguished Who's Who in America members honored with Lifetime Achievement Awards, all having an article of recognition appearing in the Wall Street Journal.

Jay Dubya's books are sold on the Internet at online Walmart, Barnes and Noble, Books-a-million, Amazon, Powell's Books, Bookdepository UK, Fishpond Australia, Loot ZA (South Africa), Bookswagon.com (India) and at other large retail Internet buying portals.

Google: Jay Dubya books
Google: Walmart.com, Jay Dubya

CPSIA information can be obtained
at www.ICGtesting.com
Printed in the USA
BVHW070553150223
658552BV00009B/187